W9-CSN-797

WHISPERING SMITH

Following the trail itself, Whispering Smith rode slowly.

[Page 406]

WHISPERING SMITH

BY

FRANK H. SPEARMAN

ILLUSTRATED BY

N. C. WYETH

Whispering Smith was Frank Spearman's most successful and best known book. It was reprinted many times into at least the 1920's and in the 1940's was made into a major motion picture starring Alan Ladd. It completes what could be called the "Medicine Bend Trilogy" which began with his second collection of short stories, *Held for Orders* (1901), and continued with *The Daughter of a Magnate* (1903).　　　　　　　—F.W.

Originally published by Charles Scribner's Sons, 1906

Published by
The Paper Tiger, Inc.
335 Jefferson Avenue
Cresskill, NJ 07626
(201) 567-5620

ISBN 1-889439-02-9

TO MY SON

THOMAS CLARK SPEARMAN

IN MEMORY OF

A PIEDMONT WINTER

CONTENTS

vii

Contents

Contents

ILLUSTRATIONS

Whispering Smith

CHAPTER I

THE WRECKING BOSS

NEWS of the wreck at Smoky Creek reached Medicine Bend from Point of Rocks at five o'clock. Sinclair, in person, was overseeing the making up of his wrecking train, and the yard, usually quiet at that hour of the morning, was alive with the hurry of men and engines. In the train-master's room of the weather-beaten headquarters building, nicknamed by railroad men " The Wicki-up," early comers—sleepy-faced, keen-eyed train-men—lounged on the tables and in chairs discussing the reports from Point of Rocks, and among them crew-callers and messengers moved in and out. From the door of the big operators' room, pushed at intervals abruptly open, burst a blaze of light and the current crash of many keys; within, behind glass screens, alert, smooth-faced boys in shirt sleeves rained calls over the wires or bent with flying pens above clips, taking incoming messages.

Whispering Smith

At one end of the room, heedless of the strain on the division, press despatches and cablegrams clicked in monotonous relay over commercial wires; while at the other, operators were taking from the despatchers' room the train orders and the hurried dispositions made for the wreck emergency by Anderson, the assistant superintendent. At a table in the alcove the chief operator was trying to reach the division superintendent, McCloud, at Sleepy Cat; at his elbow, his best man was ringing the insistent calls of the despatcher and clearing the line for Sinclair and the wrecking gang. Two minutes after the wrecking train reported ready they had their orders and were pulling out of the upper yard, with right of way over everything to Point of Rocks.

The wreck had occurred just west of the creek. A fast east-bound freight train, double-headed, had left the track on the long curve around the hill, and when the wrecking train backed through Ten Shed Cut the sun streamed over the heaps of jammed and twisted cars strung all the way from the point of the curve to the foot of Smoky Hill. The crew of the train that lay in the ditch walked slowly up the track to where the wreckers had pulled up, and the freight conductor asked for Sinclair. Men rigging the derrick pointed to the hind car. The conductor, swinging up the caboose steps, made his

The Wrecking Boss

way inside among the men that were passing out tools. The air within was bluish-thick with tobacco smoke, but through the haze the freightman saw facing him, in the far corner of the den-like interior, a man seated behind an old dining-car table, finishing his breakfast; one glimpse was enough to identify the dark beard of Sinclair, foreman of the bridges and boss of the wrecking gang.

Beside him stood a steaming coffee-tank, and in his right hand he held an enormous tin cup that he was about to raise to his mouth when he saw the freight conductor. With a laugh, Sinclair threw up his left hand and beckoned him over. Then he shook his hair just a little, tossed back his head, opened an unusual mouth, drained the cup at a gulp, and cursing the freightman fraternally, exclaimed, " How many cars have you ditched this time? "

The trainman, a sober-faced fellow, answered dryly, " All I had."

" Running too fast, eh? " glared Sinclair.

With the box cars piled forty feet high on the track, the conductor was too old a hand to begin a controversy. " Our time's fast," was all he said.

Sinclair rose and exclaimed, " Come on! " And the two, leaving the car, started up the track. The wrecking boss paid no attention to his companion as they forged ahead, but where the train had hit the curve he scanned the track as he would a blue print. "They'll have your scalp for this," he declared abruptly.

"I reckon they will."

"What's your name?"

"Stevens."

"Looks like all day for you, doesn't it? No matter; I guess I can help you out."

Where the merchandise cars lay, below the switch, the train crew knew that a tramp had been caught. At intervals they heard groans under the wreckage, which was piled high there. Sinclair stopped at the derrick, and the freight conductor went on to where his brakeman had enlisted two of Sinclair's giants to help get out the tramp. A brake beam had crushed the man's legs, and the pallor of his face showed that he was hurt internally, but he was conscious and moaned softly. The men had started to carry him to the way car when Sinclair came up, asked what they were doing, and ordered them back to the wreck. They hastily laid the tramp down. "But he wants water," protested a brakeman who was walking behind, carrying his arm in a sling.

"Water!" bawled Sinclair. "Have my men got nothing to do but carry a tramp to water? Get ahead there and help unload those refrigerators.

The Wrecking Boss

He'll find water fast enough. Let the damned hobo crawl down to the creek after it."

The tramp was too far gone for resentment; he had fainted when they laid him down, and his half-glazed eyes, staring at the sky, gave no evidence that he heard anything.

The sun rose hot, for in the Red Desert sky there is rarely a cloud. Sinclair took the little hill nearest the switch to bellow his orders from, running down among the men whenever necessary to help carry them out. Within thirty minutes, though apparently no impression had been made on the great heaps of wrenched and splintered equipment, Sinclair had the job in hand.

Work such as this was the man's genius. In handling a wreck Sinclair was a marvel among mountain men. He was tall but not stout, with flashing brown eyes and a strength always equal to that of the best man in his crew. But his inspiration lay in destruction, and the more complete the better. There were no futile moves under Sinclair's quick eyes, no useless pulling and hauling, no false grappling; but like a raven at a feast, every time his derrick-beak plucked at the wreck he brought something worth while away. Whether he was righting a tender, rerailing an engine, tearing out a car-body, or swinging a set of trucks into the clear, Sinclair, men said, had

Whispering Smith

luck, and no confusion in day or night was great enough to drown his heavy tones or blur his rapid thinking.

Just below where the wrecking boss stood lay the tramp. The sun scorched his drawn face, but he made no effort to turn from it. Sometimes he opened his eyes, but Sinclair was not a promising source of help, and no one that might have helped dared venture within speaking distance of the injured man. When the heat and the pain at last extorted a groan and an appeal, Sinclair turned. "Damn you, ain't you dead yet? What? Water?" He pointed to a butt standing in the shade of a car that had been thrown out near the switch. "There's water; go get it!" The cracking of a box car as the derrick wrenched it from the wreck was engaging the attention of the boss, and as he saw the grapple slip he yelled to his men and pointed to the chains.

The tramp lay still a long time. At last he began to drag himself toward the butt. In the glare of the sun timbers strained and snapped, and men with bars and axes chopped and wrenched at the massive frames and twisted iron on the track. The wrecking gang moved like ants in and out of the shapeless *débris,* and at intervals, as the sun rose higher, the tramp dragged himself nearer the butt. He lay on the burning sand like a crippled insect,

The Wrecking Boss

crawling, and waiting for strength to crawl. To him there was no railroad and no wreck, but only the blinding sun, the hot sand, the torture of thirst, and somewhere water, if he could reach it.

The freight conductor, Stevens, afraid of no man, had come up to speak to Sinclair, and Sinclair, with a smile, laid a cordial hand on his shoulder. " Stevens, it's all right. I'll get you out of this. Come here." He led the conductor down the track where they had walked in the morning. He pointed to flange-marks on the ties. " See there— there's where the first wheels left the track, and they left on the inside of the curve; a thin flange under the first refrigerator broke. I've got the wheel itself back there for evidence. They can't talk fast running against that. Damn a private car-line, anyway! Give me a cigar—haven't got any? Great guns, man, there's a case of Key Wests open up ahead; go fill your pockets and your grip. Don't be bashful; you've got friends on the division if you are Irish, eh? "

" Sure, only I don't smoke," said Stevens, with diplomacy.

" Well, you drink, don't you? There's a barrel of brandy open at the switch."

The brandy-cask stood up-ended near the water-butt, and the men dipped out of both with cups. They were working now half naked at the wreck.

Whispering Smith

The sun hung in a cloudless sky, the air was still, and along the right of way huge wrecking fires added to the scorching heat. Ten feet from the water-butt lay a flattened mass of rags. Crusted in smoke and blood and dirt, crushed by a vise of beams and wheels out of human semblance, and left now an aimless, twitching thing, the tramp clutched at Stevens's foot as he passed. " Water! "

" Hello, old boy, how the devil did you get here? " exclaimed Stevens, retreating in alarm.

" Water! "

Stevens stepped to the butt and filled a cup. The tramp's eyes were closed. Stevens poured the water over his face; then he lifted the man's head and put a cupful to his lips.

" Is that hobo alive yet? " asked Sinclair, coming back smoking a cigar. " What does he want now? Water? Don't waste any time on him."

" It's bad luck refusing water," muttered Stevens, holding the cup.

" He'll be dead in a minute," growled Sinclair. The sound of his voice roused the failing man to a fury. He opened his bloodshot eyes, and with the dregs of an ebbing vitality cursed Sinclair with a frenzy that made Stevens draw back. If Sinclair was startled he gave no sign. " Go to hell! " he exclaimed harshly.

With a ghastly effort the man made his retort.

8

The Wrecking Boss

He held up his blood-soaked fingers. " I'm going all right—I know that," he gasped, with a curse, " but I'll come back for you! "

Sinclair, unshaken, stood his ground. He repeated his imprecation more violently; but Stevens, swallowing, stole out of hearing. As he disappeared, a train whistled in the west.

CHAPTER II

KARG, Sinclair's crew foreman, came running over to him from a pile of merchandise that had been set off the right of way on the wagon-road for loot. " That's the superintendent's car coming, ain't it, Murray ? " he cried, looking across the creek at the approaching train.

" What of it ? " returned Sinclair.

" Why, we're just loading the team."

The incoming train, an engine with a way car, two flats, and the Bear Dance derrick, slowed up at one end of the wreck while Sinclair and his foreman talked. Three men could be seen getting out of the way car—McCloud and Reed Young, the Scotch roadmaster, and Bill Dancing. A gang of trackmen filed slowly out after them.

The leaders of the party made their way down the curve, and Sinclair, with Karg, met them at the point. McCloud asked questions about the wreck and the chances of getting the track clear, and while they talked Sinclair sent Karg to get the new derrick into action. Sinclair then asked McCloud to walk with him up the track to see where the cars had left the rail. The two men showed in contrast as they stepped along the ties. McCloud was not alone younger and below Sinclair's height: his broad Stetson hat flattened him somewhat. His movement was deliberate beside Sinclair's litheness, and his face, though burned by sun and wind, was boyish, while Sinclair's was strongly lined.

"Just a moment," suggested McCloud mildly, as Sinclair hastened past the goods piled in the wagon-road. "Whose team is that, Sinclair?" The road followed the right of way where they stood, and a four-horse team of heavy mules was pulling a loaded ranch-wagon up the grade when McCloud spoke.

Sinclair answered cordially. "That's my team from over on the Frenchman. I picked them up at Denver. Nice mules, McCloud, ain't they? Give me mules every time for heavy work. If I had just a hundred more of 'em the company could have my job—what?"

"Yes. What's that stuff they are hauling?"

"That's a little stuff mashed up in the merchandise car; there's some tobacco there and a little wine, I guess. The cases are all smashed."

"Let's look at it."

"Oh, there's nothing there that's any good, McCloud."

Whispering Smith

" Let's look at it."

As Bill Dancing and Young walked behind the two men toward the wagon, Dancing made extraordinary efforts to wink at the roadmaster. " That's a good story about the mules coming from Denver, ain't it? " he muttered. Young, unwilling to commit himself, stopped to light his pipe. When he and Dancing joined Sinclair and McCloud the talk between the superintendent and the wrecking boss had become animated.

" I always do something for my men out of a wreck when I can; that's the way I get the work out of them," Sinclair was saying. " A little stuff like this," he added, nodding toward the wagon, " comes handy for presents, and the company wouldn't get any salvage out of it, anyway. I get the value a dozen times over in quick work. Look there! " Sinclair pointed to where the naked men heaved and wrenched in the sun. " Where could you get white men to work like that if you didn't jolly them along once in a while? What? You haven't been here long, McCloud," smiled Sinclair, laying a hand with heavy affection on the young man's shoulder. " Ask any man on the division who gets the work out of his men—who gets the wrecks cleaned up and the track cleared. Ain't that what you want? "

" Certainly, Sinclair; no man that ever saw

12

you handle a wreck would undertake to do it better."

" Then what's all this fuss about? "

" We've been over all this matter before, as you know. The claim department won't stand for this looting; that's the whole story. Here are ten or twelve cases of champagne on your wagon— soiled a little, but worth a lot of money."

" That was a mistake loading that up; I admit it; it was Karg's carelessness."

" Here is one whole case of cigars and part of another," continued McCloud, climbing from one wheel to another of the wagon. " There is a thousand dollars in this load! I know you've got good men, Sinclair. If they are not getting paid as they should be, give them time and a half or double time, but put it in the pay checks. The freight loss and damage account increased two hundred per cent last year. No railroad company can keep that rate up and last, Sinclair."

" Hang the company! The claim agents are a pack of thieves," cried Sinclair. " Look here, Mc-Cloud, what's a pay check to a man that's sick, compared with a bottle of good wine? "

" When one of your men is sick and needs wine, let me know," returned McCloud; " I'll see that he gets it. Your men don't wear silk dresses, do they? " he asked, pointing to another case of goods

Whispering Smith

under the driver's seat. "Have that stuff all hauled back and loaded into a box car on track."

"Not by a damned sight!" exclaimed Sinclair. He turned to his ranch driver, Barney Rebstock. "You haul that stuff where you were told to haul it, Barney." Then, "you and I may as well have an understanding right here," he said, as McCloud walked to the head of the mules.

"By all means, and I'll begin by countermanding that order right now. Take your load straight back to that car," directed McCloud, pointing up the track. Barney, a ranch hand with a cigarette face looked surlily at McCloud.

Sinclair raised a finger at the boy. "You drive straight ahead where I told you to drive. I don't propose to have my affairs interfered with by you or anybody else, Mr. McCloud. You and I can settle this thing ourselves," he added, walking straight toward the superintendent.

"Get away from those mules!" yelled Barney at the same moment, cracking his whip.

McCloud's dull eyes hardly lightened as he looked at the driver. "Don't swing your whip this way, my boy," he said, laying hold quietly of the near bridle.

"Drop that bridle!" roared Sinclair.

"I'll drop your mules in their tracks if they move one foot forward. Dancing, unhook those

14

At Smoky Creek

traces," said McCloud peremptorily. "Dump the wire out of that wagon-box, Young." Then he turned to Sinclair and pointed to the wreck. "Get back to your work."

The sun marked the five men rooted for an instant on the hillside. Dancing jumped at the traces, Reed Young clambered over the wheel, and Sinclair, livid, faced McCloud. With a bitter denunciation of interlopers, claim agents, and "fresh" railroad men generally, Sinclair swore he would not go back to work, and a case of wine crashing to the ground infuriated him. He turned on his heel and started for the wreck. "Call off the men!" he yelled to Karg at the derrick. The foreman passed the word. The derrickmen, dropping their hooks and chains in some surprise, moved out of the wreckage. The axemen and laborers gathered around the foreman and followed him toward Sinclair.

"Boys," cried Sinclair, "we've got a new superintendent, a college guy. You know what they are; the company has tried 'em before. They draw the salaries and we do the work. This one down here now is making his little kick about the few pickings we get out of our jobs. You can go back to your work or you can stand right here with me till we get our rights. What?"

Half a dozen men began talking at once. The

15

Whispering Smith

derrickman from below, a hatchet-faced wiper, with the visor of a greasy cap cocked over his ear, stuck his head between the uprights and called out shrilly, " What's er matter, Murray? " and a few men laughed. Barney had deserted the mules. Dancing and Young, with small regard for loss or damage, were emptying the wagon like deckhands, for in a fight such as now appeared imminent, possession of the goods even on the ground seemed vital to prestige. McCloud waited only long enough to assure the emptying of the wagon, and then followed Sinclair to where he had assembled his men. " Sinclair, put your men back to work."

" Not till we know just how we stand," Sinclair answered insolently. He continued to speak, but McCloud turned to the men. " Boys, go back to your work. Your boss and I can settle our own differences. I'll see that you lose nothing by working hard."

" And you'll see we make nothing, won't you? " suggested Karg.

" I'll see that every man in the crew gets twice what is coming to him—all except you, Karg. I discharge you now. Sinclair, will you go back to work? "

" No! "

" Then take your time. Any men that want to

At Smoky Creek

go back to work may step over to the switch," added McCloud.

Not a man moved. Sinclair and Karg smiled at each other, and with no apparent embarrassment McCloud himself smiled. " I like to see men loyal to their bosses," he said good-naturedly. " I wouldn't give much for a man that wouldn't stick to his boss if he thought him right. But a question has come up here, boys, that must be settled once for all. This wreck-looting on the mountain division is going to stop—right here—at this particular wreck. On that point there is no room for discussion. Now, any man that agrees with me on that matter may step over here and I'll discuss with him any other grievance. If what I say about looting is a grievance, it can't be discussed. Is there any man that wants to come over? " No man stirred.

" Sinclair, you've got good men," continued McCloud, unmoved. " You are leading them into pretty deep water. There's a chance yet for you to get them out of serious trouble if you think as much of them as they do of you. Will you advise them to go back to work—all except Karg? "

Sinclair glared in high humor. " Oh, I couldn't do that! I'm discharged! " he protested, bowing low.

" I don't want to be over-hasty," returned Mc-

Whispering Smith

Cloud. " This is a serious business, as you know better than they do, and there will never be as good a time to fix it up as now. There is a chance for you, I say, Sinclair, to take hold if you want to now."

" Why, I'll take hold if you'll take your nose out of my business and agree to keep it out."

" Is there *any* man here that wants to go back to work for the company? " continued McCloud evenly. It was one man against thirty; McCloud saw there was not the shadow of a chance to win the strikers over. " This lets all of you out, you understand, boys," he added; " and you can never work again for the company on this division if you don't take hold now."

" Boys," exclaimed Sinclair, better-humored every moment, " I'll guarantee you work on this division when all the fresh superintendents are run out of the country, and I'll lay this matter before Bucks himself, and don't you forget it ! "

" You will have a chilly job of it," interposed McCloud.

" So will you, my hearty, before you get trains running past here," retorted the wrecking boss. " Come on, boys."

The disaffected men drew off. The emptied wagon, its load scattered on the ground, stood deserted on the hillside, and the mules drooped in the

18

heat. Bill Dancing, a giant and a dangerous one, stood lone guard over the loot, and Young had been called over by McCloud. " How many men have you got with you, Reed? "

" Eleven."

" How long will it take them to clean up this mess with what help we can run in this afternoon? "

Young studied the prospect before replying. " They're green at this sort of thing, of course; they might be fussing here till to-morrow noon, I'm afraid; perhaps till to-morrow night, Mr. Mc-Cloud."

" That won't do! " The two men stood for a moment in a study. " The merchandise is all unloaded, isn't it? " said McCloud reflectively. " Get your men here and bring a water-bucket with you."

McCloud walked down to the engine of the wrecking train and gave orders to the train and engine crews. The best of the refrigerator cars had been rerailed, and they were pulled to a safe distance from the wreck. Young brought the bucket, and McCloud pointed to the caskful of brandy. " Throw that brandy over the wreckage, Reed."

The roadmaster started. " Burn the whole thing up, eh? "

" Everything on the track."

Whispering Smith

"Bully! It's a shame to waste the liquor, but it's Sinclair's fault. Here, boys, scatter this stuff where it will catch good, and touch her off. Everything goes—the whole pile. Burn up everything; that's orders. If you can get a few rails here, now, I'll give you a track by sundown, Mr. McCloud, in spite of Sinclair and the devil."

The remains of many cars lay in heaps along the curve, and the trackmen like firebugs ran in and out of them. A tongue of flame leaped from the middle of a pile of stock cars. In five minutes the wreck was burning; in ten minutes the flames were crackling fiercely; then in another instant the wreck burst into a conflagration that rose hissing and seething a hundred feet straight up in the air.

From where they stood, Sinclair's men looked on. They were nonplussed, but their boss had not lost his nerve. He walked back to McCloud. "You're going to send us back to Medicine Bend with the car, I suppose?"

McCloud spoke amiably. "Not on your life. Take your personal stuff out of the car and tell your men to take theirs; then get off the train and off the right of way."

"Going to turn us loose on Red Desert, are you?" asked Sinclair steadily.

"You've turned yourselves loose."

"Wouldn't give a man a tie-pass, would you?"

At Smoky Creek

" Come to my office in Medicine Bend and I'll talk to you about it," returned McCloud impassively.

" Well, boys," roared Sinclair, going back to his followers, " we can't ride on this road now! But I want to tell you there's something to eat for every one of you over at my place on the Crawling Stone, and a place to sleep—and something to drink," he added, cursing McCloud once more. The superintendent eyed him, but made no response. Sinclair led his men to the wagon, and they piled into it till the box was filled. Barney Rebstock had the reins again, and the mules groaned as the whip cracked. Those that could not climb into the wagon as it moved off straggled along behind, and the air was filled with cheers and curses.

The wreck burned furiously, and the column of black smoke shot straight up. Sinclair, as his cavalcade moved over the hill, followed on foot, grimly. He was the last to cross the divide that shut the scene on the track away from the striking wreckers, and as he reached the crest he paused and looked back, standing for a moment like a statue outlined in the vivid sunshine. For all his bravado, something told him he should never handle another wreck on the mountain division—that he stood a king dethroned. Uninviting enough to many men, this had been his kingdom, and he loved the power it gave him. He had run it like many a reckless potentate, but no one could say he had not been royal in his work as well as in his looting. It was impossible not to admire the man, his tremendous capacity, his extraordinary power as a leader; and no one liked his better traits more than McCloud himself. But Sinclair never loved McCloud. Long afterward he told Whispering Smith that he made his first mistake in a long and desperate game in not killing McCloud when he laid his hand that morning on the bridle of the mules; it would have been easy then. Sinclair might have been thinking of it even as he stood looking back. But he stood only for a moment, then turned and passed over the hill.

CHAPTER III

DICKSIE

THE wreckers, drifting in the blaze of the sun across the broad alkali valley, saw the smoke of the wreck-fire behind them. No breath of wind stirred it. With the stillness of a signal column it rose, thin and black, and high in the air spread motionless, like a huge umbrella, above Smoky Creek. Reed Young had gone with an engine to wire reënforcements, and McCloud, active among the trackmen until the conflagration spent itself, had retired to the shade of the hill.

Reclining against a rock with his legs crossed, he had clasped his hands behind his head and sat looking at the iron writhing in the dying heat of the fire. The sound of hoofs aroused him, and looking below he saw a horsewoman reining up near his men at the wreck. She rode an American horse, thin and rangy, and the experienced way in which she checked him drew him back almost to his haunches. But McCloud's eyes were fixed on the slender figure of the rider. He was wholly at a loss to account, at such a time and in such a

Whispering Smith

place, for a visitor in gauntleted gloves and a banded Panama hat. He studied her with growing amazement. Her hair coiled low on her neck supported the very free roll of the hat-brim. Her black riding-skirt clung to her waist to form its own girdle, and her white stock, rolled high on her neck, rose above a heavy shirtwaist of white linen, and gave her an air of confident erectness. The trackmen stopped work to look, but her attitude in their gaze was one of impatience rather than of embarrassment. Her boot flashed in the stirrup while she spoke to the nearest man, and her horse stretched his neck and nosed the brown alkali-grass that spread thinly along the road.

To McCloud she was something like an apparition. He sat spellbound until the trackman indiscreetly pointed him out, and the eyes of the visitor, turning his way, caught him with his hands on the rock in an attitude openly curious. She turned immediately away, but McCloud rose and started down the hill. The horse's head was pulled up, and there were signs of departure. He quickened his steps. Once he saw, or thought he saw, the rider's head so turned that her eyes might have commanded one approaching from his quarter; yet he could catch no further glimpse of her face. A second surprise awaited him. Just as she seemed about to ride away, she dropped lightly from the

24

horse to the ground, and he saw how confident in figure she was. As she began to try her saddle-girths, McCloud attempted a greeting. She could not ignore his hat, held rather high above his head as he approached, but she gave him the slightest nod in return—one that made no attempt to explain why she was there or where she had come from.

"Pardon me," ventured McCloud, "have you lost your way?"

He was immediately conscious that he had said the wrong thing. The expression of her eyes implied that it was foolish to suppose she was lost, but she only answered, "I saw the smoke and feared the bridge was on fire."

Something in her voice made him almost sorry he had intervened; if she stood in need of help of any sort it was not apparent, and her gaze was confusing. He became conscious that he was at the worst for an inspection; his face felt streaky with smoke, his hat and shirt had suffered severely in directing the fire, and his hands were black. He said to himself in revenge that she was not pretty, despite the fact that she seemed completely to take away his consequence. He felt, while she inspected him, like a brakeman.

"I presume Mr. Sinclair is here?" she said presently.

"I am sorry to say he is not."

Whispering Smith

" He usually has charge of the wrecks, I think. What a dreadful fire!" she murmured, looking down the track. She stood beside the horse with one hand resting on her girdle. Around the hand that held the bridle her quirt lay coiled in the folds of her glove, and, though seemingly undecided as to what to do, her composure did not lessen. As she looked at the wreckage, a breath of wind lifted the hair that curled around her ear. The mountain wind playing on her neck had left it brown, and above, the pulse of her ride rose red in her cheek. " Was it a passenger wreck?" She turned abruptly on McCloud to ask the question. Her eyes were brown, too, he saw, and a doubt assailed him. Was she pretty?

" Only a freight wreck," he answered.

" I thought if there were passengers hurt I could send help from the ranch. Were you the conductor?"

" Fortunately not."

" And no one was hurt?"

" Only a tramp. We are burning the wreck to clear the track."

" From the divide it looked like a mountain on fire. I'm sorry Mr. Sinclair is not here."

" Why, indeed, yes, so am I."

" Because I know him. You are one of his men, I presume."

"And whom may I say the message is from?"

Dicksie

"Not exactly; but is there anything I can do——"

"Oh, thank you, nothing, except that you might tell him the pretty bay colt he sent over to us has sprung his shoulder."

"He will be sorry to hear it, I'm sure."

"But we are doing everything possible for him. He is going to make a perfectly lovely horse."

"And whom may I say the message is from?" Though disconcerted, McCloud was regaining his wits. He felt perfectly certain there was no danger, if she knew Sinclair and lived in the mountains, but that she would sometime find out he was not a conductor. When he asked his question she appeared slightly surprised and answered easily, "Mr. Sinclair will know it is from Dicksie Dunning."

McCloud knew her then. Every one knew Dicksie Dunning in the high country. This was Dicksie Dunning of the great Crawling Stone ranch, most widely known of all the mountain ranches. While his stupidity in not guessing her identity before overwhelmed him, he resolved to exhaust the last effort to win her interest.

"I don't know just when I shall see Mr. Sinclair," he answered gravely, "but he shall certainly have your message."

A doubt seemed to steal over Dicksie at the

Whispering Smith

change in McCloud's manner. " Oh, pardon me
—I thought you were working for the company."

" You are quite right, I am; but Mr. Sinclair is
not."

Her eyebrows rose a little. " I think you are
mistaken, aren't you? "

" It is possible I am; but if he is working for the
company, it is pretty certain that I am not," he continued, heaping mystification on her. " However,
that will not prevent my delivering the message.
By the way, may I ask which shoulder? "

" Shoulder! "

" Which shoulder is sprung."

" Oh, of course! The right shoulder, and it is
sprung pretty badly, too, Cousin Lance says. How
very stupid of me to ride over here for a freight
wreck! "

McCloud felt humiliated at having nothing better worth while to offer. " It was a very bad one,"
he ventured.

" But not of the kind I can be of any help at, I
fear."

McCloud smiled. " We are certainly short of
help."

Dicksie brought her horse's head around. She
felt again of the girth as she replied, " Not such
as I can supply, I'm afraid." And with the words
she stepped away, as if preparing to mount.

28

Dicksie

McCloud intervened. " I hope you won't go away without resting your horse. The sun is so hot. Mayn't I offer you some sort of refreshment? "

Dicksie Dunning thought not.

" The sun is very warm," persisted McCloud.

Dicksie smoothed her gauntlet in the assured manner natural to her. " I am pretty well used to it."

But McCloud held on. " Several cars of fruit were destroyed in the wreck. I can offer you any quantity of grapes—crates of them are spoiling over there—and pears."

" Thank you, I am just from luncheon."

" And I have cooled water in the car. I hope you won't refuse that, so far out in the desert."

Dicksie laughed a little. " Do you call this far? I don't; and I don't call this desert by any means. Thank you ever so much for the water, but I'm not in the least thirsty."

" It was kind of you even to think of extending help. I wish you would let me send some fruit over to your ranch. It is only spoiling here."

Dicksie stroked the neck of her horse. " It is about eighteen miles to the ranch house."

" I don't call that far."

" Oh, it isn't," she returned hastily, professing not to notice the look that went with the words,

" except for perishable things ! " Then, as if ac-
knowledging her disadvantage, she added, swinging her bridle rein around, " I am under obliga-
tions for the offer, just the same."

" At least, won't you let your horse drink ? "
McCloud threw the force of an appeal into his
words, and Dicksie stopped her preparations and
appeared to waver.

" Jim *is* pretty thirsty, I suppose. Have you
plenty of water ? "

" A tender full. Had I better lead him down
while you wait up on the hill in the shade ? "

" Can't I ride him down ? "

" It would be pretty rough riding."

" Oh, Jim goes anywhere," she said, with her
attractive indifference to situations. " If you don't
mind helping me mount."

" With pleasure."

She stood waiting for his hand, and McCloud
stood, not knowing just what to do. She glanced
at him expectantly. The sun grew intensely hot.

" You will have to show me how," he stammered
at last.

" Don't you know ? "

He mentally cursed the technical education that
left him helpless at such a moment, but it was useless to pretend. " Frankly, I don't ! "

" Just give me your hand. Oh, not in that way !

Dicksie

But never mind, I'll walk," she suggested, catching up her skirt.

" The rocks will cut your boots all to pieces. Suppose you tell me what to do this once," he said, assuming some confidence. " I'll never forget."

" Why, if you will just give me your hand for my foot, I can manage, you know."

He did not know, but she lifted her skirt graciously, and her crushed boot rested easily for a moment in his hand. She rose in the air above him before he could well comprehend. He felt the quick spring from his supporting hand, and it was an instant of exhilaration. Then she balanced herself with a flushed laugh in the saddle, and he guided her ahead among the loose rocks, the horse nosing at his elbow as they picked their way.

Crossing the track, they gained better ground. As they reached the switch and passed a box car, Jim shied, and Dicksie spoke sharply to him. McCloud turned.

In the shade of the car lay the tramp.

" That man lying there frightened him," explained Dicksie. " Oh," she exclaimed suddenly, " he has been hurt ! " She turned away her head. " Is that the man who was in the wreck? "

" Yes."

" Do something for him. He must be suffering terribly."

Whispering Smith

"The men gave him some water awhile ago, and when we moved him into the shade we thought he was dead."

"He isn't dead yet!" Dicksie's face, still averted, had grown white. "I saw him move. Can't you do something for him?"

She reined up at a little distance. McCloud bent over the man a moment and spoke to him. When he rose he called to the men on the track. "You are right," he said, rejoining Dicksie; "he is very much alive. His name is Wickwire; he is a cowboy."

"A cowboy!"

"A tramp cowboy."

"What can you do with him?"

"I'll have the men put him in the caboose and send him to Barnhardt's hospital at Medicine Bend when the engine comes back. He may live yet. If he does, he can thank you for it."

CHAPTER IV

GEORGE McCLOUD

McCLOUD was an exception to every tradition that goes to make up a mountain railroad man. He was from New England, with a mild voice and a hand that roughened very slowly. McCloud was a classmate of Morris Blood's at the Boston " Tech," and the acquaintance begun there continued after the two left school, with a scattering fire of letters between the mountains and New England, as few and as far between as men's letters usually scatter after an ardent school acquaintance.

There were just two boys in the McCloud family—John and George. One had always been intended for the church, the other for science. Somehow the boys got mixed in their cradles, or, what is the same matter, in their assignments, and John got into the church. For George, who ought to have been a clergyman, nothing was left but a long engineering course for which, after he got it, he appeared to have no use. However, it seemed a little late to shift the life alignments. John had

33

Whispering Smith

the pulpit and appeared disposed to keep it, and George was left, like a New England farm, to wonder what had become of himself.

It is, nevertheless, odd how matters come about. John McCloud, a prosperous young clergyman, stopped on a California trip at Medicine Bend to see brother George's classmate and something of a real Western town. He saw nothing sensational —it was there, but he did not see it—but he found both hospitality and gentlemen, and, if surprised, was too well-bred to admit it. His one-day stop ran on to several days. He was a guest at the Medicine Bend Club, where he found men who had not forgotten the Harvard Greek plays. He rode in private cars and ate antelope steak grilled by Glover's own darky boy, who had roasted buffalo hump for the Grand Duke Alexis as far back as 1871, and still hashed his browned potatoes in ragtime; and with the sun breaking clear over the frosty table-lands, a ravenous appetite, and a day's shooting in prospect, the rhythm had a particularly cheerful sound. John was asked to occupy a Medicine Bend pulpit, and before Sunday the fame of his laugh and his marksmanship had spread so far that Henry Markover, the Yale cowboy, rode in thirty-two miles to hear him preach. In leaving, John McCloud, in a seventh heaven of enthusiasm over the high country, asked Morris Blood

George McCloud

why he could not find something for George out there; and Blood, not even knowing the boy wanted to come, wrote for him, and asked Bucks to give him a job. Possibly, being over-solicitous, George was nervous when he talked to Bucks; possibly the impression left by his big, strong, bluff brother John made against the boy; at all events, Bucks, after he talked with George, shook his head. " I could make a first-class railroad man out of the preacher, Morris, but not out of the brother. Yes, I've talked with him. He can't do anything but figure elevations, and, by heaven, we can't feed our own engineers here now." So George found himself stranded in the mountains.

Morris Blood was cut up over it, but George McCloud took it quietly. " I'm no worse off here than I was back there, Morris." Blood, at that, plucked up courage to ask George to take a job in the Cold Springs mines, and George jumped at it. It was impossible to get a white man to live at Cold Springs after he could save money enough to get away, so George was welcomed as assistant superintendent at the Number Eight Mine, with no salary to speak of and all the work.

In one year everybody had forgotten him. Western men, on the average, show a higher heart temperature than Eastern men, but they are tolerably busy people and have their own troubles.

Whispering Smith

"Be patient," Morris Blood had said to him. "Sometime there will be more railroad work in these mountains; then, perhaps, your darned engineering may come into play. I wish you knew how to sell cigars."

Meantime, McCloud stuck to the mine, and insensibly replaced his Eastern tissue with Western. In New England he had been carefully moulded by several generations of gentlemen, but never baked hard. The mountains put the crust on him. For one thing, the sun and wind, best of all hemlocks, tanned his white skin into a tough all-American leather, seasoned his muscles into rawhide sinews, and, without burdening him with an extra ounce of flesh, sprinkled the red through his blood till, though thin, he looked apoplectic.

Insensibly, too, something else came about. George McCloud developed the rarest of all gifts of temperament, even among men of action—the ability to handle men. In Cold Springs, indeed, it was a case either of handling or of being handled. McCloud got along with his men and, with the tough element among them, usually through persuasion; but he proved, too, that he could inspire confidence even with a club.

One day, coming down "special" from Bear Dance, Gordon Smith, who bore the nickname Whispering Smith, rode with President Bucks in

George McCloud

the privacy of his car. The day had been long, and the alkali lay light on the desert. The business in hand had been canvassed, and the troubles put aside for chicken, coffee, and cigars, when Smith, who did not smoke, told the story of something he had seen the day before at Cold Springs that pleased him.

The men in the Number Eight Mine had determined to get rid of some Italians, and after a good deal of rowing had started in to catch one of them and hang him. They had chosen a time when McCloud, the assistant superintendent of the mine, was down with mountain fever. It was he who had put the Italians into the mine. He had already defended them from injury, and would be likely, it was known, to do so again if he were able. On this day a mob had been chasing the Dagos, and had at length captured one. They were running him down street to a telegraph pole when the assistant superintendent appeared in scant attire and stopped them. Taking advantage of the momentary confusion, he hustled their victim into the only place of refuge at hand, a billiard hall. The mob rushed the hall. In the farthest corner the unlucky Italian, bleeding like a bullock and insane with fright, knelt, clinging to McCloud's shaky knees. In trying to make the back door the two had been cut off, and the sick boss had got into a corner behind a pool-table to make his stand.

37

Whispering Smith

In his pocket he had a pistol, knowing that to use it meant death to him as well as to the wretch he was trying to save. Fifty men were yelling in the room. They had rope, hatchets, a sprinkling of guns, and whiskey enough to burn the town, and in the corner behind a pool-table stood the mining boss with mountain fever, the Dago, and a broken billiard-cue.

Bucks took the cigar from his mouth, leaned forward in his chair, and stretched his heavy chin out of his neck as if the situation now promised a story. The leader, Smith continued, was the mine blacksmith, a strapping Welshman, from whom McCloud had taken the Italian in the street. The blacksmith had a revolver, and was crazy with liquor. McCloud singled him out in the crowd, pointed a finger at him, got the attention of the men, and lashed him across the table with his tongue until the blacksmith opened fire on him with his revolver, McCloud all the while shaking his finger at him and abusing him like a pickpocket. "The crowd couldn't believe its eyes," Gordon Smith concluded, "and McCloud was pushing for the blacksmith with his cue when Kennedy and I squirmed through to the front and relieved the tension. McCloud wasn't hit."

"What is that mining man's name?" asked Bucks, reaching for a message clip.

George McCloud

" McCloud."

" First name? " continued Bucks mechanically.

" George."

Bucks looked at his companion in surprise.
Then he spoke, and a feeling of self-abasement
was reflected in his words. " George McCloud,"
he echoed. " Did you say George? Why, I must
know that man. I turned him down once for a
job. He looked so peaceable I thought he was
too soft for us." The president laid down his cigar
with a gesture of disgust. " And yet there really
are people along this line that think I'm clever. I
haven't judgment enough to operate a trolley car.
It's a shame to take the money they give me for
running this system, Gordon. Hanged if I didn't
think that fellow was too soft." He called the
flagman over. " Tell Whitmyer we will stay at
Cold Springs to-night."

" I thought you were going through to Medicine
Bend," suggested Smith as the trainman disappeared.

" McCloud," repeated Bucks, taking up his
cigar and throwing back his head in a cloud of
smoke.

" Yes," assented his companion; " but I am
going through to Medicine Bend, Mr. Bucks."

" Do."

" How am I to do it? "

Whispering Smith

" Take the car and send it back to-morrow on Number Three."

" Thank you, if you won't need it to-night."

" I sha'n't. I am going to stay at Cold Springs to-night and hunt up McCloud."

" But that man is in bed in a very bad way; you can't see him. He is going to die."

" No, he isn't. I am going to hunt him up and have him taken care of."

That night Bucks, in the twilight, was sitting by McCloud's bed, smoking and looking him over. " Don't mind me," he said when he entered the room, lifted the ill-smelling lamp from the table, and, without taking time to blow it out, pitched it through the open window. " I heard you were sick, and just looked in to see how they were taking care of you. Wilcox," he added, turning to the nurse he had brought in—a barber who wanted to be a railroad man, and had agreed to step into the breach and nurse McCloud—"have a box of miner's candles sent up from the roundhouse. We have some down there; if not, buy a box and send me the bill."

McCloud, who after the rioting had crawled back to bed with a temperature of 105 degrees, knew the barber, but felt sure that a lunatic had wandered in with him, and immediately bent his feeble mental energies on plans for getting rid of

George McCloud

a dangerous man. When Bucks sat down by him and continued talking at the nurse, McCloud caught nothing of what was said until Bucks turned quietly toward him. " They tell me, McCloud, you have the fever."

The sick man, staring with sunken eyes, rose half on his elbow in astonishment to look again at his visitor, but Bucks eased him back with an admonition to guard his strength. McCloud's temperature had already risen with the excitement of seeing a man throw his lamp out of the window. Bucks, meantime, working carefully to seem unconcerned and incensing McCloud with great clouds of smoke, tried to discuss his case with him as he had already done with the mine surgeon. McCloud, thinking it best to humor a crazy man, responded quietly. " The doctor said yesterday," he explained, " it was mountain fever, and he wants to put me into an ice-pack."

Bucks objected vigorously to the ice-pack.

" The doctor tells me that it is the latest treatment for that class of fevers in the Prussian army," answered McCloud feebly, but getting interested in spite of himself.

" That's a good thing, no doubt, for the Prussian army," replied Bucks, " but, McCloud, in the first place, you are not a Dutchman; in the second,

Whispering Smith

you have not got mountain fever—not in my judgment."

McCloud, confident now that he had an insane man on his hands, held his peace.

"Not a symptom of mountain fever," continued Bucks calmly; "you have what looks to me like gastritis, but the homeopaths," he added, "have a better name for it. Is it stomatitis, McCloud? I forget."

The sick man, confounded by such learning, determined to try one question, and, if he was at fault, to drag his gun from under his pillow and sell his life as dearly as possible. Summoning his waning strength, he looked hard at Bucks. "Just let me ask you one question. I never saw you before. Are you a doctor?"

"No, I'm a railroad man; my name is Bucks." McCloud rose half up in bed with amazement. "They'll kill you if you lie here a week," continued Bucks. "In just a week. Now I'll tell you my plan. I'll take you down in the morning in my car to Medicine Bend; this barber will go with us. There in the hospital you can get everything you need, and I can make you comfortable. What do you say?"

McCloud looked at his benefactor solemnly, but if hope flickered for an instant in his eyes it soon died. Bucks said afterward that he looked like a

George McCloud

cold-storage squab, just pinfeathers and legs. "Shave him clean," said he, " and you could have counted his teeth through his cheeks."

The sick man turned his face to the wall. " It's kind enough," he muttered, " but I guess it's too late."

Bucks did not speak for some time. Twilight had faded above the hills, and only the candle lighted the room. Then the master of mountain men, grizzled and brown, turned his eyes again to the bed. McCloud was staring at the ceiling. " We have a town of your name down on the plains, McCloud," said Bucks, blowing away the cigar smoke after the long silence. " It is one of our division points, and a good one."

" I know the town," responded McCloud. " It was named after one of our family."

" I guess not."

" It was, though," said McCloud wearily.

" I think," returned Bucks, " you must be mistaken. The man that town was named after belonged to the fighting McClouds."

" That is my family."

" Then where is your fight? When I propose to put you into my car and pull you out of this, why do you say it is too late? It is never too late."

McCloud made no answer, and Bucks ran on: " For a man that worked out as well as you did

43

yesterday in a trial heat with a billiard-cue, I should say you could turn a handspring or two yet if you had to. For that matter, if you don't want to be moved, I can run a spur in here to your door in three hours in the morning. By taking out the side-wall we can back the car right up to the bed. Why not? Or we can stick a few hydraulic jacks under the sills, raise the house, and push your bed right on the observation platform." He got Mc-Cloud to laughing, and lighted a fresh cigar. A framed photograph hung on one of the bare walls of the room, and it caught the eye of the railroad man. He walked close to it, disinfected it with smoke, brushed the dust from the glass, and examined the print. " That looks like old Van Dyne College campus, hanged if it doesn't! "

McCloud was watching him. " It is a photograph of the campus."

" McCloud, are you a Van Dyne man? "

" I did my college work there before I went to Boston."

Bucks stood motionless. " Poor little old Van Dyne! Why, my brother Sam taught at Van Dyne. No, you would not have known him; he's dead. Never before west of the Missouri River have I seen a Van Dyne man. You are the first." He shook his head as he sat down again. " It is crowded out now: no money, no prestige, half-

44

George McCloud

starved professors with their elbows out, the president working like a dog all the week and preaching somewhere every Sunday to earn five dollars. But, by Heaven, they turned out men! Did you know Bug Robinson?" he asked suddenly.

" He gave me my degree."

" Old Bug! He was Sam's closest friend, McCloud. It's good to see him getting the recognition he deserves, isn't it? Do you know, I send him an annual every year? Yes, sir! And one year I had the whole blooming faculty out here on a fossil expedition; but, by Heaven, McCloud, some of them looked more like megatheriums than what they dug up did."

" I heard about that expedition."

" I never got to college. I had to hustle. I'll get out of here before I tire you. Wilcox will be here all night, and my China boy is making some broth for you now. You'll feel better in the morning."

Ten weeks later McCloud was sent from Medicine Bend up on the Short Line as trainmaster, and on the Short Line he learned railroading.

" That's how I came here," said George McCloud to Farrell Kennedy a long time afterward, at Medicine Bend. " I had shrivelled and starved three years out there in the desert. I lived with those cattle underground till I had forgotten my

Whispering Smith

own people, my own name, my own face—and
Bucks came along one day with Whispering Smith
and dragged me out of my coffin. They had it ordered, and it being a small size and ' onhandy,' as
the undertaker said, I paid for it and told him to
store it for me. Well, do you think I ever could
forget either of those men, Farrell ? "

McCloud's fortunes thus threw him first into the
operating department of the mountain lines, but
his heart was in the grades and the curves. To him
the interest in the trainwork was the work of the
locomotives toiling with the heavy loads up the
canyons and across the uneven plateaus and through
the deep gorges of the inner range, where the pant-
ing exhaust, choked between sheer granite walls,
roared in a mighty protest against the burden put
by the steep grades on the patient machines.

In all the group of young men then on the mountain division, obscure and unknown at the time, but
destined within so few years to be scattered far and
wide as constructionists with records made in the
rebuilding operations through the Rocky Mountains, none was less likely to attract attention than
McCloud. Bucks, who, indeed, could hardly be
reckoned so much of the company as its head, was
a man of commanding proportions physically.
Like Glover, Bucks was a giant in stature, and
the two men, when together, could nowhere escape

George McCloud

notice; they looked, in a word, their part, fitted to cope with the tremendous undertakings that had fallen to their lot. Callahan, the chess-player on the Overland lines, the man who could hold large combinations of traffic movement constantly in his head and by intuition reach the result of a given problem before other men could work it out, was, like Morris Blood, the master of tonnage, of middle age. But McCloud, when he went to the mountain division, in youthfulness of features was boyish, and when he left he was still a boy, bronzed, but young of face in spite of a lifetime's pressure and worry crowded into three years. He himself counted this physical make-up as a disadvantage. " It has embroiled me in no end of trouble, because I couldn't convince men I was in earnest until I made good in some hard way," he complained once to Whispering Smith. " I never could acquire even a successful habit of swearing, so I had to learn to fight."

When, one day in Boney Street in Medicine Bend, he threw open the door of Marion Sinclair's shop, flung his hat sailing along the show-case with his war-cry, and called to her in the back rooms, she thought he had merely run in to say he was in town.

" How do you do? What do you think? You're going to have an old boarder back," he cried. "I'm coming to Medicine Bend, superintendent of the division!"

"Mr. McCloud!" Marion Sinclair clasped her hands and dropped into a chair. "Have they made you superintendent already?"

"Well, I like that! Do you want them to wait till I'm gray-headed?"

Marion threw her hands to her own head. "Oh, don't say anything about gray hairs. My head won't bear inspection. But I can't get over this promotion coming so soon—this whole big division! Well, I congratulate you very sincerely——"

"Oh, but that isn't it! I suppose anybody will congratulate me. But where am I to board? Have you a cook? You know how I went from bad to worse after you left Cold Springs. May I have my meals here with you as I used to there?"

"Why, I suppose you can, yes, if you can stand the cooking. I have an apprentice, Mr. Dancing's daughter, who does. pretty well. She lives here with me, and is learning the business. But I sha'n't take as much as you used to pay me, for I'm doing so much better down here."

"Let me run that end of it, will you? I shall be doing better down here myself."

They laughed as they bantered. Marion Sinclair wore gold spectacles, but they did not hide the

George McCloud

delightful good-nature in her eyes. On the third finger of her slender left hand she wore, too, a gold band that explained the gray in her hair at twenty-six.

This was the wife of Murray Sinclair, whom he had brought to the mountains from her far-away Wisconsin home. Within a year he had broken her heart so far as it lay in him to do it, but he could not break her charm nor her spirit. She was too proud to go back, when forced to leave him, and had set about earning her own living in the country to which she had come as a bride. She put on spectacles, she mutilated her heavy brown hair and to escape notice and secure the obscurity that she craved, her name, Marion, became, over the door of her millinery shop and in her business, only " M. Sinclair."

Cold Springs, where Sinclair had first brought her when he had headquarters there as foreman of bridges, had proved a hopeless place for the millinery business—at least, in the way that Marion ran it. The women that had husbands had no money to buy hats with, and the women without husbands wore gaudy headgear, and were of the kind that made Marion's heart creep when they opened the shop door. What was worse, they were inclined to joke with her, as if there must be a community of interest between a deserted woman and women who

49

had deserted womanhood. To this business Marion would not cater, and in consequence her millinery affairs sometimes approached collapse. She could, however, cook extraordinarily well, and, with the aid of a servant-maid, could always provide for a boarder or two—perhaps a railroad man or a mine superintendent to whom she could serve meals, and who, like all mountain men, were more than generous in their accounting with women. Among these standbys of hers was McCloud. McCloud had always been her friend, and when she left Cold Springs and moved to Medicine Bend to set up her little shop in Boney Street near Fort, she had lost him. Yet somehow, to compensate Marion for other cruel things in the mountains, Providence seemed to raise up a new friend for her wherever she went. In Medicine Bend she did not know a soul, but almost the first customer that walked into her shop—and she was a customer worth while—was Dicksie Dunning of the Crawling Stone.

CHAPTER V

THE CRAWLING STONE

WHERE the mountain chains of North America have been flung up into a continental divide, the country in many of its aspects is still terrible. In extent alone this mountain empire is grandiose. The swiftest transcontinental trains approaching its boundaries at night find night falling again before they have fairly penetrated it. Geologically severe, this region in geological store is the richest of the continent; physically forbidding beyond all other stretches of North America, the Barren Land alone excepted, in this region lie its gentlest valleys. Here the desert is most grotesque, and here are pastoral retreats the most secluded. It is the home of the Archean granite, and its basins are of a fathomless dust. Under its sagebrush wastes the skeletons of earth's hugest mammals lie beside behemoth and the monsters of the deep. The eternal snow, the granite peak, the sandstone butte, the lava-bed, the gray desert, the far horizon are familiar here. With the sunniest and bluest of skies, this is the range of the deadliest storms, and its delightful summers contrast with the dreadest cold.

Here the desert of death simulates a field of cooling snow, green hills lie black in the dazzling light of day, limpid waters run green over arsenic stone, and sunset betricks the fantastic rock with column and capital and dome. Clouds burst here above arid wastes, and where dew is precious the skies are most prodigal in their downpour. If the torrent bed is dry, distrust it.

This vast mountain shed parts rivers whose waters find two oceans, and their valleys are the natural highways up which railroads wind to the crest of the continent. To the mountain engineer the waterway is the sphinx that holds in its silence the riddle of his success; with him lies the problem of providing a railway across ranges which often defy the hoofs of a horse.

The construction engineer studies the course of the mountain water. The water is both his ally and his enemy—ally because it alone has made possible his undertakings; enemy because it fights to destroy his puny work, just as it fights to level the barriers that oppose him. Like acid spread on copperplate, water etches the canyons in the mountain slopes and spreads wide the valleys through the plains. Among these scarcely known ranges of the Rocky Mountain chain the Western rivers

The Crawling Stone

have their beginnings. When white men crowded the Indian from the plains he retreated to the mountains, and in their valleys made his final stand against the aggressor. The scroll of this invasion of the mountain West by the white man has been unrolled, read, and put away within a hundred years, and of the agencies that made possible the swiftness of the story transportation overshadows all others. The first railroad put across those mountains cost twenty-five thousand miles of reconnoissances and fifteen thousand miles of instrument surveys. Since the day of that undertaking a generation of men has passed, and in the interval the wilderness that those men penetrated has been transformed. The Indian no longer extorts terms from his foe: he is not.

Where the tepee stood the rodman drives his stakes, and the country of the great Indian rivers, save one, has been opened for years to the railroad. That one is the Crawling Stone. The valley of Crawling Stone River marked for more than a decade the dead line between the Overland Route of the white man and the last country of the Sioux. It was long after the building of the first line before even an engineer's reconnoissance was made in the Crawling Stone country. Then, within ten years, three surveys were made, two on the north side of the river and one on the south

53

Whispering Smith

side, by interests seeking a coast outlet. Three
reports made in this way gave varying estimates of
the expense of putting a line up the valley, but
the three coincided in this, that the cost would
be prohibitive. Engineers of reputation had in
this respect agreed, but Glover, who looked after
such work for Bucks, remained unconvinced, and
before McCloud was put into the operating department on the Short Line he was asked by Glover to
run a preliminary up Crawling Stone Valley. Before the date of his report the conclusions reached
by other engineers had stood unchallenged.

The valley was not unknown to McCloud.
His first year in the mountains, in which, fitted as
thoroughly as he could fit himself for his profes-
sion, he had come West and found himself unable
to get work, had been spent hunting, fishing, and
wandering, often cold and often hungry, in the
upper Crawling Stone country. The valley in
itself offers to a constructionist no insuperable
obstacles; the difficulty is presented in the canyon
where the river bursts through the Elbow Mountains. South of this canyon, McCloud, one day on
a hunting trip, found himself with two Indians
pocketed in the rough country, and was planning
how to escape passing a night away from camp
when his companions led him past a vertical wall
of rock a thousand feet high, split into a narrow

54

The Crawling Stone

defile down which they rode, as it broadened out, for miles. They emerged upon an open country that led without a break into the valley of the Crawling Stone below the canyon. Afterward, when he had become a railroad man, McCloud, sitting at a camp-fire with Glover and Morris Blood, heard them discussing the coveted and impossible line up the valley. He had been taken into the circle of constructionists and was told of the earlier reports against the line. He thought he knew something about the Elbow Mountains, and disputed the findings, offering in two days' ride to take the men before him to the pass called by the Indians The Box, and to take them through it. Glover called it a find, and a big one, and though more immediate matters in the strategy of territorial control then came before him, the preliminary was ordered and McCloud's findings were approved. McCloud himself was soon afterward engrossed in the problems of operating the mountain division; but the dream of his life was to build the Crawling Stone Line with a maximum grade of eight tenths through The Box.

The prettiest stretch of Crawling Stone Valley lies within twenty miles of Medicine Bend. There it lies widest, and has the pick of water and grass between Medicine Bend and the Mission Mountains. Cattlemen went into the Crawling Stone country before the Indians had wholly left it. The first house in the valley was the Stone Ranch, built by Richard Dunning, and it still stands overlooking the town of Dunning at the junction of the Frenchman Creek with the Crawling Stone. The Frenchman is fed by unfailing springs, and when by summer sun and wind every smaller stream in the middle basin has been licked dry, the Frenchman runs cold and swift between its russet hills. Richard Dunning, being on the border of the Indian country, built for his ranch-house a rambling stone fortress. He had chosen, it afterward proved, the choice spot in the valley, and he stocked it with cattle when yearlings could be picked up in Medicine Bend at ten dollars a head. He got together a great body of valley land when it could be had for the asking, and became the rich man of the Long Range.

The Dunnings were Kentuckians. Richard was a bridge engineer and builder, and under Brodie built some of the first bridges on the mountain division, notably the great wooden bridge at Smoky Creek. Richard brought out his nephew, Lance Dunning. He taught Lance bridge-building, and Murray Sinclair, who began as a cowboy on the Stone Ranch, learned bridge-building from Richard Dunning. The Dunnings both came West, though at different times, as young men and unmarried,

The Crawling Stone

and, as far as Western women were concerned, might always have remained so. But a Kentucky cousin, Betty, one of the Fairfield Dunnings, related to Richard within the sixth or eighth degree, came to the mountains for her health. Betty's mother had brought Richard up as a boy, and Betty, when he left Fairfield, was a baby. But Dick—as they knew him at home—and the mother wrote back and forth, and he persuaded her to send Betty out for a trip, promising he would send her back in a year a well woman.

Betty came with only her colored maid, old Puss Dunning, who had taken her from the nurse's arms when she was born and taken care of her ever since. The two—the tall Kentucky girl and the bent mammy—arrived at the Stone Ranch one day in June, and Richard, done then with bridges and looking after his ranch interests, had already fallen violently in love with Betty. She was delicate, but, if those in Medicine Bend who remembered her said true, a lovely creature. Remaining in the mountains was the last thing Betty had ever thought of, but no one, man or woman, could withstand Dick Dunning. She fell quite in love with him the first time she set eyes on him in Medicine Bend, for he was very handsome in the saddle, and Betty was fairly wild about horses. So Dick Dunning wooed a fond mistress and married her and buried her, and all within hardly more than a year.

But in that year they were very happy, never two happier, and when she slept away her suffering she left him, as a legacy, a tiny baby girl. Puss brought the mite of a creature in its swaddling-clothes to the sick mother,—very, very sick then,—and poor Betty turned her dark eyes on it, kissed it, looked at her husband and whispered " Dicksie," and died. Dicksie had been Betty's pet name for her mountain lover, so the father said the child's name should be Dicksie and nothing else; and his heart broke and soon he died. Nothing else, storm or flood, death or disaster, had ever moved Dick Dunning; then a single blow killed him. He rode once in a while over the ranch, a great tract by that time of twenty thousand acres, all in one body, all under fence, up and down both sides of the big river, in part irrigated, swarming with cattle—none of it stirred Dick! and with little Dicksie in his arms he slept away *his* suffering.

So Dicksie was left, as her mother had been, to Puss, while Lance looked after the ranch, swore at the price of cattle, and played cards at Medicine Bend. At ten, Dicksie, as thoroughly spoiled as a pet baby could be by a fool mammy, a fond cousin, and a galaxy of devoted cowboys, was sent, in spite of crying and flinging, to a far-away convent—her

The Crawling Stone

father had planned everything—where in many tears she learned that there were other things in the world besides cattle and mountains and sunshine and tall, broad-hatted horsemen to swing from their stirrups and pick her hat from the ground— just to see little Dicksie laugh—when they swooped past the house to the corrals. When she came back from Kentucky, her grandmother dead and her schooldays finished, all the land she could see in the valley was hers, and all the living creatures in the fields. It seemed perfectly natural, because since childhood even the distant mountains and their snows had been Dicksie's.

CHAPTER VI

THE FINAL APPEAL

SINCLAIR'S discharge was a matter of comment for the whole country, from the ranchhouses to the ranges. For a time Sinclair himself refused utterly to believe that McCloud could keep him off the division. His determination to get back led him to carry his appeal to the highest quarters, to Glover and to Bucks himself. But Sinclair, able as he was, had passed the limit of endurance and had long been marked for an accounting. He had been a railroad man to whom the West spelled license, and, while a valuable man, had long been a source of demoralization to the forces of the division. In the railroad life clearly defined plans are often too deeply laid to fathom, and it was impossible for even so acute a man as Sinclair to realize that he was not the victim of an accident, but that he must look to his own record for the real explanation of his undoing. He was not the only man to suffer in the shake-out that took place under the new superintendent; but he seemed the only one unable to realize that Bucks,

The Final Appeal

patient and long-suffering, had put McCloud into the mountain saddle expressly to deal with cases such as his. In the West sympathy is quick but not always discerning. Medicine Bend took Sinclair's grievance as its own. No other man in the service had Sinclair's following, and within a week petitions were being circulated through the town not asking merely but calling for his reinstatement. The sporting element of the community to a man were behind Sinclair because he was a sport; the range men were with him because his growing ranch on the Frenchman made him one of them; his own men were with him because he was a far-seeing pirate and divided liberally. Among the railroad men, too, he had much sympathy. Sinclair had always been lavish with presents; brides were remembered by Sinclair, and babies were not forgotten. He could sit up all night with a railroad man that had been hurt, and he could play poker all night with one that was not afraid of getting hurt. In his way, he was a division autocrat, whose vices were varnished by virtues such as these. His hold on the people was so strong that they could not believe the company would not reinstate him. In spite of the appointment of his successor, Phil Hailey, a mountain boy and the son of an old-time bridge foreman, rumor assigned again and again definite dates for Sinclair's return to work; but the dates never materialized. The bridge machinery of the big division moved on in even rhythm. A final and determined appeal from the deposed autocrat for a hearing at last brought Glover and Morris Blood, the general manager, to Medicine Bend for a final conference. Callahan too was there with his pipe, and they talked quietly with Sinclair—reminded him of how often he had been warned, showed him how complete a record they had of his plundering, and Glover gave to him Bucks's final word that he could never again work on the mountain division.

A pride grown monstrous with prestige long undisputed broke under the final blow. The big fellow put his face in his hands and burst into tears, and the men before him sat confused and uncomfortable at his outburst of feeling. It was only for a moment. Sinclair raised his hand, shook his long hair, and swore an oath against the company and the men that curled the very smoke in Callahan's pipe. Callahan, outraged at the insolence, sprang to his feet, resenting Sinclair's fury. Choking with anger he warned him not to go too far. The two were ready to spring at each other's throat when Farrell Kennedy stepped between them. Sinclair, drunk with rage, called for McCloud; but he submitted quietly to Kennedy's

The Final Appeal

reproof, and with a semblance of self-control begged that McCloud be sent for. Kennedy, without complying, gradually pushed Sinclair out of the room and, without seeming officious, walked with him down the hall and quite out of the building.

CHAPTER VII

IN Boney Street, Medicine Bend, stands an early-day row of one-story buildings; they once made up a prosperous block, which has long since fallen into the decay of paintless days. There is in Boney Street a livery stable, a second-hand store, a laundry, a bakery, a moribund grocery, and a bicycle shop, and at the time of this story there was also Marion Sinclair's millinery shop; but the better class of Medicine Bend business, such as the gambling houses, saloons, pawnshops, restaurants, barber shops, and those sensitive, clean-shaven, and alert establishments known as "gents' stores," had deserted Boney Street for many years. Bats fly in the dark of Boney Street while Front Street at the same hour is a blaze of electricity and frontier hilarity. The millinery store stood next to the corner of Fort Street. The lot lay in an "L," and at the rear of the store the first owner had built a small connecting cottage to live in. This faced on Fort Street, so that Marion had her shop and living-rooms communicating,

64

In Marion's Shop

and yet apart. The store building is still pointed out as the former shop of Marion Sinclair, where George McCloud boarded when the Crawling Stone Line was built, where Whispering Smith might often have been seen, where Sinclair himself was last seen alive in Medicine Bend, where Dicksie Dunning's horse dragged her senseless one wild mountain night, and where, indeed, for a time the affairs of the whole mountain division seemed to tangle in very hard knots.

As to the millinery business, it was never, after Marion bought the shop, more than moderately successful. The demand that existed in Medicine Bend for red hats of the picture sort Marion declined to recognize. For customers who sought these she turned out hats of sombre coloring calculated to inspire gloom rather than revelry, and she naturally failed to hold what might be termed the miscellaneous business. But after Dicksie Dunning of the Stone Ranch, fresh from the convent, rode into the shop, or if not into it nearly so, and, gliding through the door, ordered a hat out of hand, Marion always had some business. All Medicine Bend knew Dicksie Dunning, who dressed stunningly, rode famously, and was so winningly democratic that half the town never called her anything, at a distance, but Dicksie.

The first hat was a small affair but haughty.

Whispering Smith

The materials were unheard of in Marion's stock and had to be sent for. Marion's arrangements with the jobbing houses always had a C. O. D. complexion; the jobbers maintained that this saved book-keeping, and Marion, who of course never knew any better, paid the double express charges like a lamb. She acted, too, as banker for the other impecunious tradespeople in the block, and as this included nearly all of them she was often pressed for funds herself. McCloud undertook sometimes to intervene and straighten out her millinery affairs. One evening he went so far as to attempt an inventory of her stock and some schedule of her accounts; but Marion, with the front-shop curtains closely drawn and McCloud perspiring on a step-ladder, inspecting boxes of feathers and asking stern questions, would look so pathetically sweet and helpless when she tried to recall what things cost that McCloud could not be angry with her; indeed, the pretty eyes behind the patient spectacles would disarm any one. In the end he took inventory on the basis of the retail prices, dividing it afterward by five, as Marion estimated the average profit in the business at five hundred per cent.—this being what the woman she bought out had told her.

How then, McCloud asked himself, could Marion be normally hard pressed for money? He talked to her learnedly about fixed charges, but even these seemed difficult to arrive at. There was no rent, because the building belonged to the railroad company, and when the real-estate and tax man came around and talked to McCloud about rent for the Boney Street property, McCloud told him to chase himself. There was no insurance, because no one would dream of insuring Marion's stock boxes; there were no bills payable, because no travelling man would advise a line of credit to an inexperienced and, what was worse, an unpractical milliner. Marion did her own trimming, so there were no salaries except to Katie Dancing. It puzzled McCloud to find the leak. How could he know that Marion was keeping nearly all the block supplied with funds? So McCloud continued to raise the price of his table-board, and, though Marion insisted he was paying her too much, held that he must be eating her out of house and home.

In her dining-room, which connected through a curtained door with the shop, McCloud sat one day alone eating his dinner. Marion was in front serving a customer. McCloud heard voices in the shop, but gave no heed till a man walked through the curtained doorway and he saw Murray Sinclair standing before him. The stormy interview with Callahan and Blood at the Wickiup

Whispering Smith

had taken place just a week before, and McCloud, after what Sinclair had then threatened, though not prepared, felt as he saw him that anything might occur. McCloud being in possession of the little room, however, the initiative fell on Sinclair, who, looking his best, snatched his hat from his head and bowed ironically. " My mistake," he said blandly.

" Come right in," returned McCloud, not knowing whether Marion had a possible hand in her husband's unexpected appearance. " Do you want to see me? "

" I don't," smiled Sinclair; " and to be perfectly frank," he added with studied consideration, " I wish to God I never had seen you. Well—you've thrown me, McCloud."

" You've thrown yourself, haven't you, Murray? "

" From your point of view, of course. But, McCloud, this is a small country for two points of view. Do you want to get out of it, or do you want me to? "

" The country suits me, Sinclair."

" No man that has ever played me dirt can stay here while I stay." Sinclair, with a hand on the portière, was moving from the doorway into the room. McCloud in a leisurely way rose, though with a slightly flushed face, and at that

68

In Marion's Shop

juncture Marion ran into the room and spoke abruptly. "Here is the silk, Mr. Sinclair," she exclaimed, handing to him a package she had not finished wrapping. "I meant you to wait in the other room."

"It was an accidental intrusion," returned Sinclair, maintaining his irony. "I have apologized, and Mr. McCloud and I understand one another better than ever."

"Please say to Miss Dunning," continued Marion, nervous and insistent, "that the band for her riding-hat hasn't come yet, but it should be here to-morrow."

As she spoke McCloud leaned across the table, resolved to take advantage of the opening, if it cost him his life. "And by the way, Mr. Sinclair, Miss Dunning wished me to say to you that the lovely bay colt you sent her had sprung his shoulder badly, the hind shoulder, I think, but they are doing everything possible for it and they think it will make a great horse."

Sinclair's snort at the information was a marvel of indecision. Was he being made fun of? Should he draw and end it? But Marion faced him resolutely as he stood, and talking in the most business-like way she backed him out of the room and to the shop door. Balked of his opportunity, he retreated stubbornly but with the utmost politeness, and left with a grin, lashing his tail, so to speak.

Coming back, Marion tried to hide her uneasiness under even tones to McCloud. " I'm sorry he disturbed you. I was attending to a customer and had to ask him to wait a moment."

" Don't apologize for having a customer."

" He lives over beyond the Stone Ranch, you know, and is taking some things out for the Dunnings to-day. He likes an excuse to come in here because it annoys me. Finish your dinner, Mr. McCloud."

" Thank you, I'm done."

" But you haven't eaten anything. Isn't your steak right? "

" It's fine, but that man—well, you know how I like him and how he likes me. I'll content myself with digesting my temper."

CHAPTER VIII

SMOKY CREEK BRIDGE

IT was not alone that a defiance makes a bad dinner sauce: there was more than this for McCloud to feed on. He was forced to confess to himself as he walked back to the Wickiup that the most annoying feature of the incident was the least important, namely, that his only enemy in the country should be intrusted with commissions from the Stone Ranch and be carrying packages for Dicksie Dunning. It was Sinclair's trick to do things for people, and to make himself so useful that they must like first his obligingness and afterward himself. Sinclair, McCloud knew, was close in many ways to Lance Dunning. It was said to have been his influence that won Dunning's consent to sell a right of way across the ranch for the new Crawling Stone Line. But McCloud felt it useless to disguise the fact to himself that he now had a second keen interest in the Crawling Stone country—not alone a dream of a line, but a dream of a girl. Sitting moodily in his office, with his feet on the desk, a few nights after his encounter with Sinclair, he

recalled her nod as she said good-by. It had
seemed the least bit encouraging, and he meditated
anew on the only twenty minutes of real pleasur-
able excitement he had ever felt in his life, the
twenty minutes with Dicksie Dunning at Smoky
Creek. Her intimates, he had heard, called her
Dicksie, and he was vaguely envying her intimates
when the night despatcher, Rooney Lee, opened the
door and disturbed his reflections.

"How is Number One, Rooney?" called Mc-
Cloud, as if nothing but the thought of a
train movement ever entered his head.

Rooney Lee paused. In his hand he held a message. Rooney's cheeks were hollow and his sunken
eyes were large. His face, which was singularly
a night face, would shock a stranger, but any man
on the division would have given his life for
Rooney. The simple fellow had but two living
interests—his train-sheets and his chewing tobacco.
Sometimes I think that every railroad man earns
his salary—even the president. But Rooney was
a Past Worthy Master in that unnumbered lodge
of railroad slaves who do killing work and have
left, when they die, only a little tobacco to show
for it. It was on Rooney's account that Mc-
Cloud's order banishing cuspidors from his office
had been rescinded. A few evenings of agony
on the despatcher's part when in consultation

Smoky Creek Bridge

with his chief, the mournful wandering of his uncomplaining eyes, his struggle to raise an obstinate window before he could answer a question, would have moved a heart harder than McCloud's. The cuspidor had been restored to one corner of the large room, and to this corner Rooney, like a man with a jaw full of birdshot, always walked first. When he turned back to face his chief his face had lost its haunted expression, and he answered with solemn cheer, "On time," or "Fourteen minutes late," as the case might be. This night his face showed something out of the ordinary, and he faced McCloud with evident uneasiness. "Holy smoke, Mr. McCloud, here's a ripper! We've lost Smoky Creek Bridge."

"Lost Smoky Creek Bridge?" echoed McCloud, rising in amazement.

"Burned to-night. Seventy-seven was flagged by the man at the pump station."

"That's a tie-up for your life!" exclaimed McCloud, reaching for the message. "How could it catch fire? Is it burned up?"

"I can't get anything on that yet; this came from Canby. I'll have a good wire in a few minutes and get it all for you."

"Have Phil Hailey and Hyde notified, Rooney, and Reed and Brill Young, and get up a train. Smoky Creek Bridge! By heavens, we are ripped

Whispering Smith

up the back now! What can we do there,
Rooney?" He was talking to himself. "There
isn't a thing for it on God's earth but switchbacks
and five-per-cent. grades down to the bottom of the
creek and cribbing across it till the new line is
ready. Wire Callahan and Morris Blood, and get
everything you can for me before we start."

Ten hours later and many hundreds of miles
from the mountain division, President Bucks and a
companion were riding in the peace of a June morning down the beautiful Mohawk Valley with an
earlier and illustrious railroad man, William C.
Brown. The three men were at breakfast in
Brown's car. A message was brought in for Bucks.
He read it and passed it to his companion, Whispering Smith, who sat at Brown's left hand. The
message was from Callahan with the news of the
burning of Smoky Creek Bridge. Details were
few, because no one on the West End could suggest a plausible cause for the fire.

"What do you think of it, Gordon?" demanded
Bucks bluntly.

Whispering Smith seemed at all times bordering
on good-natured surprise, and in that normal condition he read Callahan's message. Everything
surprised Whispering Smith, even his salary; but
an important consequence was that nothing excited him. He seemed to accommodate himself

to the unexpected through habitual surprise. It showed markedly in his eyes, which were bright and quite wide open, and, save for his eyes, no feature about him would fix itself in the memory. His round, pleasant face, his heavy brown mustache, the medium build that concealed under its commonplace symmetry an unusual strength, his slightly rounding shoulders bespeaking a not too serious estimate of himself—every characteristic, even to his unobtrusive suit and black hat, made him distinctly an ordinary man—one to be met in the street to-day and passed, and forgotten to-morrow.

He was laughing under Bucks's scrutiny when he handed the message back. " Why, I don't know a thing about it, not a thing; but taking a long shot and speaking by and far, I should say it looks something like first blood for Sinclair," he suggested, and to change the subject lifted his cup of coffee.

" Then it looks like you for the mountains to-night instead of for Weber and Fields's," retorted Bucks, reaching for a cigar. " Brown, why have you never learned to smoke ? "

CHAPTER IX

NO attempt was made to minimize the truth that the blow to the division was a staggering one. The loss of Smoky Creek Bridge put almost a thousand miles of the mountain division out of business. Perishable freight and time freight were diverted to other lines. Passengers were transferred; lunches were served to them in the deep valley, and they were supplied by an ingenuous advertising department with pictures of the historic bridge as it had long stood, and their addresses were taken with the promise of a picture of the ruins. Smoky Creek Bridge had long been famous in mountain song and story. For one generation of Western railroad men it had stood as a monument to the earliest effort to conquer the Rockies with a railroad. Built long before the days of steel, this high and slender link in the first transcontinental line had for thirty years served faithfully at its danger-post, only to fall in the end at the hands of a bridge assassin; nor has the mystery of its fate ever completely been solved, though

The Misunderstanding

it is believed to lie with Murray Sinclair in the Frenchman hills. The engineering department and the operating department united in a tremendous effort to bring about a resumption of traffic. Glover's men, pulled off construction, were sent forward in trainloads. Dancing's linemen strung arc-lights along the creek until the canyon twinkled at night like a mountain village, and men in three shifts worked elbow to elbow unceasingly to run the switchbacks down to the creek-bed. There, by cribbing across the bottom, they got in a temporary line.

Train movement was thrown into a spectacle of confusion. Upon the incessant and well-ordered activities of the road the burning of the bridge fell like the heel of a heavy boot on an ant-hill; but the railroad men like ants rose to the emergency, and, where the possible failed, achieved the impossible.

McCloud spent his days at the creek and his nights at Medicine Bend with his assistant and his chief despatcher, advising, counselling, studying out trouble reports, and steadying wherever he could the weakened lines of his operating forces. He was getting his first taste of the trials of the hardest-worked and poorest-paid man in the operating department of a railroad—the division superintendent.

To these were added personal annoyances. A

trainload of Duck Bar steers, shipped by Lance Dunning from the Crawling Stone Ranch, had been caught west of the bridge the very night of the fire. They had been loaded at Tipton and shipped to catch a good market, and under extravagant promises from the live-stock agent of a quick run to Chicago. When Lance Dunning learned that his cattle had been caught west of the break and would have to be unloaded, he swore up a horse in hot haste and started for Medicine Bend. Mc-Cloud, who had not closed his eyes for sixty hours, had just got into Medicine Bend from Smoky Creek and was sitting at his desk buried in a mass of papers, but he ordered the cattleman admitted. He was, in fact, eager to meet the manager of the big ranch and the cousin of Dicksie. Lance Dunning stood above six feet in height, and was a handsome man, in spite of the hard lines around his eyes, as he walked in; but neither his manner nor his expression was amiable.

"Are you Mr. McCloud? I've been here three times this afternoon to see you," said he, ignoring McCloud's answer and a proffered chair. "This is your office, isn't it?"

McCloud, a little surprised, answered again and civilly: "It certainly is; but I have been at Smoky Creek for two or three days."

"What have you done with my cattle?"

The Misunderstanding

" The Duck Bar train was run back to Point of Rocks and the cattle were unloaded at the yard."

Lance Dunning spoke with increasing harshness: " By whose order was that done? Why wasn't I notified? Have they had feed or water? "

" All the stock caught west of the bridge was sent back for feed and water by my orders. It has all been taken care of. You should have been notified, certainly; it is the business of the stock agent to see to that. Let me inquire about it while you are here, Mr. Dunning," suggested McCloud, ringing for his clerk.

Dunning lost no time in expressing himself. " I don't want my cattle held at Point of Rocks! " he said angrily. " Your Point of Rocks yards are infected. My cattle shouldn't have been sent there."

" Oh, no! The old yards where they had a touch of fever were burned off the face of the earth a year ago. The new yards are perfectly sanitary. The loss of the bridge has crippled us, you know. Your cattle are being well cared for, Mr. Dunning, and if you doubt it you may go up and give our men any orders you like in the matter at our expense."

" You're taking altogether too much on yourself when you run my stock over the country in this way," exclaimed Dunning, refusing to be placated.

Whispering Smith

" How am I to get to Point of Rocks—walk there? "

" Not at all," returned McCloud, ringing up his clerk and asking for a pass, which was brought back in a moment and handed to Dunning. " The cattle," continued McCloud, " can be run down, unloaded, and driven around the break to-morrow —with the loss of only two days."

" And in the meantime I lose my market."

" It is too bad, certainly, but I suppose it will be several days before we can get a line across Smoky Creek."

" Why weren't the cattle sent through that way yesterday? What have they been held at Point of Rocks for? I call the thing badly managed."

" We couldn't get the empty cars up from Piedmont for the transfer until to-day; empties are very scarce everywhere now."

" There always have been empties here when they were wanted until lately. There's been no head or tail to anything on this division for six months."

" I'm sorry that you have that impression."

" That impression is very general," declared the stockman, with an oath, " and if you keep on discharging the only men on this division that are competent to handle a break like this, it is likely to continue! "

The Misunderstanding

"Just a moment!" McCloud's finger rose pointedly. "My failure to please you in caring for your stock in an emergency may be properly a matter for comment; your opinion as to the way I am running this division is, of course, your own: but don't attempt to criticise the retention or discharge of any man on my payroll!"

Dunning strode toward him. "I'm a shipper on this line; when it suits me to criticise you or your methods, or anybody else's, I expect to do so," he retorted in high tones.

"But you cannot tell me how to run my business!" thundered McCloud, leaning over the table in front of him.

As the two men glared at each other Rooney Lee opened the door. His surprise at the situation amounted to consternation. He shuffled to the corner of the room, and while McCloud and Dunning engaged hotly again, Rooney, from the corner, threw a shot of his own into the quarrel. "On time!" he roared.

The angry men turned. "What's on time?" asked McCloud curtly.

"Number One; she's in and changing engines. I told them you were going West," declared Rooney in so deep tones that his fiction would never have been suspected. If his cue had been,

Whispering Smith

" My lord, the conductor waits," it could not have been rung in more opportunely.

Dunning, to emphasize, without a further word, his disgust for the situation and his contempt for the management, tore into scraps the pass that had been given him, threw the scraps on the floor, took a cigar from his pocket and lighted it; insolence could do no more.

McCloud looked over at the despatcher. " No, I am not going West, Rooney. But if you will be good enough to stay here and find out from this man just how this railroad ought to be run, I will go to bed. He can tell you; the microbe seems to be working in his mind right now," said McCloud, slamming down the roll-top of his desk. And with Lance Dunning glaring at him, somewhat speechless, he put on his hat and walked out of the room.

It was but one of many disagreeable incidents due to the loss of the bridge. Complications arising from the tie-up followed him at every turn. It seemed as if he could not get away from trouble following trouble. After forty hours further of toil, relieved by four hours of sleep, McCloud found himself, rather dead than alive, back at Medicine Bend and in the little dining-room at Marion's. Coming in at the cottage door on Fort Street, he dropped into a chair. The cottage rooms were

The Misunderstanding

empty. He heard Marion's voice in the front shop; she was engaged with a customer. Putting his head on the table to wait a moment, nature asserted itself and McCloud fell asleep. He woke hearing a voice that he had heard in dreams. Perhaps no other voice could have wakened him, for he slept for a few minutes a death-like sleep. At all events, Dicksie Dunning was in the front room and McCloud heard her. She was talking with Marion about the burning of Smoky Creek Bridge.

"Every one is talking about it yet," Dicksie was saying. "If I had lost my best friend I couldn't have felt worse; you know, my father built it. I rode over there the day of the fire, and down into the creek, so I could look up where it stood. I never realized before how high and how long it was; and when I remembered how proud father always was of his work there—Cousin Lance has often told me—I sat down right on the ground and cried. Really, the ruins were the most pathetic thing you ever saw, Marion, with great clouds of smoke rolling up from the canyon that day; the place looked so lonely when I rode away that every time I turned to look back my eyes filled with tears. Poor daddy! I am almost glad he didn't live to see it. How times have changed in railroading, haven't they? Mr. Sinclair was over just the other night, and he said if they kept using this new

83

coal in the engines they would burn up everything on the division. Do you know, I have been waiting in town three or four hours now for Cousin Lance? I feel almost like a tramp. He is coming from the West with the stock train. It was due here hours ago, but they never seem to know when anything is to get here the way things are run on the railroad now. I want to give Cousin Lance some mail before he goes through."

"The passenger trains crossed the creek over the switchbacks hours ago, and they say the emergency grades are first-rate," said Marion Sinclair, on the defensive. "The stock trains must have followed right along. Your cousin is sure to be here pretty soon. Probably Mr. McCloud will know which train he is on, and Mr. Lee telephoned that Mr. McCloud would be over here at three o'clock for his dinner. He ought to be here now."

"Oh, dear, then I must go!"

"But he can probably tell you just when your cousin will be in."

"I wouldn't meet him for worlds!"

"You wouldn't? Why, Mr. McCloud is delightful."

"Oh, not for worlds, Marion! You know he is discharging all the best of the older men, the men that have made the road everything it is, and of course we can't help sympathizing with them

The Misunderstanding

over our way. For my part, I think it is terrible, after a man has given all of his life to building up a railroad, that he should be thrown out to starve in that way by new managers, Marion."

McCloud felt himself shrinking within his weary clothes. Resentment seemed to have died. He felt too exhausted to undertake controversy, even if it were to be thought of, and it was not.

Nothing further was needed to complete his humiliation. He picked up his hat and with the thought of getting out as quietly as he had come in. In rising he swept a tumbler at his elbow from the table. The glass broke on the floor, and Marion exclaimed, "What is that?" and started for the dining-room.

It was too late to get away. McCloud stepped to the portières of the trimming-room door and pushed them aside. Marion stood with a hat in her hand, and Dicksie, sitting at the table, was looking directly at the intruder as he appeared in the doorway. She saw in him her pleasant acquaintance of the wreck at Smoky Creek, whose name she had not learned. In her surprise she rose to her feet, and Marion spoke quickly: " Oh, Mr. McCloud, is it you? I did not hear you come in."

Dicksie's face, which had lighted, became a spectacle of confusion after she heard the name.

Whispering Smith

McCloud, conscious of the awkwardness of his position and the disorder of his garb, said the worst thing at once: " I fear I am inadvertently overhearing your conversation."

He looked at Dicksie as he spoke, chiefly because he could not help it, and this made matters hopeless.

She flushed more deeply. " I cannot conceive why our conversation should invite a listener."

Her words did not, of course, help to steady him. " I tried to get away," he stammered, " when I realized I was a part of it."

" In any event," she exclaimed hastily, " if you are Mr. McCloud I think it unpardonable to do anything like that! "

" I am Mr. McCloud, though I should rather be anybody else; and I am sorry that I was unable to help hearing what was said; I——"

" Marion, will you be kind enough to give me my gloves? " said Dicksie, holding out her hand.

Marion, having tried once or twice to intervene, stood between the firing-lines in helpless amazement. Her exclamations were lost; the two before her gave no heed to ordinary intervention.

McCloud flushed at being cut off, but he bowed. " Of course," he said, " if you will listen to no explanation I can only withdraw."

He went back, dinnerless, to work all night;

The Misunderstanding

but the switchbacks were doing capitally, and all night long, trains were rolling through Medicine Bend from the West in an endless string. In the morning the yard was nearly cleared of westbound tonnage. Moreover, the mail in the morning brought compensation. A letter came from Glover telling him not to worry himself to death over the tie-up, and one came from Bucks telling him to make ready for the building of the Crawling Stone Line.

McCloud told Rooney Lee that if anybody asked for him to report him dead, and going to bed slept twenty-four hours.

CHAPTER X

THE burning of Smoky Creek Bridge was hardly off the minds of the mountain men when a disaster of a different sort befell the division. In the Rat Valley east of Sleepy Cat the main line springs between two ranges of hills with a dip and a long supported grade in each direction. At the point of the dip there is a switch from which a spur runs to a granite quarry. The track for two miles is straight and the switch-target and lights are seen easily from either direction save at one particular moment of the day—a moment which is in the valley neither quite day nor quite night. Even this disadvantage occurs to trains east-bound only, because due to unusual circumstances. When the sun in a burst of dawning glory shows itself above the crest of the eastern range an engineman, east-bound, may be so blinded by the rays streaming from the rising sun that he cannot see the switch at the foot of the grade. For these few moments he is helpless should anything be wrong with the quarry switch.

Sweeping Orders

Down this grade, a few weeks after the Smoky Creek fire, came a double-headed stock train from the Short Line with forty cars of steers. The switch stood open; this much was afterward abundantly proved. The train came down the grade very fast to gain speed for the hill ahead of it. The head engineman, too late, saw the open target. He applied the emergency air, threw his engine over, and whistled the alarm. The mightiest efforts of a dozen engines would have been powerless to check the heavy train. On the quarry track stood three flat cars loaded with granite blocks for the abutment of the new Smoky Creek Bridge. On a sanded track, rolling at thirty miles an hour and screaming in the clutches of the burning brakes, the heavy engines struck the switch like an avalanche, reared upon the granite-laden flats, and with forty loads of cattle plunged into the canyon below; not a car remained on the rails. The head brakeman, riding in the second cab, was instantly killed, and the engine crews, who jumped, were badly hurt.

The whole operating department of the road was stirred. What made the affair more dreadful was that it had occurred on the time of Number Six, the east-bound passenger train, held that morning at Sleepy Cat by an engine failure. Glover came to look into the matter. The testimony of all tended to one conclusion—that the quarry switch had been thrown at some time between four-thirty and five o'clock that morning. Inferences were many: tramps during the early summer had been unusually troublesome and many of them had been rigorously handled by trainmen; robbery might have been a motive, as the express cars on train Number Six carried heavy specie shipments from the coast.

Yet a means so horrible as well as so awkward and ineffective seemed unlike mountain outlaws. Strange men from headquarters were on the ground as soon as they could reach the wreck, men from the special-service department, and a stock inspector who greatly resembled Whispering Smith was on the ground looking into the brands of the wrecked cattle. Glover was much in consultation with him, and there were two or three of the division men, such as Anderson, Young, McCloud, and Lee, who knew him but could answer no inquiries concerning his long stay at the wreck.

A third and more exciting event soon put the quarry wreck into the background. Ten days afterward an east-bound passenger train was flagged in the night at Sugar Buttes, twelve miles west of Sleepy Cat. When the heavy train slowed up, two men boarded the engine and with pistols compelled the engineman to cut off the express cars and pull them to the water-tank a mile east of the station. Three men there in waiting forced the express car, blew open the safe, and the gang rode away half an hour later loaded with gold coin and currency.

Had a stick of dynamite been exploded under the Wickiup there could not have been more excitement at Medicine Bend. Within three hours after the news reached the town a *posse* under Sheriff Van Horn, with a carload of horseflesh and fourteen guns, was started for Sugar Buttes. The trail led north and the pursuers rode until nearly nightfall. They crossed Dutch Flat and rode single file into a wooded canyon, where they came upon traces of a camp-fire. Van Horn, leading, jumped from his horse and thrust his hand into the ashes; they were still warm, and he shouted to his men to ride up. As he called out, a rifle cracked from the box-elder trees ahead of him. The sheriff fell, shot through the head, and a deputy springing from his saddle to pick him up was shot in precisely the same way, through the head. The riderless horses bolted; the *posse*, thrown into a panic, did not fire a shot, and for an hour dared not ride back for the bodies. After dark they got the two dead men and at midnight rode with them into Sleepy Cat.

When the news reached McCloud he was talk-

Whispering Smith

ing with Bucks over the wires. Bucks had got into headquarters at the river late that night, and was getting details from McCloud of the Sugar Buttes robbery when the superintendent sent him the news of the killing of Van Horn and the deputy. In the answer that Bucks sent came a name new to the wires of the mountain division and rarely seen even in special correspondence, but Hughie Morrison, who took the message, never forgot that name; indeed, it was soon to be thrown sharply into the spotlight of the mountain railroad stage. Hughie repeated the message to get it letter-perfect; to handle stuff at the Wickiup signed " J. S. B." was like handling diamonds on a jeweller's tongs or arteries on a surgeon's hook; and, in truth, Bucks's words were the arteries and pulse-beat of the mountain division. Hughie handed the message to McCloud and stood by while the superintendent read:

Whispering Smith is due in Cheyenne to-morrow. Meet him at the Wickiup Sunday morning; he has full authority. I have told him to get these fellows, if it takes all the money in the treasury, and not to stop till he cleans them out of the Rocky Mountains. J. S. B.

CHAPTER XI

AT THE THREE HORSES

"CLEAN them out of the Rocky Mountains; that is a pretty good contract," mused the man in McCloud's office on Sunday morning. He sat opposite McCloud in Bucks's old easy chair and held in his hand Bucks's telegram. As he spoke he raised his eyebrows and settled back, but the unusual depth of the chair and the shortness of his legs left his chin helpless in his black tie, so that he was really no better off except that he had changed one position of discomfort for another. " I wonder, now," he mused, sitting forward again as McCloud watched him, " I wonder—you know, George, the Andes are, strictly speaking, a part of the great North American chain—whether Bucks meant to include the South American ranges in that message? " and a look of mildly good-natured anticipation overspread his face.

"Suppose you wire him and find out," suggested McCloud.

" No, George, no! Bucks never was accurate in geographical expressions. Besides, he is shifty

93

and would probably cover his tracks by telling me to report progress when I got to Panama."

A clerk opened the outer office door. " Mr. Dancing asks if he can see you, Mr. McCloud."

" Tell him I am busy."

Bill Dancing, close on the clerk's heels, spoke for himself. " I know it, Mr. McCloud, I know it! " he interposed urgently, " but let me speak to you just a moment." Hat in hand, Bill, because no one would knock him down to keep him out, pushed into the room. " I've got a plan," he urged, " in regards to getting these hold-ups."

" How are you, Bill? " exclaimed the man in the easy chair, jumping hastily to his feet and shaking Dancing's hand. Then quite as hastily he sat down, crossed his knees violently, stared at the giant lineman, and exclaimed, " Let's have it! "

Dancing looked at him in silence and with some contempt. The trainmaster had broken in on the superintendent for a moment and the two were conferring in an undertone. " What might your name be, mister? " growled Dancing, addressing with some condescension the man in the easy chair.

The man waved his hand as if it were immaterial and answered with a single word: " Forgotten! "

" How's that? "

At the Three Horses

" Forgotten ! "

" That's a blamed queer name——"

" On the contrary, it's a very common name and that is just the trouble: it's forgotten."

" What do you want, Bill? " demanded Mc-Cloud, turning to the lineman.

" Is this man all right? " asked Dancing, jerking his thumb toward the easy chair.

" I can't say; you'll have to ask him."

" I'll save you that trouble, Bill, by saying that if it's for the good of the division I *am* all right. Death to its enemies, damme, say I. Now go on, William, and give us your plan in regards to getting these hold-ups—yes."

Dancing looked from one man to the other, but McCloud appeared preoccupied and his visitor seemed wholly serious. " I don't want to take too much on myself—" Bill began, speaking to McCloud.

" You look as if you could carry a fair-sized load, William, provided it bore the right label," suggested the visitor, entirely amiable.

" —But nobody has felt worse over this thing and recent things——"

" Recent things," echoed the easy chair.

" —happening to the division that I have. Now I know there's been trouble on the division——"

Whispering Smith

"I think you are putting it too strong there, Bill, but let it pass."

"—there's been differences; misunderstandings and differences. So I says to myself maybe something might be done to get everybody together and bury the differences, like this: Murray Sinclair is in town; he feels bad over this thing, like any railroad man would. He's a mountain man, quick as the quickest with a gun, a good trailer, rides like a fiend, and can catch a streak of sunshine travelling on a pass. Why not put him at the head of a party to run 'em down?"

"Run 'em down," nodded the stranger.

"Differences such as be or may be——"

"May be——"

"Being discussed when he brings 'em in dead or alive, and not before. That's what I said to Murray Sinclair, and Murray Sinclair is ready for to take hold this minute and do what he can if he's asked. I told him plain I could promise no promises; that, I says, lays with George McCloud. Was I right, was I wrong? If I was wrong, right me; if I was right, say so. All I want is harmony."

The new man nodded approval. "Bully, Bill!" he exclaimed heartily.

"Mister," protested the lineman, with simple dignity, "I'd just a little rather you wouldn't bully me nor Bill me."

At the Three Horses

"All in good part, Bill, as you shall see; all in good part. Now before Mr. McCloud gives you his decision I want to be allowed a word. Your idea looks good to me. At first I may say it didn't. I am candid; I say it didn't. It looked like setting a dog to catch his own tail. Mind you, I don't say it can't be done. A dog *can* catch his own tail; *they do do it*," proclaimed the stranger in a low and emphatic undertone. " But," he added, moderating his utterance, " when they succeed— who gets anything out of it but the dog?" Bill Dancing, somewhat clouded and not deeming it well to be drawn into any damaging admissions, looked around for a cigar, and not seeing one, looked solemnly at the new Solomon and stroked his beard. " That is how it looked to me at first," concluded the orator; " *but*, I say now it looks good to me, and as a stranger I may say I favor it."

Dancing tried to look unconcerned and seemed disposed to be friendly. " What might be your line of business?"

" Real estate. I am from Chicago. I sold everything that was for sale in Chicago and came out here to stake out the Spanish Sinks and the Great Salt Lake—yes. It's drying up and there's an immense opportunity for claims along the shore. I've been looking into it."

Whispering Smith

" Into the claims or into the lake? " asked Mc-Cloud.

" Into both; and, Mr. McCloud, I want to say I favor Mr. Dancing's idea, that's all. Right wrongs no man. Let Bill see Sinclair and see what they can figure out." And having spoken, the stranger sank back and tried to look comfortable.

" I'll talk with you later about it, Bill," said McCloud briefly.

" Meantime, Bill, see Sinclair and report," suggested the stranger.

" It's as good as done," announced Dancing, taking up his hat, " and, Mr. McCloud, might I have a little advance for cigars and things? "

" Cigars and ammunition—of course. See Sykes, William, see Sykes; if the office is closed go to his house—and see what will happen to you—" added the visitor in an aside, " and tell him to telephone up to Mr. McCloud for instruction," he concluded unceremoniously.

" Now why do you want to start Bill on a fool business like that? " asked McCloud, as Bill Dancing took long steps from the room toward the office of Sykes, the cashier.

" He didn't know me to-day, but he will to-morrow," said the stranger reflectively. " Gods, what I've seen that man go through in the days of the giants! Why, George, this will keep the boys talking, and they have to do something. Spend the money; the company is making it too fast anyway; they moved twenty-two thousand cars one day last week. Personally I'm glad to have a little fun out of it; it will be hell pure and undefiled long before we get through. This will be an easy way of letting Sinclair know I am here. Bill will report me confidentially to him as a suspicious personage."

To the astonishment of Sykes, the superintendent confirmed over the telephone Dancing's statement that he was to draw some expense money. Bill asked for twenty-five dollars. Sykes offered him two, and Bill with some indignation accepted five. He spent all of this in trying to find Sinclair, and on the strength of his story to the boys borrowed five dollars more to prosecute the search. At ten o'clock that night he ran into Sinclair playing cards in the big room above the Three Horses.

The Three Horses still rears its hospitable two-story front in Fort Street, the only one of the Medicine Bend gambling houses that goes back to the days of '67; and it is the boast of its owners that since the key was thrown away, thirty-nine years ago, its doors have never been closed, night or day, except once for two hours during the funeral of Dave Hawk. Bill Dancing drew Sinclair from his game and told him of the talk with McCloud,

Whispering Smith

touching it up with natural enthusiasm. The bridgeman took the news in high good humor and slapped Dancing on the back. "Did you see him alone, Bill?" asked Sinclair, with interest. "Come over here, come along. I want you to meet a good friend. Here, Harvey, shake hands with Bill Dancing. Bill, this is old Harvey Du Sang, meanest man in the mountains to his enemies and the whitest to his friends—eh, Harvey?"

Harvey seemed uncommunicative. Studying his hand, he asked in a sour way whether it was a jack-pot, and upon being told that it was not, pushed forward some chips and looked stupidly up—though Harvey was by no means stupid. "Proud to know you, sir," said Bill, bending frankly as he put out his hand. "Proud to know any friend of Murray Sinclair's. What might be your business?"

Again Du Sang appeared abstracted. He looked up at the giant lineman, who, in spite of his own size and strength, could have crushed him between his fingers, and hitched his chair a little, but got no further toward an answer and paid no attention whatever to Bill's extended hand.

"Cow business, Bill," interposed Sinclair. "Where? Why, up near the park, Bill, up near the park. Bill is an old friend of mine, Harvey. Shake hands with George Seagrue, Bill, and you

100

At the Three Horses

know Henry Karg—and old Stormy Gorman—well, I guess you know him too," exclaimed Sinclair, introducing the other players. "Look here a minute, Harvey."

Harvey, much against his inclination, was drawn from the table and retired with Sinclair and Dancing to an empty corner, where Dancing told his story again. At the conclusion of it Harvey rather snorted. Sinclair asked questions. "Was anybody else there when you saw McCloud, Bill?"

"One man," answered Bill impressively.

"Who?"

"A stranger to me."

"A stranger? What did he look like?"

"Slender man and kind of odd talking, with a sandy mustache."

"Hear his name?"

"He told me his name, but it's skipped me, I declare. He's kind of dark-complected like."

"Stranger, eh?" mused Du Sang; his eyes were wandering over the room.

"Slender man," repeated Bill, "but I didn't take much notice of him. Said he was in the' real-estate business."

"In the real-estate business? And did he sit there while you talked this over with the college guy?" muttered Du Sang.

Whispering Smith

" He is all right, boys, and he said you'd know his name if I could speak it," declared Bill.

" Look anything like that man standing with his hands in his pockets over there by the wheel? " asked Du Sang, turning his back carefully on a new-comer as he made the suggestion.

" Where—there? No! Yes, hold on, that's the man there now! Hold on, now! " urged Bill, struggling with the excitement of ten hours and ten dollars all in one day. " His name sounded like Fogarty."

As Dancing spoke, Sinclair's eyes riveted on the new face at the other side of the gambling-room. " Fogarty, hell! " he exclaimed, starting. " Stand right still, Du Sang; don't look around. That man is Whispering Smith."

CHAPTER XII

PARLEY

IT was recalled one evening not long ago at the Wickiup that the affair with Sinclair had all taken place within a period of two years, and that practically all of the actors in the event had been together and in friendly relation on a Thanksgiving Day at the Dunning ranch not so very long before the trouble began. Dicksie Dunning was away at school at the time, and Lance Dunning was celebrating with a riding and shooting fest and a barbecue.

The whole country had been invited. Bucks was in the mountains on an inspection trip, and Bill Dancing drove him with a party of railroad men over from Medicine Bend. The mountain men for a hundred and fifty miles around were out. Gene and Bob Johnson, from Oroville and the Peace River, had come with their friends. From Williams Cache there was not only a big delegation—more of one than was really desirable—but it was led by old John Rebstock himself. When the invitation is general, lines cannot be too closely drawn. Not only was Lance Dunning something of a sport himself, but on the Long Range it is part of a stockman's creed to be on good terms with his neighbors. At a Thanksgiving Day barbecue not even a mountain sheriff would ask questions, and Ed Banks, though present, respected the holiday truce. Cowboys rode that day in the roping contest who were from Mission Creek and from Two Feather River.

Among the railroad people were George Mc-Cloud, Anderson, the assistant superintendent, Farrell Kennedy, chief of the special service, and his right-hand man, Bob Scott. In especial, Sinclair's presence at the barbecue was recalled. He had some cronies with him from among his up-country following, and was introducing his new bridge foreman, Karg, afterward known as Flat Nose, and George Seagrue, the Montana cowboy. Sinclair fraternized that day with the Williams Cache men, and it was remarked even then that though a railroad man he appeared somewhat outside the railroad circle. When the shooting matches were announced a brown-eyed railroad man was asked to enter. He had been out of the mountains for some time and was a comparative stranger in the gathering, but the Williams Cache men had not forgotten him; Rebstock, especially, wanted to see him shoot. While much of the time out of the

Parley

mountains on railroad business, he was known to be closely in Bucks's counsels, and as to the mountains themselves, he was reputed to know them better than Bucks or Glover himself knew them. This was Whispering Smith; but, beyond a low-voiced greeting or an expression of surprise at meeting an old acquaintance, he avoided talk. When urged to shoot he resisted all persuasion and backed up his refusal by showing a bruise on his trigger finger. He declined even to act as judge in the contest, suggesting the sheriff, Ed Banks, for that office.

The rifle matches were held in the hills above the ranch-house, and in the contest between the ranches, for which a sweepstakes had been arranged, Sinclair entered Seagrue, who was then working for him. Seagrue shot all the morning and steadily held up the credit of the Frenchman Valley Ranch against the field. Neither continued shooting nor severe tests availed to upset Sinclair's entry, and riding back after the matches with the prize purse in his pocket, Seagrue, who was tall, light-haired, and perfectly built, made a new honor for himself on a dare from Stormy Gorman, the foreman of the Dunning ranch. Gorman, who had ridden a race back with Sinclair, was at the foot of the long hill, down which the crowd was riding, when he stopped, yelled back at Seagrue,

Whispering Smith

and, swinging his hat from his head, laid it on a sloping rock beside the trail.

" You'd better not do that, Stormy," said Sinclair. " Seagrue will put a hole through it."

Gorman laughed jealously. " If he can hit it, let him hit it."

At the top of the hill Seagrue had dismounted and was making ready to shoot. Whispering Smith, at his side, had halted with the party, and the cowboy knelt to adjust his sights. On his knee he turned to Whispering Smith, whom he seemed to know, with an abrupt question: " How far do you call it?"

The answer was made without hesitation: " Give it seven hundred and fifty yards, Seagrue."

The cowboy made ready, brought his rifle to his shoulder, and fired. The slug passed through the crown of the hat, and a shower of splinters flying back from the rock blew the felt into a sieve. Gorman's curiosity, as well as that of everybody else, seemed satisfied, and, gaining the level ground, the party broke into a helter-skelter race for the revolver-shooting.

In this Sinclair himself had entered, and after the early matches found only one troublesome contestant—Du Sang from the Cache, who was present under Rebstock's wing. After Sinclair and Du Sang had tied in test after test at shooting out

Parley

of the saddle, Whispering Smith, who lost sight of
nothing in the gun-play, called for a pack of cards,
stripped the aces from the deck, and had a little
conference with the judge. The two contestants,
Sinclair and Du Sang, were ordered back thirty-
five paces on their horses, and the railroad man,
walking over to the targets, held out between the
thumb and forefinger of his left hand the ace
of clubs. The man that should first spot the
pip out of the card was to take the prize, a
Cheyenne saddle. Sinclair shot, and his horse,
perfectly trained, stood like a statue. The card
flew from Smith's hand, but the bullet had struck
the ace almost an inch above the pip, and a second
ace was held out for Du Sang. As he raised his
gun his horse moved. He spurred angrily, circled
quickly about, halted, and instantly fired. It was
not alone that his bullet cut the shoulder of the
club pip on the card: the whole movement, beginning with the circling dash of the horse under
the spur, the sudden halt, and the instantly accurate
aim, raised a quick, approving yell for the new-
comer. The signal was given for Sinclair, and a
third ace went up. In the silence Sinclair, with
deliberate care, brought his gun down on the card,
fired, and cut the pip cleanly from the white field.
Du Sang was urged to shoot again, but his horse
annoyed him and he would not.

Whispering Smith

With a little speech the prize was given by Ed Banks to Sinclair. "Here's hoping your gun will never be trained on me, Murray," smiled the modest sheriff.

Sinclair responded in high humor. He had every reason to feel good. His horses had won the running races, and his crowd had the honors with the guns. He turned on Du Sang, who sat close by in the circle of horsemen, and, holding the big prize out toward him on his knee, asked him to accept it. "It's yours by rights anyway, Du Sang," declared Sinclair. "You're a whole lot better shot than I am, every turn of the road. You've shot all day from a nervous horse."

Not only would Sinclair not allow a refusal of his gift, but, to make his generosity worth while, he dispatched Flat Nose to the corral, and the foreman rode back leading the pony that had won the half-mile dash. Sinclair cinched the prize saddle on the colt with his own hands, led the beast to Du Sang, placed the bridle in his hand, and bowed. "From a jay to a marksman," he said, saluting.

Du Sang, greatly embarrassed by the affair—he had curious pink eyes—blinked and got away to the stables. When Rebstock joined him the Williams Cache party were saddling to go home. Du Sang made no reference to his gift horse and

Parley

saddle, but spoke of the man that had held the
target aces. "He must be a sucker!" declared
Du Sang, with an oath. "I wouldn't do that for
any man on top of ground. Who is he?"

"That man?" wheezed Rebstock. "Never
have no dealings with him. He plays 'most any
kind of a game. He's always ready to play, and
holds aces most of the time. Don't you remember
my telling about the man that got Chuck Williams
and hauled him out of the Cache on a buckboard?
That's the man. Here, he give me this for you;
it's your card." Rebstock handed Du Sang the
target ace of clubs. "Why didn't you thank Murray Sinclair, you mule?"

Du Sang, whose eyelashes were white, blinked
at the hole through the card, and looked around
as he rode back across the field for the man
that had held it; but Whispering Smith had disappeared.

He was at that moment walking past the barbecue pit with George McCloud. "Rebstock
talks a great deal about your shooting, Gordon,"
said McCloud to his companion.

"He and I once had a little private match of
our own. It was on the Peace River, over a bunch
of steers. Since then we have got along very well,
though he has an exaggerated opinion of my ability. Rebstock's worst failing is his eyesight. It

bothers him in seeing brands. He's liable to
brand a critter half a dozen times. That albino,
Du Sang, is a queer duck. Sinclair gave him a
fine horse. There they go." The Cache riders
were running their horses and whooping across the
creek. "What a hand a State's prison warden at
Fort City could draw out of that crowd, George!"
continued McCloud's companion. "If the right
man should get busy with that bunch of horses Sinclair has got together, and organize those up-country fellows for mischief, wouldn't it make things
hum on the mountain division for a while?"

McCloud did not meet the host, Lance Dunning,
that day, nor since the day of the barbecue had
Du Sang or Sinclair seen Whispering Smith until
the night Du Sang spotted him near the wheel in
the Three Horses. Du Sang at once drew out
of his game and left the room. Sinclair in the
meantime had undertaken a quarrelsome interview
with Whispering Smith.

"I supposed you knew I was here," said Smith
to him amiably. "Of course I don't travel in a
private car or carry a bill-board on my back, but I
haven't been hiding."

"The last time we talked," returned Sinclair,
measuring words carefully, "you were going to
stay out of the mountains."

"I should have been glad to, Murray. Affairs

Parley

are in such shape on the division now that somebody had to come, so they sent for me."

The two men were sitting at a table. Whispering Smith was cutting and leisurely mixing a pack
of cards.

"Well, so far as I'm concerned, I'm out of it,"
Sinclair went on after a pause, "but, however that
may be, if you're back here looking for trouble
there's no reason, I guess, why you can't find it."

"That's not it. I'm not here looking for
trouble; I'm here to fix this thing up. What do
you want?"

"Not a thing."

"I'm willing to do anything fair and right," declared Whispering Smith, raising his voice a little
above the hum of the rooms.

"Fair and right is an old song."

"And a good one to sing in this country just
now. I'll do anything I can to adjust any grievance, Murray. What do you want?"

Sinclair for a moment was silent, and his answer
made plain his unwillingness to speak at all.
"There never would have been a grievance if I'd
been treated like a white man." His eyes burned
sullenly. "I've been treated like a dog."

"That is not it."

"That is it," declared Sinclair savagely, "and
they'll find it's it."

Whispering Smith

"Murray, I want to say only this—only this to make things clear. Bucks feels that he's been treated worse than a dog."

"Then let him put me back where I belong."

"It's a little late for that, Murray; a *little* late," said Smith gently. "Shouldn't you rather take good money and get off the division? Mind you, I say good money, Murray—and peace."

Sinclair answered without the slightest hesitation: "Not while that man McCloud is here."

Whispering Smith smiled. "I've got no authority to kill McCloud."

"There are plenty of men in the mountains that don't need any."

"But let's start fair," urged Whispering Smith softly. He leaned forward with one finger extended in confidence. "Don't let us have any misunderstanding on the start. Let McCloud alone. If he is killed—now I'm speaking fair and open and making no threats, but I know how it will come out—there will be nothing but killing here for six months. We will make just that memorandum on McCloud. Now about the main question. Every sensible man in the world wants something."

"I know men that have been going a long time without what they wanted."

Smith flushed and nodded. "You needn't have

Parley

said that, but no matter. Every sensible man wants something Murray. This is a big country. There's a World's Fair running somewhere all the time in it. Why not travel a little? What do you want?"

"I want my job, or I want a new superintendent here."

"Just exactly the two things, and, by heavens! the only two, I can't manage. Come once more and I'll meet you."

"No!" Sinclair rose to his feet. "No—damn your money! This is my home. The high country is my country; it's where my friends are."

"It's filled with your friends; I know that. But don't put your trust in your friends. They will stay by you, I know; but once in a long while there will be a false friend, Murray, one that will sell you—remember that."

"I stay."

Whispering Smith looked up in admiration. "I know you're game. It isn't necessary for me to say that to you. But think of the fight you are going into against this company. You can worry them; you've done it. But a bronco might as well try to buck a locomotive as for one man or six or six hundred to win out in the way you are playing."

"I will look out for my friends; others—" Sinclair hitched his belt and paused, but Whispering Smith, cutting and running the cards, gave no heed. His eyes were fixed on the green cloth under his fingers. " Others—" repeated Sinclair.

" Others? " echoed Whispering Smith good-naturedly.

" May look out for themselves."

" Of course, of course! Well, if this is the end of it, I'm sorry."

" You will be sorry if you mix in a quarrel that is none of yours."

" Why, Murray, I never had a quarrel with a man in my life."

" You are pretty smooth, but you can't drive me out of this country. I know how well you'd like to do it; and, take notice, there's one trail you can't cross even if you stay here. I suppose you understand that."

Smith felt his heart leap. He sat in his chair turning the pack slowly, but with only one hand now; the other hand was free. Sinclair eyed him sidewise. Smith moistened his lips and when he replied spoke slowly: " There is no need of dragging any allusion to her into it. For that matter, I told Bucks he should have sent any man but me. If I'm in the way, Sinclair, if my presence here is all that stands in the way, I'll go back and stay back as before, and send any one else you like or

Parley

Bucks likes. Are you willing to say that I stand in the way of a settlement?"

Sinclair sat down and put his hands on the table. "No; your matter and mine is another affair. All I want between you and me is fair and right."

Whispering Smith's eyes were on the cards. "You've always had it."

"Then keep away from *her*."

"Don't tell me what to do."

"Then don't tell me."

"I'm not telling you. You will do as you please; so will I. I left here because Marion asked me to. I am here now because I have been sent here. It is in the course of my business. I have my living to earn and my friends to protect. Don't dictate to me, because it would be of no use."

"Well, you know now how to get into trouble."

"Every one knows that; few know how to keep out."

"You can't lay your finger on me at any turn of the road."

"Not if you behave yourself."

"And you can't bully me."

"Surely not. No hard feelings, Murray. I came for a friendly talk, and if it's all the same to you I'll watch this wheel awhile and then go over to the Wickiup. I leave first—that's understood, I

hope—and if your pink-eyed friend is waiting outside tell him there is nothing doing, will you, Murray? Who is the albino, by the way? You don't
know him? I think I do. Fort City, if I remember. Well, good-night, Murray."

It was after twelve o'clock and the room had
filled up. Roulette-balls were dropping, and above
the faro-table the extra lights were on. The deal-
ers, fresh from supper, were putting things in order
for the long trick.

At the Wickiup Whispering Smith found Mc-
Cloud in the office signing letters. "I can do
nothing with him," said Smith, drawing down a
window-shade before he seated himself to detail
his talk with Sinclair. "He wants a fight."

McCloud put down his pen. "If I am the dis-
turber it would be better for me to get out."

"That would be hauling down the flag across
the whole division. It is too late for that. If he
didn't centre the fight on you he would centre it
somewhere else. The whole question is, who is
going to run this division, Sinclair and his gang
or the company? and it is as easy to meet them on
one point as another. I know of no way of making this kind of an affair pleasant. I am going to
do some riding, as I told you. Kennedy is working up through the Deep Creek country, and has
three men with him. I shall ride toward the

Parley

Cache and meet him somewhere near South Mission Pass."

"Gordon, would it do any good to ask a few questions?"

"Ask as many as you like, my dear boy, but don't be disappointed if I can't answer them. I can look wise, but I don't know anything. You know what we are up against. This fellow has grown a tiger among the wolves, and he has turned the pack loose on us. One thing I ask you to do. Don't expose yourself at night. Your life isn't worth a coupling-pin if you do."

McCloud raised his hand. "Take care of *your*self. If you are murdered in this fight I shall know I got you in and that I am to blame."

"And suppose you were?" Smith had risen from his chair. He had few mannerisms, and recalling the man the few times I have seen him, the only impression he has left on me is that of quiet and gentleness. "Suppose you were?" He was resting one arm on top of McCloud's desk. "What of it? You have done for me up here what I couldn't do, George. You have been kind to Marion when she hadn't a friend near. You have stood between him and her when I couldn't be here to do it, and when she didn't want me to—helped her when I hadn't the privilege of doing it." McCloud put up his hand in protest, but it was unheeded. " How many times it has been in my heart to kill that man. She knows it; she prays it may never happen. That is why she stays here and has kept me out of the mountains. She says they would talk about her if I lived in the same town, and I have stayed away." He threw himself back into the chair. " It's going beyond both of us now. I've kept the promise I made to her to-day to do all in my power to settle this thing without bloodshed. It will not be settled in that way, George."

" Was he at Sugar Buttes ? "

" If not, his gang was there. The quick getaway, the short turn on Van Horn, killing two men to rattle the *posse*—it all bears Sinclair's ear-marks. He has gone too far. He has piled up plunder till he is reckless. He is crazy with greed and insane with revenge. He thinks he can gallop over this division and scare Bucks till he gets down on his knees to him. Bucks will never do it. I know him, and I tell you Bucks will never do it. He is like that man in Washington: he will fight it to the death. He would fight Sinclair if he had to come up here and meet him single-handed, but he will never have to do it. He put you here, George, to round that man up. This is the price for your advancement, and you must pay it."

" It is all right for me to pay it, but I don't want

Parley

you to pay it. Will you have a care for yourself, Gordon? "

" Will you? "

" Yes."

" You need never ask me to be careful," Smith went on. " That is my business. I asked you to watch your window-shades at night, and when I came in just now I found one up. It is you who are likely to forget, and in this kind of a game a man never forgets but once. I'll lie down on the Lincoln lounge, George."

" Get into the bed."

" No; I like the lounge, and I'm off early."

In the private room of the superintendent, provided as a sleeping apartment in the old headquarters building many years before hotel facilities reached Medicine Bend, stood the only curio the Wickiup possessed—the Lincoln lounge. When the car that carried the remains of Abraham Lincoln from Washington to Springfield was dismantled, the Wickiup fell heir to one piece of its elaborate furnishings, the lounge, and the lounge still remains as an early-day relic. Whispering Smith walked into the bedroom and disposed himself in an incredibly short time. " I've borrowed one of your pillows, George," he called out presently.

" Take both."

Whispering Smith

" One's enough. I hope," he went on, rolling himself like a hen into the double blanket, " the horse Kennedy has left me will be all right; he got three from Bill Dancing. Bill Dancing," he snorted, driving his nose into the pillow as if in final memorandum for the night, " he will get himself killed if he fools around Sinclair too much now."

McCloud, under a light shaded above his desk, opened a roll of blue-prints. He was going to follow a construction gang up the Crawling Stone in the morning and wanted to look over the surveys. Whispering Smith, breathing regularly, lay not far away. It was late when McCloud put away his maps, entered the inner room, and looked at his friend.

He lay like a boy asleep. On the chair beside his head he had placed his old-fashioned hunting-case watch, as big as an alarm-clock, the kind a railroad man would wind up with a spike-maul. Beside the watch he had laid his huge revolver in its worn leather scabbard. Breathing peacefully, he lay quite at his companion's mercy, and McCloud, looking down on this man who never made a mistake, never forgot a danger, and never took an unnecessary chance, thought of what between men confidence may sometimes mean. He sat a moment with folded arms on the side of

Parley

his bed, studying the tired face, defenceless in the slumber of fatigue. When he turned out the light and lay down, he wondered whether, somewhere in the valley of the great river to which he was to take his men in the morning, he should encounter the slight and reckless horsewoman who had blazed so in anger when he stood before her at Marion's. He had struggled against her charm too long. She had become, how or when he could not tell, not alone a pretty woman but a fascinating one—the creature of his constant thought. Already she meant more to him than all else in the world. He well knew that if called on to choose between Dicksie and all else he could only choose her. But as he drew together the curtains of thought and sleep stole in upon him, he was resolved first to have Dicksie; to have all else if he could, but, in any case, Dicksie Dunning. When he awoke day was breaking in the mountains. The huge silver watch, the low-voiced man, and the formidable six-shooter had disappeared. It was time to get up, and Marion Sinclair had promised an early breakfast.

CHAPTER XIII

THE TURN IN THE STORM

THE beginning of the Crawling Stone Line marked the first determined effort under President Bucks, while undertaking the reconstruction of the system for through traffic, to develop the rich local territory tributary to the mountain division. New policies in construction dated from the same period. Glover, with an enormous capital staked for the new undertakings, gave orders to push the building every month in the year, and for the first time in mountain railroad-building winter was to be ignored. The older mountain men met the innovation as they met any departure from their traditions, with curiosity and distrust. On the other hand, the new and younger blood took hold with confidence, and when Glover called, " Yo, heave ho! " at headquarters, they bent themselves clear across the system for a hard pull together.

McCloud, resting the operating on the shoulders of his assistant Anderson, devoted himself wholly to forwarding the construction plans, and his first clash over winter road-building in the Rockies came

The Turn in the Storm

with his own right-hand man, Mears. McCloud
put in a switch below Piedmont, opened a material-
yard, and began track-laying toward the lower
Crawling Stone Valley, when Mears said it was
time to stop work till spring. When McCloud
told him he wanted track across the divide and
into the lower valley by spring, Mears threw up
his hands. But there was metal in the old man,
and he was for orders all the time. He kept up
a running fire of protests and forebodings about
the danger of exposing men during the winter season, but stuck to his post. Glover sent along the
men, and although two out of every three deserted
the day after they arrived, Mears kept a force in
hand, and crowded the track up the new grade as
fast as the ties and steel came in, working day in
and day out with one eye on the clouds and one on
the tie-line and hoping every day for orders to stop.

December slipped away to Christmas with the
steel still going down and the disaffected element
among the railroad men at Medicine Bend waiting
for disaster. The spectacle of McCloud handling
a flying column on the Crawling Stone work in the
face of the most treacherous weather in the mountain year was one that brought out constant criti-
cism of him among Sinclair's sympathizers and
friends, and while McCloud laughed and pushed
ahead on the work, they waited only for his dis-

comfiture. Christmas Day found McCloud at the front, with men still very scarce, but Mears's gang at work and laying steel. The work train was in charge of Stevens, the freight conductor, who had been set back after the Smoky Creek wreck and was slowly climbing back to position. They were working in the usual way, with the flat cars ahead pushed by the engine, the caboose coupled to the tender being on the extreme hind end of the train.

At two o'clock on Christmas afternoon, when there was not a cloud in the sky, the horizon thickened in the east. Within thirty minutes the mountains from end to end of the sky-line were lost in the sweep of a coming wind, and at three o'clock snow struck the valley like a pall. Mears, greatly disturbed, ordered the men off the grade and into the caboose. McCloud had been inspecting culverts ahead, and had started for the train when the snow drove across the valley. It blotted the landscape from sight so fast that he was glad after an anxious five minutes to regain the ties and find himself safely with his men.

But when McCloud came in the men were bordering on a panic. Mears, with his two foremen, had gone ahead to hunt McCloud up, and had passed him in the storm; it was already impossible to see, or to hear an ordinary sound ten yards away. McCloud ordered the flat cars cut off the train and

The Turn in the Storm

the engine whistle sounded at short intervals, and, taking Stevens, buttoned his reefer and started up the grade after the three trackmen. They fired their revolvers as they went on, but the storm tossed their signals on the ears of Mears and his companions from every quarter of the compass. McCloud was standing on the last tie and planning with his companion how best to keep the grade as the two advanced, when the engine signals suddenly changed. "Now that sounds like one of Bill Dancing's games," said McCloud to his companion. "What the deuce is it, Stevens?"

Stevens, who knew a little of everything, recognized the signals in an instant and threw up his hands. "It's Morse code, Mr. McCloud, and they are in—Mears and the foremen—and us for the train as quick as the Lord will let us; that's what they're whistling."

"So much for an education, Stevens. Bully for you! Come on!"

They regained the flat cars and made their way back to the caboose and engine, which stood uncoupled. McCloud got into the cab with Dancing and Stevens. Mears, from the caboose ahead, signalled all in, and, with a whistling scream, the engine started to back the caboose to Piedmont. They had hardly more than got under full headway when a difficulty became ap-

Whispering Smith

parent to the little group around the superintendent. They were riding an unballasted track and using such speed as they dared to escape from a situation that had become perilous. But the light caboose, packed like a sardine-box with men, was dancing a hornpipe on the rail-joints. McCloud felt the peril, and the lurching of the car could be seen in the jerk of the engine tender to which it was coupled. Apprehensive, he crawled back on the coal to watch the caboose himself, and stayed long enough to see that the rapidly drifting snow threatened to derail the outfit any minute. He got back to the cab and ordered a stop. " This won't do ! " said he to Stevens and the engineman. " We can't back that caboose loaded with men through this storm. We shall be off the track in five minutes."

" Try it slow," suggested Stevens.

" If we had the time," returned McCloud; " but the snow is drifting on us. We've got to make a run for it if we ever get back, and we must have the engine in front of that way car with her pilot headed for the drifts. Let's look at things."

Dancing and Stevens, followed by McCloud, dropped out of the gangway. Mears opened the caboose door and the four men went forward to inspect the track and the trucks. In the lee of the caboose a council was held. The roar of the wind

The Turn in the Storm

was like the surge of many waters, and the snow had whitened into storm. They were ten miles from a habitation, and, but for the single track they were travelling, might as well have been a hundred miles so far as reaching a place of safety was concerned. They were without food, with a caboose packed with men on their hands, and they realized that their supply of fuel for either engine or caboose was perilously slender.

"Get your men ready with their tools, Pat," said McCloud to Mears.

"What are you going to do?"

"I'm going to turn the train around and put the nose of the engine into it."

"Turn the train around—why, yes, that would make it easy. I'd be glad to see it turned around. But where's your turntable, Mr. McCloud?" asked Mears.

"How are·you going to turn your train around on a single track?" asked Stevens darkly.

"I'm going to turn the track around. I know about where we are, I think. There's a little stretch just beyond this curve where the grade is flush with the ground. Ask your engineman to run back very slowly and watch for the bell-rope. I'll ride on the front platform of the caboose till we get to where we want to go to work. Lose no time, Pat; tell your men it's now or never. If we are caught here we may stay till they carry us home, and the success of this little game depends on having everything ready and working quick."

Stevens, who stayed close to McCloud, pulled the cord within five minutes, and before the caboose had stopped the men were tumbling out of it. Mc-Cloud led Mears and his foreman up the track. They tramped a hundred yards back and forth, and, with steel tapes for safety lines, swung a hundred feet out on each side of the track to make sure of the ground. "This will do," announced McCloud; "you waited here half a day for steel a week ago; I know the ground. Break that joint, Pat." He pointed to the rail under his foot. "Pass ahead with the engine and car about a thousand feet," he said to the conductor, "and when I give you a signal back up slow and look out for a thirty-degree curve—without any elevation, either. Get out all your men with lining-bars."

The engine and caboose faded in the blur of the blizzard as the break was made in the track. "Take those bars and divide your men into batches of ten with foremen that can make signs, if they can't talk English," directed McCloud. "Work lively now, and throw this track to the south!"

Pretty much everybody—Japs, Italians, and Greeks—understood the game they were playing. McCloud said afterward he would match his Pied-

The Turn in the Storm

mont hundred in making a movable Y against any two hundred experts Glover could pick; they had had the experience, he added, when the move meant their last counter in the game of mountain life or death. The Piedmont "hundred," to Mc-Cloud's mind, were after that day past masters in the art of track-shifting. Working in a driving cloud of grit and snow, the ignorant, the dull, and the slow rose to the occasion. Bill Dancing, Pat Mears and his foreman, and Stevens moved about in the driving snow like giants. The howling storm rang with the shouting of the foremen, the guttural cries of the Japs, and the clank of the lining-bars as rail-length after rail-length of the heavy track was slued bodily from the grade alignment and swung around in a short curve to a right angle out on the open ground.

McCloud at last gave the awaited signal, and, with keen-eyed, anxious men watching every revolution of the cautious driving-wheels, the engine, hissing and pausing as the air-brakes went off and on, pushed the light caboose slowly out on the rough spur to its extreme end and stopped with the pilot facing the main track at right angles; but before it had reached its halting-place spike-mauls were ringing at the fish-plates where a moment before it had left the line on the curve. The track at that point was cut again, and under a long line of

bars and a renewed shouting it was thrown gradually quite across the long gap in the main line, and
the new joints in a very rough curve were made fast
just as the engine, running now with its pilot ahead,
steamed slowly around the new curve and without
accident regained the regular grade.   It was
greeted by a screeching yell as the men climbed
into the caboose, for the engine stood safely headed
into the teeth of the storm for Piedmont.   The
ten miles to cover were now a matter of less than
thirty minutes, and the construction train drew into
the Piedmont yards just as the telegraph wires were
heating from headquarters with orders annulling
freights, ordering ploughs on outgoing engines,
and battening the division hatches for·a grapple
with a Christmas blizzard.

No man came back better pleased than Stevens.
" That man is all right," said he to Mears, nodding his head toward McCloud, as they walked up
from the caboose.   " That's all I want to say.
Some of these fellows have been a little shy about
going out with him; they've hounded me for
months about stepping over his way when Sinclair
and his mugs struck.   I reckon I played my hand
about right."

CHAPTER XIV

SPRING found the construction of the valley line well advanced, and the grades nearing the lands of the Dunning ranch. Right-of-way men had been working for months with Lance Dunning, over the line, and McCloud had been called frequently into consultation to adjust the surveys to objections raised by Dicksie's cousin to the crossing of the ranch lands. Even when the proceedings had been closed, a strong current of discontent set from the managing head of the Stone Ranch. Rumors of Lance Dunning's dissatisfaction often reached the railroad people. Vague talk of an extensive irrigation scheme planned by Sinclair for the Crawling Stone Valley crept into the newspapers, and it was generally understood that Lance Dunning had expressed himself favorably to the enterprise.

Dicksie gave slight heed to matters as weighty as these. She spent much of her time on horseback, with Jim under the saddle; and in Medicine

131

Bend, where she rode with frequency, Marion's shop became her favorite abiding-place. Dicksie ordered hats until Marion's conscience rose and she practically refused to supply any more. But the spirited controversy on this point, as on many others—Dicksie's haughtiness and Marion's restraint, quite unmoved by any show of displeasure —ended always in drawing the two closer to each other.

At home Dicksie's fancies, at that time ran to chickens, and crate after crate of thoroughbreds and clutch after clutch of eggs were brought over the pass from far-away countries. But the coyotes stole the chickens and kept the hens in such a state of excitement that they could not be got to sit effectively. Nest after nest Dicksie had the mortification of seeing deserted at critical moments and left to furred prowlers of the foothills and canyons. Once she had managed to shoot a particularly bold coyote, only to be overcome with remorse at seeing its death-struggle. She gained reputation with her cousin and the men, but was ever afterward assailed with the reflection that the poor fellow might have been providing for a hungry family. Housekeeping cares rested lightly on Dicksie. Puss had charge of the house, and her mistress concerned herself more with the setting of Jim's shoes than with the dust on the elk heads

These three carried rifles slung across their pommels, and in
front of them rode the stranger.

The Quarrel

over the fireplace in the dining-room. Her Medicine Bend horseshoer stood in much greater awe of her than Puss did, because if he ever left a mistake on Jim's heels Dicksie could, and would, point it coldly out.

One March afternoon, coming home from Medicine Bend, she saw at some distance before her a party of men on horseback. She was riding a trail leading from the pass road that followed the hills, and the party was coming up the bridge road from the lower ranch. Dicksie had good eyes, and something unusual in the riding of the men was soon apparent to her. Losing and regaining sight of them at different turns in the trail, she made out, as she rode among the trees, that they were cowboys of her own ranch, and riding, under evident excitement, about a strange horseman. She recognized in the escort Stormy Gorman, the ferocious foreman of the ranch, and Denison and Jim Baugh, two of the most reckless of the men. These three carried rifles slung across their pommels, and in front of them rode the stranger.

Fragments of the breakfast-table talk of the morning came back to Dicksie's mind. The railroad graders were in the valley below the ranch, and she had heard her cousin say a good deal on a point she cared little about, as to where the railroad should cross the Stone Ranch. Approaching the fork of the two roads toward which she and the cowboys were riding, she checked her horse in the shade of a cotton-wood tree, and as the party rode up the draw she saw the horseman under surveillance. It was George McCloud.

Unluckily, as she caught a glimpse of him she was conscious that he was looking at her. She bent forward to hide a momentary confusion, spoke briskly to her horse, and rode out of sight. At Marion's she had carefully avoided him. Her precipitancy at their last meeting had seemed, on reflection, unfortunate. She felt that she must have appeared to him shockingly rude, and there was in her recalling of the scene an unconfessed impression that she had been to blame. Often when Marion spoke of him, which she did without the slightest reserve and with no reference as to whether Dicksie liked it or not, it had been in Dicksie's mind to bring up the subject of the disagreeable scene, hoping that Marion would suggest a way for making some kind of unembarrassing amends. But such opportunities had slipped away unimproved, and here was the new railroad superintendent, whom their bluff neighbor Sinclair never referred to other than as the college guy, being brought apparently as a prisoner to the Stone Ranch.

The Quarrel

Busied with her thoughts, Dicksie rode slowly along the upper trails until a long *détour* brought her around the corrals and in at the back of the house. Throwing her lines to the ground, she alighted and through the back porch door made her way unobserved to her room. From the office across the big hall she heard men's voices in dispute, and she slipped into the dining-room, where she could hear and might see without being seen. The office was filled with cowboys. Lance Dunning, standing with a cigar in his hand and one leg thrown over a corner of the table, was facing Mc-Cloud, who stood before him with his hand on a chair. Lance was speaking as Dicksie looked into the room, and in curt tones: "My men were acting under my orders."

"You have no right to give such orders," Mc-Cloud said distinctly, "nor to detain me, nor to obstruct our free passage along the right of way you have agreed to convey to us under our survey."

"Damn your survey! I never had a plat of any such survey. I don't recognize any such survey. And if your right-of-way men had ever said a word about crossing the creek above the flume I never would have given you a right of way at all."

"There were never but two lines run below the creek; after you raised objection I ran them both, and both were above the flume."

Whispering Smith

" Well, you can't put a grade there. I and some of my neighbors are going to dam up that basin, and the irrigation laws will protect our rights."

" I certainly can't put a grade in below the flume, and you refuse to talk about our crossing above it."

" I certainly do."

" Why not let us cross where we are, and run a new level for your ditch that will put the flume higher up? "

" You will have to cross below the flume where it stands, or you won't cross the ranch at all."

McCloud was silent for a moment. " I am using a supported grade there for eight miles to get over the hill within a three-tenths limit. I can't drop back there. We might as well not build at all if we can't hold our grade, whereas it would be very simple to run a new line for your ditch, and my engineers will do it for you without a dollar of expense to you, Mr. Dunning."

Lance Dunning waved his hand as an ultimatum. " Cross where I tell you to cross, or keep off the Stone Ranch. Is that English? "

" It certainly is. But in matter of fact we must cross on the survey agreed on in the contract for a right-of-way deed."

" I don't recognize any contract obtained under false representations."

" Do you accuse me of false representations? "

136

The Quarrel

Lance Dunning flipped the ash from his cigar. "Who are you?"

"I am just a plain, every-day civil engineer, but you must not talk false representations in any contract drawn under my hand."

"I am talking facts. Whispering Smith may have rigged the joker—I don't know. Whoever rigged it, it has been rigged all right."

"Any charge against Whispering Smith is a charge against me. He is not here to defend himself, but he needs no defence. You have charged me already with misleading surveys. I was telephoned for this morning to come over to see why you had held up our work, and your men cover me with rifles while I am riding on a public road."

"You have been warned, or your men have, to keep off this ranch. Your man Stevens cut our wires this morning——"

"As he had a perfect right to do on our right of way."

"If you think so, stranger, go ahead again!"

"Oh, no! We won't have civil war—not right away, at least. And if you and your men have threatened and browbeaten me enough for to-day, I will go."

"Don't set foot on the Stone Ranch again, and don't send any men here to trespass, mark you!"

" I mark you perfectly. I did not set foot willingly on your ranch to-day. I was dragged on it. Where the men are grading now, they will finish their work."

" No, they won't."

" What, would you drive us off land you have already deeded? "

" The first man that cuts our wires or orders them cut where they were strung yesterday will get into trouble."

" Then don't string any wires on land that belongs to us, for they will certainly come down if you do."

Lance Dunning turned in a passion. " I'll put a bullet through you if you touch a barb of Stone Ranch wire! "

Stormy Gorman jumped forward with his hand covering the grip of his six-shooter. " Yes, damn you, and I'll put another! "

" Cousin Lance! " Dicksie Dunning advanced swiftly into the room. " You are under our own roof, and you are wrong to talk in that way."

Her cousin stared at her. " Dicksie, this is no place for you! "

" It is when my cousin is in danger of forgetting he is a gentleman."

" You are interfering with what you know nothing about! " exclaimed Lance angrily.

The Quarrel

"I know what is due to every one under this roof."

"Will you be good enough to leave this room?"

"Not if there is to be any shooting or threats of shooting that involve my cousin."

"Dicksie, leave the room!"

There was a hush. The cowboys dropped back. Dicksie stood motionless. She gave no sign in her manner that she heard the words, but she looked very steadily at her cousin. "You forget yourself!" was all she said.

"I am master here!"

"Also my cousin," murmured Dicksie evenly.

"You don't understand this matter at all!" declared Lance Dunning vehemently.

"Nothing could justify your language."

"Do you think I am going to allow this railroad company to ruin this ranch while I am responsible here? You have no business interfering, I say!"

"I think I have."

"These matters are not of your affair!"

"Not of my affair?" The listeners stood riveted. McCloud felt himself swallowing, and took a step backward with an effort as Dicksie advanced. Her hair, loosened by her ride, spread low upon her head. She stood in her saddle habit, with her quirt still in hand. "Any affair that may lead my cousin into shooting is my affair. I make it mine. This is my father's roof. I neither know nor care anything about what led to this quarrel, but the quarrel is mine now. I will not allow my cousin to plunge into anything that may cost him his life or ruin it." She turned suddenly, and her eyes fell on McCloud. "I am not willing to leave either myself or my cousin in a false position. I regret especially that Mr. Mc-Cloud should be brought into so unpleasant a scene, because he has already suffered rudeness at my own hands——"

McCloud flushed. He raised his hand slightly.

"And I am very sorry for it," added Dicksie, before he could speak. Then, turning, she withdrew from the room.

"I am sure," said McCloud slowly, as he spoke again to her cousin, "there need be no serious controversy over the right-of-way matter, Mr. Dunning. I certainly shall not precipitate any. Suppose you give me a chance to ride over the ground with you again and let us see whether we can't arrive at some conclusion?"

But Lance was angry, and nursed his wrath a long time.

CHAPTER XV

THE SHOT IN THE PASS

DICKSIE walked hurriedly through the dining-room and out upon the rear porch.
Her horse was standing where she had left him.
Her heart beat furiously as she caught up the reins,
but she sprang into the saddle and rode rapidly
away. The flood of her temper had brought a
disregard of consequence: it was in the glow of
her eyes, the lines of her lips, and the tremor of
her nostrils as she breathed long and deeply on her
flying horse.

When she checked Jim she had ridden miles,
but not without a course nor without a purpose.
Where the roads ahead of her parted to lead down
the river and over the Elbow Pass to Medicine
Bend, she halted within a clump of trees almost
where she had first seen McCloud. Beyond the
Mission Mountains the sun was setting in a fire
like that which glowed under her eyes. She
could have counted her heart-beats as the crimson
ball sank below the verge of the horizon and the

shadows threw up the silver thread of the big river and deepened across the heavy green of the alfalfa fields. Where Dicksie sat, struggling with her bounding pulse and holding Jim tightly in, no one from the ranch or, indeed, from the up-country could pass her unseen. She was waiting for a horseman, and the sun had set but a few minutes when she heard a sharp gallop coming down the upper road from the hills.

All her brave plans, terror-stricken at the sound of the hoof-beats, fled from her utterly. She was stunned by the suddenness of the crisis. She had meant to stop McCloud and speak to him, but before she could summon her courage a tall, slender man on horseback dashed past within a few feet of her. She could almost have touched him as he flew by, and a horse less steady than Jim would have shied under her. Dicksie caught her breath. She did not know this man—she had seen only his eyes, oddly bright in the twilight as he passed—but he was not of the ranch. He must have come from the hill road, she concluded, down which she herself had just ridden. He was somewhere from the North, for he sat his horse like a statue and rode like the wind.

But the encounter nerved her to her resolve. Some leaden moments passed, and McCloud, galloping at a far milder pace toward the fork of the

The Shot in the Pass

roads, checked his speed as he approached. He saw a woman on horseback waiting in his path.

" Mr. McCloud! "

" Miss Dunning! "

" I could not forgive myself if I waited too long to warn you that threats have been made against your life. Not of the kind you heard to-day. My cousin is not a murderer, and never could be, I am sure, in spite of his talk; but I was frightened at the thought that if anything dreadful should happen his name would be brought into it. There are enemies of yours in this country to be feared, and it is against these that I warn you. Goodnight! "

" Surely you won't ride away without giving me a chance to thank you! " exclaimed McCloud. Dicksie checked her horse. " I owe you a double debt of gratitude," he added, " and I am anxious to assure you that we desire nothing that will injure your interests in any way in crossing your lands."

" I know nothing about those matters, because my cousin manages everything. It is growing late and you have a good way to go, so goodnight."

" But you will allow me to ride back to the house with you? "

" Oh, no, indeed, thank you! "

" It will soon be dark and you are alone."

143

Whispering Smith

"No, no! I am quite safe and I have only a short ride. It is you who have far to go," and she spoke again to Jim, who started briskly.

"Miss Dunning, won't you listen just a moment? Please don't run away!" McCloud was trying to come up with her. "Won't you hear me a moment? I have suffered some little humiliation to-day; I should really rather be shot up than have more put on me. I am a man and you are a woman, and it is already dark. Isn't it for me to see you safely to the house? Won't you at least pretend I can act as an escort and let me go with you? I should make a poor figure trying to catch you on horseback——"

Dicksie nodded naïvely. "With that horse."

"With any horse—I know that," said McCloud, keeping at her side.

"But I *can't* let you ride back with me," declared Dicksie, urging Jim and looking directly at McCloud for the first time. "How could I explain?"

"Let me explain. I am famous for explaining," urged McCloud, spurring too.

"And will you tell me what *I* should be doing while you were explaining?" she asked.

"Perhaps getting ready a first aid for the injured."

"I feel as if I ought to run away," declared

144

The Shot in the Pass

Dicksie, since she had clearly decided not to. " It will have to be a compromise, I suppose. You must not ride farther than the first gate, and let us take this trail instead of the road. Now make your horse go as fast as you can and I'll keep up."

But McCloud's horse, though not a wonder, went too fast to suit his rider, who divided his efforts between checking him and keeping up the conversation. When McCloud dismounted to open Dicksie's gate, and stood in the twilight with his hat in his hand and his bridle over his arm, he was telling a story about Marion Sinclair, and Dicksie in the saddle, tapping her knee with her bridle-rein, was looking down and past him as if the light upon his face were too bright. Before she would start away she made him remount, and he said good-by only after half a promise from her that she would show him sometime a trail to the top of Bridger's Peak, with a view of the Peace River on the east and the whole Mission Range and the park country on the north. Then she rode away at an amazing run, nodding back as he sat still holding his hat above his head.

McCloud galloped toward the pass with one determination—that he would have a horse, and a good one, one that could travel with Jim, if it cost him his salary. He exulted as he rode, for the day had brought him everything he wished, and humiliation had been swallowed up in triumph. It was nearly dark when he reached the crest between the hills. At this point the southern grade of the pass winds sharply, whence its name, the Elbow; but from the head of the pass the grade may be commanded at intervals for half a mile. Trotting down this road with his head in a whirl of excitement, McCloud heard the crack of a rifle; at the same instant he felt a sharp slap at his hat. Instinct works on all brave men very much alike. McCloud dropped forward in his saddle, and, seeking no explanation, laid his head low and spurred Bill Dancing's horse for life or death. The horse, quite amazed, bolted and swerved down the grade like a snipe, with his rider crouching close for a second shot. But no second shot came, and after another mile McCloud ventured to take off his hat and put his finger through the holes in it, though he did not stop his horse to make the examination. When they reached the open country the horse had settled into a fast, long stride that not only redeemed his reputation but relieved his rider's nerves.

When McCloud entered his office it was half-past nine o'clock, and the first thing he did before turning on the lights was to draw the window-shades. He examined the hat again, with sensa-

The Shot in the Pass

tions that were new to him—fear, resentment, and a hearty hatred of his enemies. But all the while the picture of Dicksie remained. He thought of her nodding to him as they parted in the saddle, and her picture blotted out all that had followed.

CHAPTER XVI

TWO nights later Whispering Smith rode into Medicine Bend. " I've been up around Williams Cache," he said, answering McCloud's greeting as he entered the upstairs office. " How goes it ? " He was in his riding rig, just as he had come from a late supper.

When he asked for news McCloud told him the story of the trouble with Lance Dunning over the survey, and added that he had referred the matter to Glover. He told then of his unpleasant surprise when riding home afterward.

" Yes," assented Smith, looking with feverish interest at McCloud's head; " I heard about it."

" That's odd, for I haven't said a word about the matter to anybody but Marion Sinclair, and you haven't seen her."

" I heard up the country. It is great luck that he missed you."

" Who missed me ? "

" The man that was after you."

" The bullet went through my hat."

At The Wickiup

" Let me see the hat."

McCloud produced it. It was a heavy, broad-brimmed Stetson, with a bullet-hole cut cleanly through the front and the back of the crown. Smith made McCloud put the hat on and describe his position when the shot was fired. McCloud stood up, and Whispering Smith eyed him and put questions.

" What do you think of it? " asked McCloud when he had done.

Smith leaned forward on the table and pushed McCloud's hat toward him as if the incident were closed. " There is no question in my mind, and there never has been, but that Stetson puts up the best hat worn on the range."

McCloud raised his eyebrows. " Why, thank you! Your conclusion clears things so. After you speak a man has nothing to do but guess."

" But, by Heaven, George," exclaimed Smith, speaking with unaccustomed fervor, " Miss Dicksie Dunning is a hummer, *isn't* she? That child will have the whole range going in another year. To think of her standing up and lashing her cousin in that way when he was browbeating a railroad man! "

" Where did you hear about that? "

" The whole Crawling Stone country is talking about it. You never told me you had a mis-

understanding with Dicksie Dunning at Marion's.
Loosen up!"

"I will loosen up in the way you do. What
scared me most, Gordon, was waiting for the second shot. Why didn't he fire again?"

"Doubtless he thought he had you the first
time. Any man big enough to start after you is
not used to shooting twice at two hundred and
fifty yards. He probably thought you were falling
out of the saddle; and it was dark. I can account
for everything but your reaching the pass so late.
How did you spend all your time between the
ranch and the foothills?"

McCloud saw there was no escape from telling of his meeting with Dicksie Dunning, of her
warning, and of his ride to the gate with her.
Every point brought a suppressed exclamation from
Whispering Smith. "So she gave you your life,"
he mused. "Good for her! If you had got into
the pass on time you could not have got away—the
cards were stacked for you. He overestimated you
a little, George; just a little. Good men make
mistakes. The sport of circumstances that we are!
The sport of circumstances!"

"Now tell me how *you* heard so much about it,
Gordon, and where?"

"Through a friend, but forget it."

"Do you know who shot at me?"

At The Wickiup

" Yes."

" I think I do, too. I think it was the fellow that shot so well with the rifle at the barbecue—what was his name? He was working for Sinclair, and perhaps is yet."

" You mean Seagrue, the Montana cowboy? No, you are wrong. Seagrue is a man-killer, but a square one."

" How do you know? "

" I will tell you sometime—but this was not Seagrue."

" One of Dunning's men, was it? Stormy Gorman? "

" No, no, a very different sort! Stormy is a wind-bag. The man that is after you is in town at this minute, and he has come to stay until he finishes his job."

" The devil! That's what makes your eyes so bright, is it? Do you know him? "

" I have seen him. You may see him yourself if you want to."

" I'd like nothing better. When? "

" To-night—in thirty minutes." McCloud closed his desk. There was a rap at the door.

" That must be Kennedy," said Smith. " I haven't seen him, but I sent word for him to meet me here." The door opened and Kennedy entered the room.

Whispering Smith

"Sit down, Farrell," said Whispering Smith easily. *"Ve gates?"*

"How's that?"

"Wie geht es? Don't pretend you can't make out my German. He is trying to let on he is not a Dutchman," observed Whispering Smith to McCloud. "You wouldn't believe it, but I can remember when Farrell wore wooden shoes and lighted his pipe with a candle. He sleeps under a feather-bed yet. Du Sang is in town, Farrell."

"Du Sang!" echoed the tall man with mild interest as he picked up a ruler and, throwing his leg on the edge of the table, looked cheerful. "How long has Du Sang been in town? Visiting friends or doing business?"

"He is after your superintendent. He has been here since four o'clock, I reckon, and I've ridden a hard road to-day to get in in time to talk it over with him. Want to go?"

Kennedy slapped his leg with the ruler. "I always want to go, don't I?"

"Farrell, if you hadn't been a railroad man you would have made a great undertaker, do you know that?" Kennedy, slapping his leg, showed his ivory teeth. "You have such an instinct for funerals," added Whispering Smith.

"Now, Mr. Smith! Well, who are we waiting

At The Wickiup

for? I'm ready," said Kennedy, taking out his revolver and examining it.

McCloud put on his new hat and asked if he should take a gun. "You are really accompanying me as my guest, George," explained Whispering Smith reproachfully. "Won't it be fun to shove this man right under Du Sang's nose and make him bat his eyes?" he added to Kennedy. "Well, put one in your pocket if you like, George, provided you have one that will go off when sufficiently urged."

McCloud opened the drawer of the table and took from it a revolver. Whispering Smith reached out his hand for the gun, examined it, and handed it back.

"You don't like it."

Smith smiled a sickly approbation. "A forty-five gun with a thirty-eight bore, George? A little light for shock; a *little* light. A bullet is intended to knock a man down; not necessarily to kill him, but, if possible, to keep him from killing you. Never mind, we all have our fads. Come on!"

At the foot of the stairs Whispering Smith stopped. "Now I don't know where we shall find this man, but we'll try the Three Horses." As they started down the street McCloud took the inside of the sidewalk, but Smith dropped behind and

brought McCloud into the middle.   They failed
to find Du Sang at the Three Horses, and leav-
ing started to round up the street.   They visited
many places, but each was entered in the same way.
Kennedy sauntered in first and moved slowly ahead.
He was to step aside only in case he saw Du Sang.
McCloud in every instance followed him, with
Whispering Smith just behind, amiably surprised.
They spent an hour in and out of the Front Street
resorts, but their search was fruitless.

" You are sure he is in town? " asked Kennedy.
The three men stood deliberating in the shadow of
a side street.

" Sure! " answered Whispering Smith.   " Of
course, if he turns the trick he wants to get away
quietly.   He is lying low.   Who is that, Farrell? "   A man passing out of the shadow of a
shade tree was crossing Fort Street a hundred
feet away.

" It looks like our party," whispered Kennedy.
" No, stop a bit! "   They drew back into the
shadow.   " That is Du Sang," said Kennedy; " I
know his hobble."

CHAPTER XVII

A TEST

DU SANG had the sidewise gait of a wolf, and crossed the street with the choppy walk of the man out of a long saddle. Being both uncertain and quick, he was a man to slip a trail easily. He travelled around the block and disappeared among the many open doors that blazed along Hill Street. Less alert trailers than the two behind him would have been at fault; but when he entered the place he was looking for, Kennedy was so close that Du Sang could have spoken to him had he turned around.

Kennedy passed directly ahead. A moment later Whispering Smith put his head inside the door of the joint Du Sang had entered, withdrew it, and, rejoining his companions, spoke in an undertone: " A negro dive; he's lying low. Now we will keep our regular order. It's a half-basement, with a bar on the left; crap games at the table behind the screen on the right. Kennedy, will you take the rear end of the bar? It covers the whole room and the back door. George, pass in ahead

of me and step just to the left of the slot machine;
you've got the front door there and everything
behind the screen, and I can get close to Du Sang.
Look for a thinnish, yellow-faced man with a
brown hat and a brown shirt—and pink eyes—
shooting craps under this window. I'll shoot craps
with him. Is your heart pumping, George?
Never mind, this is easy! Farrell, you're first!"

The dive, badly lighted and ventilated, was
counted tough among tough places. White men
and colored mixed before the bar and about the
tables. When Smith stepped around the screen
and into the flare of the hanging lamps, Du Sang
stood in the small corner below the screened street
window. McCloud, though vitally interested in
looking at the man that had come to town to kill
him, felt his attention continually wandering back
to Whispering Smith. The clatter of the rolling
dice, the guttural jargon of the negro gamblers,
the drift of men to and from the bar, and the
clouds of tobacco smoke made a hazy background
for the stoop-shouldered man with his gray hat and
shabby coat, dust-covered and travel-stained. In-
dustriously licking the broken wrapper of a cheap
cigar and rolling it fondly under his forefinger, he
was making his way unostentatiously toward Du
Sang. Thirty-odd men were in the saloon, but only
two knew what the storm centre moving slowly

A Test

across the room might develop. Kennedy, seeing everything and talking pleasantly with one of the barkeepers, his close-set teeth gleaming twenty feet away, stood at the end of the bar sliding an empty glass between his hands. Whispering Smith pushed past the on-lookers to get to the end of the table where Du Sang was shooting. He made no effort to attract Du Sang's attention, and when the latter looked up he could have pulled the gray hat from the head of the man whose brown eyes were mildly fixed on Du Sang's dice; they were lying just in front of Smith. Looking indifferently at the intruder, Du Sang reached for the dice: just ahead of his right hand, Whispering Smith's right hand, the finger-tips extended on the table, rested in front of them; it might have been through accident or it might have been through design. In his left hand Smith held the broken cigar, and without looking at Du Sang he passed the wrapper again over the tip of his tongue and slowly across his lips.

Du Sang now looked sharply at him, and Smith looked at his cigar. Others were playing around the semicircular table—it might mean nothing. Du Sang waited. Smith lifted his right hand from the table and felt in his waistcoat for a match. Du Sang, however, made no effort to take up the dice. He watched Whispering Smith scratch a match on the table, and, either because it failed to light or through design, it was scratched the second time on the table, marking a cross between the two dice.

The meanest negro in the joint would not have stood that, yet Du Sang hesitated. Whispering Smith, mildly surprised, looked up. " Hello, Pearline! You shooting here? " He pushed the dice back toward the outlaw. " Shoot again! "

Du Sang, scowling, snapped the dice and threw badly.

" Up jump the devil, is it? Shoot again! " And, pushing back the dice, Smith moved closer to Du Sang. The two men touched arms. Du Sang, threatened in a way wholly new to him, waited like a snake braved by a mysterious enemy. His eyes blinked like a badger's. He caught up the dice and threw. " Is that the best you can do? " asked Smith. " See here! " He took up the dice. " Shoot with me! " Smith threw the dice up the table toward Du Sang. Once he threw craps, but, reaching directly in front of Du Sang, he picked the dice up and threw eleven. " Shoot with me, Du Sang."

" What's your game? " snapped Du Sang, with an oath.

" What do you care, if I've got the coin? I'll throw you for twenty-dollar gold pieces."

A Test

Du Sang's eyes glittered. Unable to understand the reason for the affront, he stood like a cat waiting to spring. " This is my game! " he snarled.

" Then play it."

" Look here, what do you want? " he demanded angrily.

Smith stepped closer. " Any game you've got. I'll throw you left-handed, Du Sang." With his right hand he snapped the dice under Du Sang's nose and looked squarely into his eyes. " Got any Sugar Buttes money? "

Du Sang for an instant looked keenly back; his eyes contracted in that time to a mere narrow slit; then, sudden as thought, he sprang back into the corner. He knew now. This was the man who held the aces at the barbecue, the railroad man— Whispering Smith. Kennedy, directly across the table, watched the lightning-like move. For the first time the crap-dealer looked impatiently up.

It was a showdown. No one watching the two men under the window breathed for a moment. Whispering Smith, motionless, only watched the half-closed eyes. " You can't shoot craps," he said coldly. " What can you shoot, Pearline? You can't stop a man on horseback."

Du Sang knew he must try for a quick kill or make a retreat. He took in the field at a glance.

Whispering Smith

Kennedy's teeth gleamed only ten feet away, and with his right hand half under his coat lapel he toyed with his watch-chain. McCloud had moved in from the slot machine and stood at the point of the table, looking at Du Sang and laughing at him. Whispering Smith threw off all pretence. " Take your hand away from your gun, you albino! I'll blow your head off left-handed if you pull! Will you get out of this town to-night? If you can't drop a man in the saddle at two hundred and fifty yards, what do you think you'd look like after a break with me? Go back to the whelp that hired you, and tell him when he wants a friend of mine to send a man that can shoot. If you are within twenty miles of Medicine Bend at daylight I'll rope you like a fat cow and drag you down Front Street! "

Du Sang, with burning eyes, shrank narrower and smaller into his corner, ready to shoot if he had to, but not liking the chances. No man in Williams Cache could pull or shoot with Du Sang, but no man in the mountains had ever drawn successfully against the man that faced him.

Whispering Smith saw that he would not draw. He taunted him again in low tones, and, backing away, spoke laughingly to McCloud. While Kennedy covered the corner, Smith backed to the door and waited for the two to join him. They halted

A Test

a moment at the door, then they backed slowly up the steps and out into the street.

There was no talk till they reached the Wickiup office. " Now, will some of you tell me who Du Sang is? " asked McCloud, after Kennedy and Whispering Smith with banter and laughing had gone over the scene.

Kennedy picked up the ruler. " The wickedest, cruelest man in the bunch—and the best shot."

" Where is your hat, George—the one he put the bullet through? " asked Whispering Smith, limp in the big chair. " Burn it up; he thinks he missed you. Burn it up now. Never let him find out what a close call you had. Du Sang! Yes, he is cold-blooded as a wild-cat and cruel as a soft bullet. Du Sang would shoot a dying man, George, just to keep him squirming in the dirt. Did you ever see such eyes in a human being, set like that and blinking so in the light? It's bad enough to watch a man when you can see his eyes. Here's hoping we're done with him! "

CHAPTER XVIII

NEW PLANS

CALLAHAN crushed the tobacco under his thumb in the palm of his right hand. "So I am sorry to add," he concluded, speaking to McCloud, "that you are now out of a job." The two men were facing each other across the table in McCloud's office. "Personally, I am not sorry to say it, either," added Callahan, slowly filling the bowl of his pipe.

McCloud said nothing to the point, as there seemed to be nothing to say until he had heard more. "I never knew before that you were left-handed," he returned evasively.

"It's a lucky thing, because it won't do for a freight-traffic man, nowadays, to let his right hand know what his left hand does," observed Callahan, feeling for a match. "I am the only left-handed man in the traffic department, but the man that handles the rebates, Jimmie Black, is cross-eyed. Bucks offered to send him to Chicago to have Bryson straighten his eyes, but Jimmie thinks

New Plans

it is better to have them as they are for the present, so he can look at a thing in two different ways— one for the Interstate Commerce Commission and one for himself. You haven't heard, then?" continued Callahan, returning to his riddle about McCloud's job. "Why, Lance Dunning has gone into the United States Court and got an injunction against us on the Crawling Stone Line— tied us up tighter than zero. No more construction there for a year at least. Dunning comes in for himself and for a cousin who is his ward, and three or four little ranchers have filed bills—so it's up to the lawyers for eighty per cent. of the gate receipts and peace. Personally, I'm glad of it. It gives you a chance to look after this operating for a year yourself. We are going to be swamped with freight traffic this year, and I want it moved through the mountains like checkers for the next six months. You know what I mean, George."

To McCloud the news came, in spite of himself, as a blow. The results he had attained in building through the lower valley had given him a name among the engineers of the whole line. The splendid showing of the winter construction, on which he had depended to enable him to finish the whole work within the year, was by this news brought to naught. Those of the railroad men who said he could not deliver a completed line within the year could never be answered now. And there was some slight bitterness in the reflection that the very stumbling-block to hold him back, to rob him of his chance for a reputation with men like Glover and Bucks, should be the lands of Dicksie Dunning.

He made no complaint. On the division he took hold with new energy and bent his faculties on the operating problems. At Marion's he saw Dicksie at intervals, and only to fall more hopelessly under her spell each time. She could be serious and she could be volatile and she could be something between which he could never quite make out. She could be serious with him when he was serious, and totally irresponsible the next minute with Marion. On the other hand, when McCloud attempted to be flippant, Dicksie could be confusingly grave. Once when he was bantering with her at Marion's she tried to say something about her regret that complications over the right of way should have arisen; but McCloud made light of it, and waved the matter aside as if he were a cavalier. Dicksie did not like it, but it was only that he was afraid she would realize he was a mere railroad superintendent with hopes of a record for promotion quite blasted. And as if this obstacle to a greater reputation were not enough, a wilier enemy threatened in the spring to

New Plans

leave only shreds and patches of what he had already earned.

The Crawling Stone River is said to embody, historically, all of the deceits known to mountain streams. Below the Box Canyon it ploughs through a great bed of yielding silt, its own deposit between the two imposing lines of bluffs that resist its wanderings from side to side of the wide valley. This fertile soil makes up the rich lands that are the envy of less fortunate regions in the Great Basin; but the Crawling Stone is not a river to give quiet title to one acre of its own making. The toil of its centuries spreads beautifully green under the June skies, and the unsuspecting settler, lulled into security by many years of the river's repose, settles on its level bench lands and lays out his long lines of possession; but the Sioux will tell you in their own talk that this man is but a tenant at will; that in another time and at another place the stranger will inherit his fields; and that the Crawling Stone always comes back for its own.

This was the peril that Glover and McCloud essayed when they ran a three-tenths grade and laid an eighty-pound rail up two hundred and fifty miles of the valley. It was in local and exclusive territory a rich prize, and they brought to their undertaking not, perhaps, greater abilities than other men, but incomparably greater material resources than earlier American engineers had possessed.

Success such as theirs is cumulative: when the work is done one man stands for it, but it represents the work of a thousand men in every walk of American industry. Where the credit must lie with the engineer who achieves is in the application of these enormous reserves of industrial triumphs to the particular conditions he faces in the problem before him; in the application lies the genius called success, and this is always new. Moreover, men like Grover and McCloud were fitted for a fight with a mountain river because trained in the Western school, where poverty or resource had sharpened the wits. The building of the Crawling Stone Line came with the dawn of a new day in American capital, when figures that had slept in fairies' dreams woke into every-day use, and when enlarged calculation among men controlling hitherto unheard-of sums of money demanded the best and most permanent methods of construction to insure enduring economies in operating. Thus the constructing of the Crawling Stone Line opened in itself new chapters in Rocky Mountain railroad-building. An equipment of machinery, much of which had never before been applied to such building, had' been assembled by the engineers. Steam-shovels had been sent in battalions, grading-

New Plans

machines and dump-wagons had gone forward in trainloads, and an army of men were operating in the valley. A huge steel bridge three thousand feet long was now being thrown across the river below the Dunning ranch.

The winter had been an unusual one even in a land of winters. The season's fall of snow had not been above an average, but it had fallen in the spring and had been followed by excessively low temperatures throughout the mountains. June came again, but a strange June. The first rise of the Crawling Stone had not moved out the winter frost, and the stream lay bound from bank to bank, and for hundreds of miles, under three feet of ice. When June opened, backward and cold, there had been no spring. Heavy frosts lasting until the middle of the month gave sudden way to summer heat, and the Indians on the upper-valley reservation began moving back into the hills. Then came the rise. Creek after creek in the higher mountains, ice-bound for six months, burst without warning into flood. Soft winds struck with the sun and stripped the mountain walls of their snow. Rains set in on the desert, and far in the high northwest the Crawling Stone lifting its four-foot cap of ice like a bed of feathers began rolling it end over end down the valley. In the Box, forty feet of water struck the canyon walls and ice-floes were

Whispering Smith

hurled like torpedoes against the granite spurs:
the Crawling Stone was starting after its own.

When the river rose, the earlier talk of Dunning's men had been that the Crawling Stone
would put an end to the railroad pretensions by
washing the two hundred and fifty miles of track
back to the Peace River, where it had started.
This much in the beginning was easy to predict;
but the railroad men had turned out in force to
fight for their holdings, and while the ranchers
were laughing, the river was flowing over the bench
lands in the upper valley.

At the Dunning ranch the confidence of the
men in their own security gave way to confusion
as the river, spreading behind the ice-jams into
broad lakes and bursting in torrents through its
barriers, continued to rise. Treacherous in its
broad and yellow quiet, lifting its muddy head in
the stillness of the night, moving unheard over
broad sandy bottoms, backing noiselessly into forgotten channels, stealing through heavy alfalfa
pastures, eating a channel down a slender furrow
—then, with the soil melting from the root, the
plant has toppled at the head, the rivulet has grown
a stream; night falls, and in the morning where
yesterday smiling miles of green fields looked up
to the sun rolls a mad flood of waters: this
is the Crawling Stone.

CHAPTER XIX

THE CRAWLING STONE RISE

SO sudden was the onset of the river that the trained riders of the big ranch were taken completely aback, and hundreds of head of Dunning cattle were swept away before they could be removed to points of safety. Fresh alarms came with every hour of the day and night, and the telephones up and down the valley rang incessantly with appeals from neighbor to neighbor. Lance Dunning, calling out the reserves of his vocabulary, swore tremendously and directed the operations against the river. These seemed, indeed, to consist mainly of hard riding and hard language on the part of everybody. Murray Sinclair, although he had sold his ranch on the Crawling Stone and was concentrating his holdings on the Frenchman, was everywhere in evidence. He was the first at a point of danger and the last to ride away from the slipping acres where the muddy flood undercut; but no defiance seemed to disturb the Crawling Stone, which kept alarmingly at work.

Whispering Smith

Above the alfalfa lands on the long bench north of the house the river, in changing its course many years earlier, had left a depression known as Mud Lake. It had become separated from the main channel of the Crawling Stone by a high, narrow barrier in the form of a bench deposited by the receding waters of some earlier flood, and added to by sand-storms sweeping among the willows that overspread it. Without an effective head or definite system of work the efforts of the men at the Stone Ranch were of no more consequence than if they had spent their time in waving blankets at the river. Twenty men riding in together to tell Lance Dunning that the river was washing out the tree claims above Mud Lake made no perceptible difference in the event. Dicksie, though an inexperienced girl, saw with helpless clearness the futility of it all. The alarms and the continual failures of the army of able-bodied men directed by Sinclair and her cousin wore on her spirit. The river rose until each succeeding inch became a menace to the life and property of the ranch, and in the midst of it came the word that the river was cutting into the willows and heading for Mud Lake. All knew what that meant. If the Crawling Stone should take its old channel, not alone were the two square miles of alfalfa doomed: it would sweep away every vestige of the long stacks below the corrals,

The Crawling Stone Rise

take the barns, and lap the slope in front of the ranch-house itself.

Terror seized Dicksie. She telephoned in her distress for Marion, begging her to come up before they should all be swept away; and Marion, turning the shop over to Katie Dancing, got into the ranch-wagon that Dicksie had sent and started for the Crawling Stone. The confusion along the river road as the wagon approached the ranch showed Marion the seriousness of the situation. Settlers driven from their homes in the upper valley formed almost a procession of misery-stricken people, making their way on horseback, on foot, and in wagons toward Medicine Bend. With them they were bringing all they had saved from the flood—the little bunch of cows, the wagonload of hogs, the household effects, the ponies—as if war or pestilence had struck the valley.

At noon Marion arrived. The ranch-house was deserted, and the men were all at the river. Puss stuck her head out of the kitchen window, and Dicksie ran out and threw herself into Marion's arms. Late news from the front had been the worst: the cutting above Mud Lake had weakened the last barrier that held off the river, and every available man was fighting the current at that point.

Marion heard it all while eating a luncheon.

Whispering Smith

Dicksie, beset with anxiety, could not stay in the house. The man that had driven Marion over, saddled horses in the afternoon and the two women rode up above Mud Lake, now become through rainfall and seepage from the river a long, shallow lagoon. For an hour they watched the shovelling and carrying of sand-bags, and rode toward the river to the very edge of the disappearing willows, where the bank was melting away before the undercut of the resistless current. They rode away with a common feeling—a conviction that the fight was a losing one, and that another day would see the ruin complete.

"Dicksie," exclaimed Marion—they were riding to the house as she spoke—"I'll tell you what we *can* do!" She hesitated a moment. "I will tell you what we *can* do! Are you plucky?"

Dicksie looked at Marion pathetically.

"If you are plucky enough to do it, we can keep the river off yet. I have an idea. I will go, but you must come along."

"Marion, what do you mean? Don't you think I would go anywhere to save the ranch? I should like to know where you dare go in this country that I dare not!"

"Then ride with me over to the railroad camp by the new bridge. We will ask Mr. McCloud to

The Crawling Stone Rise

bring some of his men over. He can stop the river; he knows how."

Dicksie caught her breath. " Oh, Marion! that would do no good, even if I could do it. Why, the railroad has been all swept away in the lower valley."

" How do you know? "

" So every one says."

" Who is every one? "

" Cousin Lance, Mr. Sinclair—all the men. I heard that a week ago."

" Dicksie, don't believe it. You don't know these railroad men. They understand this kind of thing; cattlemen, you know, don't. If you will go with me we can get help. I feel just as sure that those men can control the river as I do that I am looking at you—that is, if anybody can. The question is, do you want to make the effort? "

They talked until they left the horses and entered the house. When they sat down, Dicksie put her hands to her face. " Oh, I wish you had said nothing about it! How *can* I go to him and ask for help now—after Cousin Lance has gone into court about the line and everything? And of course my name is in it all."

" Dicksie, don't raise spectres that have nothing to do with the case. If we go to him and ask him for help he will give it to us if he can; if he can't,

173

what harm is done? He has been up and down the river for three weeks, and he has an army of men camped over by the bridge. I know that, because Mr. Smith rode in from there a few days ago."

"What, Whispering Smith? Oh, if he is there I would not go for worlds!"

"Pray, why not?"

"Why, he is such an awful man!"

"That is absurd, Dicksie."

Dicksie looked grave. "Marion, no man in this part of the country has a good word to say for Whispering Smith."

"Perhaps you have forgotten, Dicksie, that you live in a very rough part of the country," returned Marion coolly. "No man that he has ever hunted down would have anything pleasant to say about him; nor would the friends of such a man be likely to say a good word of him. There are many on the range, Dicksie, that have no respect for life or law or anything else, and they naturally hate a man like Whispering Smith——"

"But, Marion, he killed——"

"I know. He killed a man named Williams a few years ago, while you were at school—one of the worst men that ever infested this country. Williams Cache is named after that man; he made the most beautiful spot in all these mountains a

The Crawling Stone Rise

nest of thieves and murderers. But did you know
that Williams shot down Gordon Smith's only
brother, a trainmaster, in cold blood in front of the
Wickiup at Medicine Bend? No, you never heard
that in this part of the country, did you? They
had a cow-thief for sheriff then, and no officer
in Medicine Bend would go after the murderer.
He rode in and out of town as if he owned it, and
no one dared say a word, and, mind you, Gordon
Smith's brother had never seen the man in his life
until he walked up and shot him dead. Oh, this
was a peaceful country a few years ago! Gordon
Smith was right-of-way man in the mountains then.
He buried his brother, and asked the officers what
they were going to do about getting the murderer.
They laughed at him. He made no protest, except
to ask for a deputy United States marshal's commission. When he got it he started for Williams
Cache after Williams in a buckboard—think of it,
Dicksie—and didn't they laugh at him! He did
not even know the trails, and imagine riding two
hundred miles in a buckboard to arrest a man in
the mountains! He was gone six weeks, and came
back with Williams's body strapped to the buckboard behind him. He never told the story; all
he said when he handed in his commission and
went back to his work was that the man was killed
in a fair fight. Hate him! No wonder they hate

him—the Williams Cache gang and all their friends on the range! Your cousin thinks it policy to placate that element, hoping that they won't steal your cattle if you are friendly with them. I know nothing about that, but I do know something about Whispering Smith. It will be a bad day for Williams Cache when they start him up again. But what has that to do with your trouble? He will not eat you up if you go to the camp, Dicksie. You are just raising bogies."

They had moved to the front porch and Marion was sitting in the rocking-chair. Dicksie stood with her back against one of the pillars and looked at her. As Marion finished Dicksie turned and, with her hand on her forehead, looked in wretchedness of mind out on the valley. As far, in many directions, as the eye could reach the waters spread yellow in the flood of sunshine across the lowlands. There was a moment of silence. Dicksie turned her back on the alarming sight. "Marion, I can't do it!"

"Oh, yes, you can if you want to, Dicksie!" Dicksie looked at her with tearless eyes. "It is only a question of being plucky enough," insisted Marion.

"Pluck has nothing to do with it!" exclaimed Dicksie in fiery tones. "I should like to know why you are always talking about my not having cour-

The Crawling Stone Rise

age! This isn't a question of courage. How can
I go to a man that I talked to as I talked to him
in your house and ask for help? How can I go
to him after my cousin has threatened to kill him,
and gone into court to prevent his coming on our
land? Shouldn't I look beautiful asking help
from him?"

Marion rocked with perfect composure. "No,
dear, you would not look beautiful asking help,
but you would look sensible. It is so easy to be
beautiful and so hard to be sensible."

"You are just as horrid as you can be, Marion
Sinclair!"

"I know that, too, dear. All I wanted to say is
that you would look very sensible just now in asking help from Mr. McCloud."

"I don't care—I won't do it. I will never do
it, not if every foot of the ranch tumbles into the
river. I hope it will! Nobody cares anything
about me. I have no friends but thieves and outlaws."

"Dicksie!" Marion rose.

"That is what you said."

"I did not. I am your friend. How dare you
call me names?" demanded Marion, taking the
petulant girl in her arms. "Don't you think I
care anything about you? There are people in this
country that you have never seen who know you

and love you almost as much as I do. Don't let any silly pride prevent your being sensible, dear." Dicksie burst into tears. Marion drew her over to the settee, and she had her cry out. When it was over they changed the subject. Dicksie went to her room. It was a long time before she came down again, but Marion rocked in patience: she was resolved to let Dicksie fight it out herself.

When Dicksie came down, Marion stood at the foot of the stairs. The young mistress of Crawling Stone Ranch descended step by step very slowly. "Marion," she said simply, "I will go with you."

CHAPTER XX

AT THE DIKE

MARION caught her closely to her heart. " I knew you would go if I got you angry, dear. But you are so slow to anger. Mr. Mc-Cloud is just the same way. Mr. Smith says when he does get angry he can do anything. He is very like you in so many ways."

Dicksie was wiping her eyes. " Is he, Marion? Well, what shall I wear? "

" Just your riding-clothes, dear, and a smile. He won't know what you have on. It is you he will want to see. But I've been thinking of something else. What will your Cousin Lance say? Suppose he should object? "

" Object! I should like to see *him* object after losing the fight himself." Marion laughed. " Well, do you think you can find the way down there for us? "

" I can find any way anywhere within a hundred miles of here."

On the 20th of June McCloud did have something of an army of men in the Crawling Stone Valley. Of these, two hundred and fifty were in the vicinity of the bridge, the abutments and piers of which were being put in just below the Dunning ranch. Near at hand Bill Dancing, with a big gang, had been for some time watching the ice and dynamiting the jams. McCloud brought in more men as the river continued to rise. The danger line on the gauges was at length submerged, and for three days the main-line construction camps had been robbed of men to guard the soft grades above and below the bridge. The new track up and down the valley had become a highway of escape from the flood, and the track patrols were met at every curve by cattle, horses, deer, wolves, and coyotes fleeing from the waste of waters that spread over the bottoms.

Through the Dunning ranch the Crawling Stone River makes a far bend across the valley to the north and east. The extraordinary volume of water now pouring through the Box Canyon exposed ten thousand acres of the ranch to the caprice of the river, and if at the point of its tremendous sweep to the north it should cut back into its old channel the change would wipe the entire body of ranch alfalfa lands off the face of the valley. With the heat of the lengthening June days a vast steam rose from the chill waters of the river, marking in ominous windings the chan-

At the Dike

nel of the main stream through a yellow sea which,
ignoring the usual landmarks of trees and dunes,
flanked the current broadly on either side. Late
in the afternoon of the day that Dicksie with Marion sought McCloud, a storm drifted down the
Topah Topah Hills, and heavy showers broke
across the valley.

At nightfall the rain had passed and the mist
lifted from the river. Above the bluffs rolling
patches of cloud obscured the face of the moon,
but the distant thunder had ceased, and at midnight the valley near the bridge lay in a stillness
broken only by the hoarse calls of the patrols and
far-off megaphones. From the bridge camp, which
lay on high ground near the grade, the distant
lamps of the track-walkers could be seen moving
dimly.

Before the camp-fire in front of McCloud's tent
a group of men, smoking and talking, sat or
lay sprawled on tarpaulins, drying themselves after
the long day. Among them were the weather-
beaten remnants of the old guard of the mountain-
river workers, men who had ridden in the caboose the night that Hailey went to his death,
and had fought the Spider Water with Glover.
Bill Dancing, huge, lumbering, awkward as a bear
and as shifty, was talking, because with no apparent effort he could talk all night, and was a valu-

able man at keeping the camp awake. Bill Dancing talked and, after Sinclair's name had been dropped from the roll, ate and drank more than any two men on the division. A little apart, Mc-Cloud lay on a leather caboose cushion trying to get a nap.

"It was the day George McCloud came," continued Dancing, spinning a continuous story. "Nobody was drinking—Murray Sinclair started that yarn. I was getting fixed up a little for to meet George McCloud, so I asked the barber for some tonic, and he understood me for to say dye for my whiskers, and he gets out the dye and begins to dye my whiskers. My cigar went out whilst he was shampooing me, and my whiskers was wet up with the dye. He turned around to put down th' bottle, and I started for to light my cigar with a parlor-match, and, by gum! away went my whiskers on fire—burnt jus' like a tumbleweed. There was the barbers all running around at once trying for to choke me with towels, and running for water, and me sitting there blazing like a tar-barrel. That's all there was to that story. I went over to Doc Torpy's and got bandaged up, and he wanted me for to go to the hospit'l—but I was going for to meet George McCloud." Bill raised his voice a little and threw his tones carelessly over toward the caboose cushion: "And I was the on'y

At the Dike

man on the platform when his train pulled in. His car was on the hind end. I walked back and waited for some one to come out. It was about seven o'clock in the evening and they was eating dinner inside, so I set up on the fence for a minute, and who do you think got out of the car? That boy laying right over there. ' Where's your dad?' says I; that's exactly what I said. ' Dead,' says he. ' Dead!' says I, surprised-like. ' Dead,' says he, ' for many years.' ' Where's the new superintendent?' says I. ' I'm the new superintendent,' says he. Well, sir, you could have blowed me over with a air-hose. ' Go 'way,' I says. ' What's the matter with your face, Bill?' he says, while I was looking at him; now that's straight. That was George McCloud, right over there, the first time I ever set eyes on him or him on me." The assertion was met with silence such as might be termed marked.

" Bucks told him," continued Bill Dancing, in corroborative detail, " that when he got to Medicine Bend one man would be waiting for to meet him. ' He met me,' says Bucks; ' he's met every superintendent since my time; he'll meet you. Go right up and speak to him,' Bucks says; ' it'll be all right.' "

" Oh, hell, Bill!" protested an indignant chorus.

" Well, what's er matter with you fellows?

Whispering Smith

Didn't you ask me to tell the story?" demanded Dancing angrily. "If you know it better than I do, tell it! Give me some tobacco, Chris," said Bill, honoring with the request the only man in the circle who had shown no scepticism, because he spoke English with difficulty. "And say, Chris, go down and read the bridge gauge, will you? It's close on twelve o'clock, and he's to be called when it reaches twenty-eight feet. I said the boy could never run the division without help from every man on it, and that's what I'm giving him, and I don't care who knows it," said Bill Dancing, raising his voice not too much. "Bucks says that any man that c'n run this division c'n run any railroad on earth. Shoo! now who's this coming here on horseback? Clouding up again, too, by gum!"

The man sent to the bridge had turned back, and behind his lantern Dancing heard the tread of horses. He stood at one side of the camp-fire while two visitors rode up; they were women. Dancing stood dumb as they advanced into the firelight. The one ahead spoke: "Mr. Dancing, don't you know me?" As she stopped her horse the light of the fire struck her face. "Why, Mis' Sinclair!"

"Yes, and Miss Dunning is with me," returned Marion. Bill staggered. "This is an awful

At the Dike

place to get to; we have been nearly drowned, and we want to see Mr. McCloud."

McCloud, roused by Marion's voice, came forward. "You were asleep," said she as he greeted her. "I am so sorry we have disturbed you!" She looked careworn and a little forlorn, yet but a little considering the struggle she and Dicksie had made to reach the camp.

Light blazed from the camp-fire, where Dicksie stood talking with Dancing about horses.

"They are in desperate straits up at the ranch," Marion went on, when McCloud had assured her of her welcome. "I don't see how they can save it. The river is starting to flow into the old channel and there's a big pond right in the alfalfa fields."

"It will play the deuce with things if it gets through there," mused McCloud. "I wonder how the river is? I've been asleep. O Bill!" he called to Dancing, "what water have you got?"

"Twenty-eight six just now, sir. She's a-raising very, very slow, Mr. McCloud."

"So I am responsible for this invasion," continued Marion calmly. "I've been up with Dicksie at the ranch; she sent for me. Just think of it —no woman but old Puss within ten miles of the poor child! And they have been trying everywhere to get bags, and you have all the bags, and the men have been buzzing around over there for a

Whispering Smith

week like bumblebees and doing just about as much good. She and I talked it all over this afternoon, and I told her I was coming over here to see you, and we started out together—and merciful goodness, such a time as we have had!"

"But you started out together; where did you leave her?"

"There she stands the other side of the fire. O Dicksie!"

"Why did you not tell me she was here!" exclaimed McCloud.

Dicksie came into the light as he hastened over. If she was uncertain in manner, he was not. He met her, laughing just enough to relieve the tension of which both for an instant were conscious. She gave him her hand when he put his out, though he felt that it trembled a little. "Such a ride as you have had! Why did you not send me word? I would have come to you!" he exclaimed, throwing reproach into the words.

Dicksie raised her eyes. "I wanted to ask you whether you would sell us some grain-sacks, Mr. McCloud, to use at the river, if you could spare them?"

"Sacks? Why, of course, all you want! But how did you *ever* get here? In all this water, and two lone women! You have been in danger tonight. Indeed you have—don't tell me! And you

At the Dike

are both wet; I know it. Your feet must be wet. Come to the fire. O Bill!" he called to Dancing, "what's the matter with your wood? Let us have a fire, won't you?—one worth while; and build another in front of my tent. I can't believe you have ridden here all the way from the ranch, two of you alone!" exclaimed McCloud, hastening boxes up to the fire for seats.

Marion laughed. "Dicksie can go anywhere! I couldn't have ridden from the house to the barns alone."

"Then tell me how *you* could do it?" demanded McCloud, devouring Dicksie with his eyes.

Dicksie looked at the fire. "I know all the roads pretty well. We did get lost once," she confessed in a low voice, "but we got out again."

"The roads are all under water, though."

"What time is it, please?"

McCloud looked at his watch. "Two minutes past twelve."

Dicksie started. "Past twelve? Oh, this is dreadful! We must start right back, Marion. I had no idea we had been five hours coming five miles."

McCloud looked at her, as if still unable to comprehend what she had accomplished in crossing the flooded bottoms. Her eyes fell back to the fire.

Whispering Smith

"What a blaze!" she murmured as the driftwood snapped and roared. "It's fine for to-night, isn't it?"

"I know you both must have been in the water," he insisted, leaning forward in front of Dicksie to feel Marion's skirt.

"I'm not wet!" declared Marion, drawing back.

"Nonsense, you are wet as a rat! Tell me," he asked, looking at Dicksie, "about your trouble up at the bend. I know something about it. Are the men there to-night? Given up, have they? Too bad! Do open your jackets and try to dry yourselves, both of you, and I'll take a look at the river."

"Suppose—I only say suppose—you first take a look at me." The voice came from behind the group at the fire, and the three turned together.

"By Heaven, Gordon Smith!" exclaimed Mc-Cloud. "Where did you come from?"

Whispering Smith stood in the gloom in patience. "Where do I look as if I had come from? Why don't you ask me whether I'm wet? And won't you introduce me—but this is Miss Dicksie Dunning, I am sure."

Marion with laughter hastened the introduction.

"And you are wet, of course," said McCloud, feeling Smith's shoulder.

"No, only soaked. I have fallen into the river

At the Dike

two or three times, and the last time a big rhinoc-
eros of yours down the grade, a section foreman
named Klein, was obliging enough to pull me out.
Oh, no! I was not looking for you," he ran on,
answering McCloud's question; "not when he
pulled me out. I was just looking for a farm or
a ladder or something. Klein, for a man named
Small, is the biggest Dutchman I ever saw. 'Tell
me, Klein,' I asked, after he had quit dragging
me out—he's a Hanoverian—'where did you get
your pull? And how about your height? Did
your grandfather serve as a grenadier under old
Frederick William and was he kidnapped?' Bill,
don't feed my horse for a while. And Klein tried
to light a cigar I had just taken from my pocket
and given him—fancy! the Germans are a remark-
able people—and sat down to tell me his history,
when some friend down the line began bawling
through a megaphone, and all that poor Klein had
time to say was that he had had no supper, nor
dinner, nor yet breakfast, and would be obliged
for some by the boat he forwarded me in." And,
in closing, Whispering Smith looked cheerfully
around at Marion, at McCloud, and last and
longest of all at Dicksie Dunning.

"Did you come from across the river?" asked
Dicksie, adjusting her wet skirt meekly over her
knees.

Whispering Smith

"You are soaking wet," observed Whispering Smith. "Across the river?" he echoed. "Well, hardly, my dear Miss Dunning! Every bridge is out down the valley except the railroad bridge and there are a few things I don't tackle; one is the Crawling Stone on a tear. No, this was across a little break in this man McCloud's track. I came, to be frank, from the Dunning Ranch to look up two women who rode away from there at seven o'clock to-night, and I want to say that they gave me the ride of my life," and Whispering Smith looked all around the circle and back again and smiled.

Dicksie spoke in amazement. "How did you know we rode away? You were not at the ranch when we left."

"Oh, don't ask him!" cried Marion.

"He knows everything," explained McCloud.

Whispering Smith turned to Dicksie. "I was interested in knowing that they got safely to their destination—whatever it might be, which was none of my business. I happened to see a man that had seen them start, that was all. You don't understand? Well, if you want it in plain English, I made it my business to see a man who made it *his* business to see them. It's all very simple, but these people like to make a mystery of it. Good women are scarcer than riches, and more to be prized than fine gold—in my judgment—so I rode after them."

Marion put her hand for a moment on his coat sleeve; he looked at Dicksie with another laugh and spoke to her because he dared not look toward Marion. "Going back to-night, do you say? You never are."

Dicksie answered quite in earnest: "Oh, but we are. We must!"

"Why did you come, then? It's taken half the night to get here, and will take a night and a half at least to get back."

"We came to ask Mr. McCloud for some grain-sacks—you know, they have nothing to work with at the ranch," said Marion; "and he said we might have some and we are to send for them in the morning."

"I see. But we may as well talk plainly." Smith looked at Dicksie. "You are as brave and as game as a girl can be, I know, or you couldn't have done this. Sacks full of sand, with the boys at the ranch to handle them, would do no more good to-morrow at the bend than bladders. The river is flowing into Squaw Lake above there now. A hundred men that know the game might check things yet if they're there by daylight. Nobody else, and nothing else on God's earth, can."

There was silence before the fire. McCloud

broke it: " I can put the hundred men there at daylight, Gordon, if Miss Dunning and her cousin want them," said McCloud.

Marion sprang to her feet. " Oh, will you do that, Mr. McCloud? "

McCloud looked at Dicksie. " If they are wanted."

Dicksie tried to look at the fire. " We have hardly deserved help from Mr. McCloud at the ranch," she said at last.

He put out his hand. " I must object. The first wreck I ever had on this division Miss Dunning rode twenty miles to offer help. Isn't that true? Why, I would walk a hundred miles to return the offer to her. Perhaps your cousin would object," he suggested, turning to Dicksie; " but no, I think we can manage that. Now what are we going to do? You two can't go back to-night, that is certain."

" We must."

" Then you will have to go in boats," said Whispering Smith.

" But the hill road? "

" There is five feet of water across it in half a dozen places. I swam my horse through, so I ought to know."

" It is all back-water, of course, Miss Dunning," explained McCloud. " Not dangerous."

At the Dike

"But moist," suggested Whispering Smith, "especially in the dark."

McCloud looked at Marion. "Then let's be sensible," he said. "You and Miss Dunning can have my tent as soon as we have supper."

"Supper!"

"Supper is served to all on duty at twelve o'clock, and we're on duty, aren't we? They're about ready to serve now; we eat in the tent," he added, holding out his hand as he heard the patter of raindrops. "Rain again! No matter, we shall be dry under canvas."

Dicksie had never seen an engineers' field headquarters. Lanterns lighted the interior, and the folding-table in the middle was strewn with papers which McCloud swept off into a camp-chest. Two double cots with an aisle between them stood at the head of the tent, and, spread with bright Hudson Bay blankets, looked fresh and undisturbed. A box-table near the head-pole held an alarm-clock, a telegraph key, and a telephone, and the wires ran up the pole behind it. Leather jackets and sweaters lay on boxes under the tent-walls, and heavy boots stood in disorderly array along the foot of the cots. These McCloud, with apologies, kicked into the corners.

"Is this where you stay?" asked Dicksie.

"Four of us sleep in the cots, when we can,

Whispering Smith

and an indefinite number lie on the ground when it rains."

Marion looked around her. " What do you do when it thunders? "

The two men were pulling boxes out for seats; McCloud did not stop to look up. " I crawl under the bed—the others don't seem to mind it."

" Which is your bed? "

" Whichever I can crawl under quickest. I usually sleep there." He pointed to the one on the right.

" I thought so. It has the blanket folded back so neatly, just as if there were sheets under it. I'll bet there aren't any."

" Do you think this is a summer resort? Knisely, my assistant, sleeps there, but of course we are never both in bed at the same time; he's down the river to-night. It's a sort of continuous performance, you know." McCloud looked at Dicksie. " Take off your coat, won't you, please? "

Whispering Smith was trying to drag a chest from the foot of the cot, and Marion stood watching. " What are you trying to do? "

" Get this over to the table for a seat."

" Silly man! why don't you move the table? "

Dicksie was taking off her coat. " How inviting

At the Dike

it all is!" she smiled. "And this is where you stay?"

"When it rains," answered McCloud. "Let me have your hat, too."

"My hair is a sight, I know. We rode over rocks and up gullies into the brush——"

"And through lakes—oh, I know! I can't conceive how you ever got here at all. Your hair is all right. This is camp, anyway. But if you want a glass you can have one. Knisely is a great swell; he's just from school, and has no end of things. I'll rob his bag."

"Don't disturb Mr. Knisely's bag for the world!"

"But you are not taking off your hat. You seem to have something on your mind."

"Help me to get it off my mind, will you, please?"

"If you will let me."

"Tell me how to thank you for your generosity. I came all the way over here to-night to ask you for just the help you have offered, and I could not—it stuck in my throat. But that wasn't what was on my mind. Tell me what you thought when I acted so dreadfully at Marion's."

"I didn't deserve anything better after placing myself in such a fool position. Why don't you ask me what I thought the day you acted so beautifully at Crawling Stone Ranch? I thought that the finest thing I ever saw."

" You were not to blame at Marion's."

" I seemed to be, which is just as bad. I am going to start the 'phones going. It's up to me to make good, you know, in about four hours with a lot of men and material. Aren't you going to take off your hat?—and your gloves are soaking wet."

McCloud took down the receiver, and Dicksie put her hands slowly to her head to unpin her hat. It was a broad hat of scarlet felt rolled high above her forehead, and an eagle's quill caught in the black rosette swept across the front. As she stood in her clinging riding-skirt and her severely plain scarlet waist with only a black ascot falling over it, Whispering Smith looked at her. His eyes did not rest on the picture too long, but his glance was searching. He spoke in an aside to Marion. Marion laughed as she turned her head from where Dicksie was talking again with McCloud. " The best of it is," murmured Marion, " she hasn't a suspicion of how lovely she really is."

CHAPTER XXI

SUPPER IN CAMP

W ILL you never be done with your telephoning?" asked Marion. McCloud was still planning the assembling of the men and teams for the morning. Breakfast and transportation were to be arranged for, and the men and teams and material were to be selected from where they could best be spared. Dicksie, with the fingers of one hand moving softly over the telegraph key, sat on a box listening to McCloud's conferences and orders.

"Cherry says everything is served. Isn't it, Cherry?" Marion called to the Japanese boy.

Cherry laughed with a guttural joy.

"We are ready for it," announced McCloud, rising. "How are we to sit?"

"You are to sit at the head of your own table," said Marion. "I serve the coffee, so I sit at the foot; and Mr. Smith may pass the beans over there, and Dicksie, you are to pour the condensed milk into the cups."

Whispering Smith

"Or into the river, just as you like," suggested Whispering Smith.

McCloud looked at Marion Sinclair. "Really," he exclaimed, "wherever you are it's fair weather! When I see you, no matter how tangled up things are, I feel right away they are coming out. And this man is another."

"Another what?" demanded Whispering Smith.

"Another care-killer." McCloud, speaking to Dicksie, nodded toward his companion. "Troubles slip from your shoulders when he swaggers in, though he's not of the slightest use in the world. I have only one thing against him. It is a physical peculiarity, but an indefensible one. You may not have noticed it, but he is bowlegged."

"From riding your scrub railroad horses. I feel like a sailor ashore when I get off one. Are you going to eat all the bacon, Mr. McCloud, or do we draw a portion of it? I didn't start out with supper to-night."

"Take it all. I suppose it would be useless to ask where you have been to-day?"

"Not in the least, but it would be useless to tell. I am violating no confidence, though, in saying I'm hungry. I certainly shouldn't eat this stuff if I weren't, should you, Miss Dunning? And I don't believe you are eating, by the way. Where

Supper in Camp

is your appetite? Your ride ought to have sharpened it. I'm afraid you are downcast. Oh, don't deny it; it is very plain: but your worry is unnecessary."

"If the rain would only stop," said Marion, "everybody would cheer up. They haven't seen the sun at the ranch for ten days."

"This rain doesn't count so far as the high water is concerned," said McCloud. "It is the weather two hundred and fifty miles above here that is of more consequence to us, and there it is clear to-night. As long as the tent doesn't leak I rather like it. Sing your song about fair weather, Gordon."

"But can the men work in such a downpour?" ventured Dicksie.

The two men looked serious and Marion laughed.

"In the morning you will see a hundred of them marching forward with umbrellas, Mr. McCloud leading. The Japs carry fans, of course."

"I wish I could forget we are in trouble at home," said Dicksie, taking the badinage gracefully. "Worrying people are such a nuisance. Don't protest, for every one knows they are."

"But we are all in trouble," insisted Whispering Smith. "Trouble! Why, bless you, it really is a blessing; pretty successfully disguised, I admit, sometimes, but still a blessing. I'm in trouble all the time, right now, up to my neck in trouble, and the water rising this minute. Look at this man," he nodded toward McCloud. "He is in trouble, and the five hundred under him, they are in all kinds of trouble. I shouldn't know how to sleep without trouble," continued Whispering Smith, warming to the contention. "Without trouble I lose my appetite. McCloud, don't be tight; pass the bread."

"Never heard him do so well," declared Mc-Cloud, looking at Marion.

"Seriously, now," Whispering Smith went on, "don't you know people who, if they were thoroughly prosperous, would be intolerable—simply intolerable? I know several such. All thoroughly prosperous people are a nuisance. That is a general proposition, and I stand by it. Go over your list of acquaintances and you will admit it is true. Here's to trouble! May it always chasten and never overwhelm us: our greatest bugbear and our best friend! It sifts our friends and unmasks our enemies. Like a lovely woman, it woos us——"

"Oh, never!" exclaimed Marion. "A lovely woman doesn't woo, she is wooed!"

"What are you looking for, perfection in rhetorical figure? This is extemporaneous."

"But it won't do!"

Supper in Camp

" And asks to be conquered," suggested Whispering Smith.

" Asks! Oh, scandalous, Mr. Smith! "

" It is easy to see why *he* never could get any one to marry him," declared McCloud over the bacon.

" Hold on, then! Like lovely woman, it does not seek us, we seek it," persisted the orator. " *That* at least is so, isn't it? "

" It is better," assented Marion.

" And it waits to be conquered. How is that? "

Marion turned to Dicksie. " You are not helping a bit. What do you think? "

" I don't think woman and trouble ought to be associated even in figure; and I think ' waits ' is horrid," and Dicksie looked gravely at Whispering Smith.

McCloud, too, looked at him. " You're in trouble now yourself."

" And I brought it on myself. So we do seek it, don't we? And trouble, I must hold, *is* like woman. ' Waits ' I strike out as unpleasantly suggestive; let it go. So, then, trouble is like a lovely woman, loveliest *when* conquered. Now, Miss Dunning, if you have a spark of human kindness you won't turn me down on that proposition. By the way, I have something put down about trouble."

Whispering Smith

He was laughing. Dicksie asked herself if this could be the man about whom floated so many accusations of coldness and cruelty and death. He drew a note-book from a waistcoat pocket.

"Oh, it's in the note-book! There comes the black note-book," exclaimed McCloud.

"Don't make fun of my note-book!"

"I shouldn't dare." McCloud pointed to it as he spoke to Dicksie. "You should see what is in that note-book: the record, I suppose, of every man in the mountains and of a great many outside."

"And countless other things," added Marion.

"Such as what?" asked Dicksie.

"Such as you, for example," said Marion.

"Am I a thing?"

"A sweet thing, of course," said Marion ironically. "Yes, you; with color of eyes, hair, length of index finger of the right hand, curvature of thumb, disposition—whether peaceable or otherwise, and prison record, if any."

"And number of your watch," added McCloud.

"How dreadful!"

Whispering Smith eyed Dicksie benignly. "They are talking this nonsense to distract us, of course, but I am bound to read you what I have here, if you will graciously submit."

"Submit? I *wait* to hear it," laughed Dicksie.

"My training in prosody is the slightest, as

202

Supper in Camp

will appear," he continued, " and *synecdoche* and *Schenectady* were always on the verge of getting mixed when I went to school. My sentiment may be termed obvious, but I want to offer a slight apology on behalf of trouble; it is abused too much. I submit this

"SONG TO TROUBLE

"Here's to the measure of every man's worth,
Though when men are wanting it grieves us.
Hearts that are hollow we're better without,
Hearts that are loyal it leaves us.

"Trouble's the dowry of every man's birth,
A nettle adversity flings us ;
It yields to the grip of the masterful hand,
When we play coward it stings us.

" Chorus."

" Don't say chorus; that's common."

" I have to say chorus. My verses don't speak for themselves, and no one would know it was a chorus if I didn't explain. Besides, I'm short a line in the chorus, and that is what I'm waiting for to finish the song.

"Chorus :

"Then here's to the bumper that proves every friend!
And though in the drinking it wrings us,
Here's to the cup that we drain to the end,
And here's to—

There I stick. I can't work out the last line."

Whispering Smith

"And here's to the hearts that it brings us!" exclaimed Dicksie.

"Fine!" cried McCloud. "'Here's to the hearts that it brings us!'"

Dicksie threw back her head and laughed with the others. Then Whispering Smith looked grave. "There is a difficulty," said he, knitting his brows. "You have spoiled my song."

"Oh, Mr. Smith, I hope not! Have I?"

"Your line is so much better than what I have that it makes my stuff sound cheap."

"Oh, no, Gordon!" interposed McCloud. "You don't see that one reason why Miss Dunning's line sounds better than yours is owing to the differences in your voices. If she will repeat the chorus, finishing with her line, you will see the difference."

"Miss Dunning, take the note-book," begged Whispering Smith.

"And rise, of course," suggested McCloud.

"Oh, the note-book! I shall be afraid to hold it. Where are the verses, Mr. Smith? Is this fine handwriting yours?

Then here's to the bumper that proves every friend!

Isn't that true?

And though when we drink it it wrings us,

—and it does sometimes!

204

Supper in Camp

Here's to the cup that we drain to the end,

Even women have to be plucky, don't they, Marion?

And here's to the hearts that it brings us!"

Whispering Smith rose before the applause subsided. " I ask you to drink this, standing, in condensed milk."

" Have we enough to stand in? " interposed Dicksie.

" If we stand together in trouble, that ought to be enough," observed McCloud.

" We're doing that without rising, aren't we? " asked Marion. " If *we* hadn't been in trouble we shouldn't have ventured to this camp to-night."

" And if you had not put me to the trouble of following you—and it was a lot of trouble!—*I* shouldn't have been in camp to-night," said Whispering Smith.

" And if *I* had not been in trouble this camp wouldn't have been here to-night," declared McCloud. " What have we to thank for it all but trouble? "

A voice called the superintendent's name through the tent door. " Mr. McCloud? "

" And there is more trouble," added McCloud. " What is it, Bill? "

Whispering Smith

"Twenty-eight and nine tenths on the gauge, sir."

McCloud looked at his companions. "I told you so. Up three tenths. Thank you, Bill; I'll be with you in a minute. Tell Cherry to come and take away the supper things, will you? That is about all the water we shall get to-night, I think. It's all we want," added McCloud, glancing at his watch. "I'm going to take a look at the river. We shall be quiet now around here until half-past three, and if you, Marion, and Miss Dunning will take the tent, you can have two hours' rest before we start. Bill Dancing will guard you against intrusion, and if you want ice-water ring twice."

CHAPTER XXII

A TALK WITH WHISPERING SMITH

WHEN Whispering Smith had followed Mc-
Cloud from the tent, Dicksie turned to
Marion and caught her hand. " Is this the terrible
man I have heard about? " she murmured. " And
I thought him ferocious! But is he as pitiless as
they say, Marion? "

Marion laughed—a troubled little laugh of surprise and sadness. " Dear, he isn't pitiless at all.
He has unpleasant things to do, and does them.
He is the man on whom the railroad relies to re-
press the lawlessness that breaks out in the mountains at times and interferes with the operating of the road. It frightens people away, and
prevents others from coming in to settle. Railroads want law and order. Robbery and murders
don't make business for railroads. They depend
on settlers for developing a country, don't you
know; otherwise they would have no traffic, not
to speak of wanting their trains and men let alone.
When Mr. Bucks undertook to open up this country to settlers, he needed a man of patience and

endurance and with courage and skill in dealing
with lawless men, and no man has ever succeeded
so well as this terrible man you have heard about.
He *is* terrible, my dear, to lawless men, not to any
one else. He is terrible in resource and in daring,
but not in anything else I know of, and I knew him
when he was a boy and wore a big pink worsted
scarf when he went skating."

"I should like to have seen that scarf," said
Dicksie reflectively. She rose and looked around
the tent. In a few minutes she made Marion lie
down on one of the cots. Then she walked to the
front of the tent, opened the flap, and looked out.

Whispering Smith was sitting before the fire.
Rain was falling, but Dicksie put on her close-
fitting black coat, raised the door-flap, and walked
noiselessly from the tent and up behind him.
"Alone in the rain?" she asked.

She had expected to see him start at her voice,
but he did not, though he rose and turned around.
"Not now," he answered as he offered her his box
with a smile.

"Are you taking your hat off for me in the rain?
Put it on again!" she insisted with a little tone of
command, and she was conscious of gratification
when he obeyed amiably.

"I won't take your box unless you can find another!" she said. "Oh, you have another! I

A Talk with Whispering Smith

came out to tell you what a dreadful man I thought
you were, and to apologize."

"Never mind apologizing. Lots of people
think worse than that of me and don't apologize.
I'm sorry I have no shelter to offer you, except to
sit on this side and take the rain."

"Why should you take the rain for me?"

"You are a woman."

"But a stranger to you."

"Only in a way."

Dicksie gazed for a moment at the fire. "You
won't think me abrupt, will you?" she said, turning to him, "but, as truly as I live, I cannot account
for you, Mr. Smith. I guess at the ranch we don't
know what goes on in the world. Everything I
see of you contradicts everything I have heard
of you."

"You haven't seen much of me yet, you know,
and you may have heard much better accounts of
me than I deserve. Still, it isn't surprising you
can't account for me; in fact, it would be surprising
if you could. Nobody pretends to do that. You
must not be shocked if I can't even account for myself. Do you know what a derelict is? A ship that
has been abandoned but never wholly sinks."

"Please don't make fun of me! How did you
happen to come into the mountains? I do want to
understand things better."

Whispering Smith

"Why, you are in real earnest, aren't you? But I am not making fun of you. Do you know President Bucks? No? Too bad! He's a very handsome old bachelor. And he is one of those men who get all sorts of men to do all sorts of things for them. You know, building and operating railroads in this part of the country is no joke. The mountains are filled with men that don't care for God, man, or the devil. Sometimes they furnish their own ammunition to fight with and don't bother the railroad for years; at such times the railroad leaves them alone. For my part, I never quarrel with a man that doesn't quarrel with the road. Then comes a time when they get after us, shooting our men or robbing our agents or stopping our trains. Of course we have to get busy then. A few years ago they worried Bucks till they nearly turned his hair gray. At that unfortunate time I happened into his office with a letter of introduction from his closest Chicago friend, Willis Howard, prince of good men, the man that made the Palmer House famous —yes. Now I had come out here, Miss Dunning —I almost said Miss Dicksie, because I hear it so much——"

"I should be greatly set up to hear you call me Dicksie. And I have wondered a thousand times about your name. Dare I ask—*why* do

A Talk with Whispering Smith

they call you Whispering Smith? You don't whisper."

He laughed with abundance of good-humor. "That is a ridiculous accident, and it all came about when I lived in Chicago. Do you know anything about the infernal climate there? Well, in Chicago I used to lose my voice whenever I caught a cold—sometimes for weeks together. So they began calling me Whispering Smith, and I've never been able to shake the name. Odd, isn't it? But I came out to go into the real-estate business. I was looking for some gold-bearing farm lands where I could raise quartz, don't you know, and such things—yes. I don't mind telling you this, though I wouldn't tell it to everybody——"

"Certainly not," assented Dicksie, drawing her skirt around to sit in closer confidence.

"I wanted to get rich quick," murmured Whispering Smith, confidentially.

"Almost criminal, wasn't it?"

"I wanted to have evening clothes."

"Yes."

"And for once in my life two pairs of suspenders—a modest ambition, but a gnawing one. Would you believe it? Before I left Bucks's office he had hired me for a railroad man. When he asked me what I could do, and I admitted a little experience in handling real estate, he brought his

Whispering Smith

fist down on the table and swore I should be his right-of-way man."

"How about the mining?"

Whispering Smith waved his hand in something of the proud manner in which Bucks could wave his presidential hand. "My business, Bucks said, need not interfere with that, not in the least; he said that I could do all the mining I wanted to, and I *have* done all the mining I wanted to. But here is the singular thing that happened: I opened up my office and had nothing to do; they didn't seem to want any right of way just then. I kept getting my check every month, and wasn't doing a hand's turn but riding over the country and shooting jack-rabbits. But, Lord, I love this country! Did you know I used to be a cowboy in the mountains years ago? Indeed I did. I know it almost as well as you do. I mined more or less in the meantime. Occasionally I would go to Bucks—you say you don't know him?—too bad!—and tell him candidly I wasn't doing a thing to earn my salary. At such times he would only ask me how I liked the job," and Whispering Smith's heavy eyebrows rose in mild surprise at the recollection. "One day when I was talking with him he handed me a telegram from the desert saying that a night operator at a lonely station had been shot and a switch misplaced and a train nearly wrecked. He asked me

A Talk with Whispering Smith

what I thought of it. I discovered that the poor fellow had shot himself, and in the end we had to put him in the insane asylum to save him from the penitentiary—but that was where my trouble began.

"It ended in my having to organize the special service on the whole road to look after a thousand and one things that nobody else had— well, let us say time or inclination to look after: fraud and theft and violence and all that sort of disagreeable thing. Then one day the cat crawled out of the bag. What do you think? That man who is now president of this road had somewhere seen a highly colored story about me in a magazine, a ten-cent magazine, you know. He had spotted me the first time I walked into his office, and told me a long time afterward it was just like seeing a man walk out of a book, and that he had hard work to keep from falling on my neck. He knew what he wanted me for; it was just this thing. I left Chicago to get away from it, and this is the result. It is not all that kind of thing, oh, no! When they want to cross a reservation I have a winter in Washington with our attorneys and dine with old friends in the White House, and the next winter I may be on snowshoes chasing a band of rustlers. I swore long ago I would do no more of it—that I couldn't and wouldn't. But it is Bucks. I can't go back on him. He is amiable and I am soft. He says he is going to have a crown and harp for me some day, but I fancy—that is, I have an intimation— that there will be a red-hot protest at the bar of Heaven," he lowered his tone, " from a certain un- mentionable quarter when I undertake to put the vestments on. By the way, I hear you are inter- ested in chickens. Oh, yes, I've heard a lot about you! Bob Johnson, over at Oroville, has some pretty bantams I want to tell you about."

Whether he talked railroad or chickens, it was all one: Dicksie sat spellbound; and when he an- nounced it was half-past three o'clock and time to rouse Marion, she was amazed.

Dawn showed in the east. The men eating breakfast in tents were to be sent on a work-train up a piece of Y-track that led as near as they could be taken to where they were needed. The train had pulled out when Dicksie, Marion, McCloud, and Whispering Smith took horses to get across to the hills and through to the ranch-house. They had ridden slowly for some distance when Mc- Cloud was called back. The party returned and rode together into the mists that hung below the bridge. They came out upon a little party of men standing with lanterns on a piece of track where the river had taken the entire grade and raced furi- ously through the gap. Fog shrouded the light of

A Talk with Whispering Smith

the lanterns and lent gloom to the silence, but the women could see the group that McCloud had joined. Standing above his companions on a pile of ties, a tall young man holding a megaphone waited. Out of the darkness there came presently a loud calling. The tall young man at intervals bawled vigorously into the fog in answer. Far away could be heard, in the intervals of silence, the faint clang of the work-train engine-bell. Again the voice came out of the fog. McCloud took the megaphone and called repeatedly. Two men rowed a boat out of the back-water behind the grade, and when McCloud stepped into it, it was released on a line while the oarsmen guided it across the flood until it disappeared. The two megaphone voices could still be heard. After a time the boat was pulled back again, and McCloud stepped out of it. He spoke a moment with the men, rejoined his party, and climbed into the saddle. " Now we are off," said he.

" What was it all about? " asked Whispering Smith.

" Your friend Klein is over there. Nobody could understand what he said except that he wanted me. When I got here I couldn't make out what he was talking about, so they let us out in the boat on a line. Half-way across the break I made out what was troubling him. He said he

Whispering Smith

was going to lose three hundred feet of track, and
wanted to know what to do."

"And you told him, of course?"

"Yes."

"What did you tell him?"

"I told him to lose it."

"I could have done that myself."

"Why didn't you?"

CHAPTER XXIII

AT THE RIVER

THEY found the ranch-house as Marion and
Dicksie had left it, deserted. Puss told
them every one was at the river. McCloud did
not approve Dicksie's plan of going down to
see her cousin first. "Why not let me ride down
and manage it without bringing you into it at all?"
he suggested. "It can be done." And after further discussion it was so arranged.

McCloud and Smith had been joined by Dancing
on horseback, and they made their way around
Squaw Lake and across the fields. The fog was
rolling up from the willows at the bend. Men were
chopping in the brush, and McCloud and his companion soon met Lance Dunning riding up the narrow strip of sand that held the river off the ranch.

McCloud greeted Dunning, regardless of his
amazement, as if he had parted from him the day
before. "How are you making it over here?"
he asked. "We are in pretty good shape at the
moment down below, and I thought I would ride
over to see if we could do anything for you. This

is what you call pretty fair water for this part of the valley, isn't it?"

Lance swallowed his astonishment. "This isn't water, McCloud; this is hell." He took off his hat and wiped his forehead. "Well, I call this white, anyway, and no mistake—I do indeed, sir! This is Whispering Smith, isn't it? Glad to see you at Crawling Stone, sir." Which served not only to surprise but to please Whispering Smith.

"Some of my men were free," continued Mc-Cloud; "I switched some mattresses and sacks around the Y, thinking they might come in play here for you at the bend. They are at your service if you think you need them."

"Need them!" Lance swore fiercely and from the bottom of his heart. He was glad to get help from any quarter and made no bones about it. Moreover, McCloud lessened the embarrassment by explaining that he had a personal interest in holding the channel where it ran, lest a change above might threaten the approaches already built to the bridge; and Whispering Smith, who would have been on terms with the catfish if he had been flung into the middle of the Crawling Stone, contributed at once, like a reënforced spring, to the ease of the situation.

Lance again took off his hat and wiped the sweat of anxiety from his dripping forehead. "What-

At the River

ever differences of opinion I may have with your damned company, I have no lack of esteem personally, McCloud, for you, sir, by Heaven! How many men did you bring?"

"And whatever wheels you Crawling Stone ranchers may have in your heads on the subject of irrigation," returned McCloud evenly, "I have no lack of esteem personally, Mr. Dunning, for you. I brought a hundred."

"Do you want to take charge here? I'm frank, sir; you understand this game and I don't."

"Suppose we look the situation over; meantime, all our supplies have to be brought across from the Y. What should you think, Mr. Dunning, of putting all the teams you can at that end of the work?"

"Every man that can be spared from the river shall go at it. Come over here and look at our work and judge for yourself."

They rode to where the forces assembled by Lance were throwing up embankments and riprapping. There was hurried running to and fro, a violent dragging about of willows, and a good deal of shouting.

Dunning, with some excitement, watched McCloud's face to note the effect of the activity on him, but McCloud's expression, naturally reserved, reflected nothing of his views on the subject. Dunning waved his hand at the lively scene. " They've been at it all night. How many would you take away, sir? "

" You might take them all away, as far as the river is concerned," said McCloud after a moment.

" What? Hell! All? "

" They are not doing anything, are they, but running around in a circle? And those fellows over there might as well be making mud pies as rip-rapping at that point. What we need there is a mattress and sandbags—and plenty of them. Bill," directed McCloud in an even tone of business as he turned to Dancing, " see how quick you can get your gangs over here with what sacks they can carry and walk fast. If you will put your men on horses, Mr. Dunning, they can help like everything. That bank won't last a great while the way the river is getting under it now." Dancing wheeled like an elephant on his bronco and clattered away through the mud. Lance Dunning, recovering from his surprise, started his men back for the wagons, and McCloud, dismounting, walked with him to the water's edge to plan the fight for what was left of the strip in front of the alfalfa fields.

When Whispering Smith got back to the house he was in good-humor. He joined Dicksie and Marion in the dining-room, where they were drink-

At the River

ing coffee. Afterward Dicksie ordered horses
saddled and the three rode to the river. Up and
down the bank as far as they could see in the misty
rain, men were moving slowly about—more men,
it seemed to Dicksie, than she had ever seen together in her life. The confusion and the noise
had disappeared. No one appeared to hurry, but
every one had something to do, and, from the
gangs who with sledges were sinking " dead-men "
among the trees to hold the cables of the mattress
that was about to be sunk, and the Japs who were
diligently preparing to float and load it, to the men
that were filling and wheeling the sandbags, no
one appeared excited. McCloud joined the visitors for a few moments and then went back to
where Dancing and his men on life-lines were
guiding the mattress to its resting-place. In spite
of the gloom of the rain, which Whispering Smith
said was breaking, Dicksie rode back to the house
in much better spirits with her two guests; and when
they came from luncheon the sun, as Smith had pre-
dicted, was shining.

"Oh, come out!" cried Dicksie, at the door.
Marion had a letter to write and went upstairs,
but Whispering Smith followed Dicksie. "Does
everything you say come true?" she demanded as
she stood in the sunshine.

She was demure with light-heartedness and he

221

looked at her approvingly. " I hope nothing I may say ever will come true unless it makes you happy," he answered lightly. " It would be a shame if it did anything else."

She pointed two accusing fingers at him. " Do you know what you promised last night? You have forgotten already! You said you would tell me why my leghorns are eating their feathers off."

" Let me talk with them."

" Just what I should like. Come on! " said Dicksie, leading the way to the chicken-yard. " I want you to see my bantams too. I have three of the dearest little things. One is setting. They are over the way. Come see them first. And, oh, you must see my new game chickens. Truly, you never saw anything as handsome as Cæsar—he's the rooster; and I have six pullets. Cæsar is perfectly superb."

When the two reached the chicken-houses Dicksie examined the nest where she was setting the bantam hen. " This miserable hen will not set," she exclaimed in despair. " See here, Mr. Smith, she has left her nest again and is scratching around on the ground. Isn't it a shame? I've tied a cord around her leg so she couldn't run away, and she is hobbling around like a scrub pony."

" Perhaps the eggs are too warm," suggested her companion. " I have had great success in cases like this with powdered ice—not using too

At the River

much, of course; just shave the ice gently and rub it over the eggs one at a time; it will often result in refreshing the attention of the hen."

Dicksie looked grave. "Aren't you ashamed to make fun of me?"

Whispering Smith seemed taken aback. "Is it really serious business?"

"Of course."

"Very good. Let me watch this hen for a few minutes and diagnose her. You go on to your other chickens. I'll stay here and think."

Dicksie went down through the yards. When she came back, Whispering Smith was sitting on a cracker-box watching the bantam. The chicken was making desperate efforts to get off Dicksie's cord and join its companions in the runway. Smith was eying the bantam critically when Dicksie rejoined him. "Do you usually," he asked, looking suddenly up, "have success in setting roosters?"

"Now you are having fun with me again."

"No, by Heaven! I am not."

"Have you diagnosed the case?"

"I have, and I have diagnosed it as a case of mistaken identity."

"Identity?"

"And misapplied energy. Miss Dicksie, you have tied up the wrong bird. This is not a ban-

tam hen at all; this is a bantam rooster. Now that
is *my* judgment. Compare him with the others.
Notice how much darker his plumage is—it's
the rooster," declared Whispering Smith, wiping
the perplexity from his brow. " Don't feel bad,
not at all. Cut him loose, Miss Dicksie—don't
hesitate; do it on my responsibility. Now let's
look at the cannibal leghorns—and great Cæsar."

CHAPTER XXIV

BETWEEN GIRLHOOD AND WOMANHOOD

ABOUT nine o'clock that night Puss ushered McCloud in from the river. Dicksie came running downstairs to meet him. " Your cousin insisted I should come up to the house for some supper," said McCloud dryly. " I could have taken camp fare with the men. Gordon stayed there with him."

Dicksie held his hat in her hand, and her eyes were bright in the firelight. Puss must have thought the two made a handsome couple, for she lingered, as she started for the kitchen, to look back.

" Puss," exclaimed her mistress, " fry a chicken right away! A big one, Puss! Mr. McCloud is very hungry, I know. And be quick, do! Oh, how is the river, Mr. McCloud? "

" Behaving like a lamb. It hasn't fallen much, but the pressure seems to be off the bank, if you know what that means? "

" You must be a magician! Things changed the minute you came! "

Whispering Smith

"The last doctor usually gets credit for the cure, you know."

"Oh, I know all about that. Don't you want to freshen up? Should you mind coming right to my room? Marion is in hers," explained Dicksie, "and I am never sure of Cousin Lance's,—he has so many boots."

When she had disposed of McCloud she flew to the kitchen. Puss was starting after a chicken. "Take a lantern, Puss!" whispered Dicksie vehemently.

"No, indeed; dis nigger don' need no lantern fo' chickens, Miss Dicksie."

"But get a good one, Puss, and make haste, do! Mr. McCloud must be starved! Where is the baking powder? I'll get the biscuits started."

Puss turned fiercely. "Now look-a heah, yo' can't make biscuits! Yo' jes' go se' down wif dat young gen'm'n! Jes' lemme lone, ef yo' please! Dis ain't de firs' time I killed chickens, Miss Dicksie, an' made biscuits. Jes' clair out an' se' down! Place f'r young ladies is in de parlor! Ol' Puss can cook supper f'r one man yet—ef she *has* to!"

"Oh, yes, Puss, certainly, I know, of course; only, get a nice chicken!" and with the parting admonition Dicksie, smoothing her hair wildly, hastened back to the living-room.

But the harm was done. Puss, more excited

than her mistress, lost her head when she got to the chicken-yard, and with sufficiently bad results. When Dicksie ran out a few moments afterward for a glass of water for McCloud, Puss was calmly wiping her hands, and in the sink lay the quivering form of young Cæsar. Dicksie caught her favorite up by the legs and suppressed a cry. There could be no mistake. She cast a burning look on Puss. It would do no good to storm now. Dicksie only wrung her hands and returned to McCloud.

He rose in the happiest mood. He could not see what a torment Dicksie was in, and took the water without asking himself why it trembled in her hand. Her restrained manner did not worry him, for he felt that his fight at the river was won, and the prospect of fried chicken composed him. Even the long hour before Puss, calm and inviting in a white cap and apron, appeared to announce supper, passed like a dream. When Dicksie rose to lead the way to the dining-room, McCloud walked on air; the high color about her eyes intoxicated him. Not till half the fried chicken, with many compliments from McCloud, had disappeared, and the plate had gone out for the second dozen biscuits, did he notice Dicksie's abstraction.

" I'm sure you need worry no longer about the

water," he observed reassuringly. "I think the worst of the danger is past."

Dicksie looked at the table-cloth with wide-open eyes. "I feel sure that it is. I am no longer worrying about that."

"It's nothing I can do or leave undone, is it?" asked McCloud, laughing a little as he implied in his tone that she must be worrying about something.

Dicksie made a gesture of alarm. "Oh, no, no; nothing!"

"It's a pretty good plan not to worry about anything."

"Do you think so?"

"Why, we all thought so last night. Heavens!" McCloud drew back in his chair. "I never offered you a piece of chicken! What have I been thinking of?"

"Oh, I wouldn't eat it anyway!" cried Dicksie.

"You wouldn't? It is delicious. Do have a plate and a wing at least."

"Really, I could not bear to think of it," she said pathetically.

He spoke lower. "Something is troubling you. I have no right to a confidence, I know," he added, taking a biscuit.

Her eyes fell to the floor. "It is nothing. Pray, don't mind me. May I fill your cup?" she asked, looking up. "I am afraid I worry too much over

Between Girlhood and Womanhood

what has happened and can't be helped. Do you never do that?"

McCloud, laughing wretchedly, tore Cæsar's last leg from his body. "No indeed. I never worry over what can't be helped."

They left the dining-room. Marion came down. But they had hardly seated themselves before the living-room fire when a messenger arrived with word that McCloud was wanted at the river. His chagrin at being dragged away was so apparent that Marion and Dicksie sympathized with him and laughed at him. "'I never worry about what can't be helped,'" Dicksie murmured.

He looked at Marion. "That's a shot at me. You don't want to go down, do you?" he asked ironically, looking from one to the other.

"Why, of course I'll go down," responded Dicksie promptly. "Marion caught cold last night, I guess, so you will excuse her, I know. I will be back in an hour, Marion, and you can toast your cold while I'm gone."

"But you mustn'c go alone!" protested Mc-Cloud.

Dicksie lifted her chin the least bit. "I shall be going with you, shall I not? And if the messenger has gone back I shall have to guide you. You never could find your way alone."

"But I can go," interposed Marion, rising.

Whispering Smith

"Not at all; you can *not* go!" announced Dicksie. "I can protect both Mr. McCloud and myself. If he should arrive down there under the wing of two women he would never hear the last of it. I am mistress here still, I think; and I sha'n't be leaving home, you know, to make the trip!"

McCloud looked at Marion. "I never worry over what can't be helped—though it is dollars to cents that those fellows don't need me down there any more than a cat needs two tails. And how will you get back?" he asked, turning to Dicksie.

"I will ride back!" returned Dicksie loftily. "But you may, if you like, help me get my horse up."

"Are you sure you can find your way back?" persisted McCloud.

Dicksie looked at him in surprise. "Find my way back?" she echoed softly. "I could not lose it. I can ride over any part of this country at noon or at midnight, asleep or awake, with a saddle or without, with a bridle or without, with a trail or without. I've ridden every horse that has ever come on the Crawling Stone Ranch. I could ride when I was three years old. Find my way back?"

The messenger had gone when the two rode from the house. The sky was heavily overcast,

230

Between Girlhood and Womanhood

and the wind blew such a gale from the south and west that one could hardly hear what the other said. McCloud could not have ridden from the house to the barn in the utter darkness, but his horse followed Dicksie's. She halted frequently on the trail for him to come up with her, and after they had crossed the alfalfa fields McCloud did not care whether they ever found the path again or not. " It's great, isn't it? " he exclaimed, coming up to her after opening a gate in the dark. " Where are you? "

" This way," laughed Dicksie. " Look out for the trail here. Give me your hand and let your horse have his head. If he slips, drop off quick on this side." McCloud caught her hand. They rode for a moment in silence, the horses stepping cautiously. " All right now," said Dicksie; " you may let go." But McCloud kept his horse up close and clung to the warm hand. " The camp is just around the hill," murmured Dicksie, trying to pull away. " But of course if you would like to ride in holding my hand you may! "

" No," said McCloud, " of course not—not for worlds! But, Miss Dicksie, couldn't we ride back to the house and ride around the other way into camp? I think the other way into the camp—say, around by the railroad bridge—would be prettier, don't you? "

Whispering Smith

For answer she touched Jim lightly with her lines and his spring released her hand very effectively. As she did so the trail turned, and the camp-fire, whipped in the high wind, blazed before them.

Whispering Smith and Lance Dunning were sitting together as the two galloped up. Smith helped Dicksie to alight. She was conscious of her color and that her eyes were now unduly bright. Moreover, Whispering Smith's glance rested so calmly on both McCloud's face and her own that Dicksie felt as if he saw quite through her and knew everything that had happened since they left the house.

Lance was talking to McCloud. " Don't abuse the wind," McCloud was saying. " It's our best friend to-night, Mr. Dunning. It is blowing the water off-shore. Where is the trouble? " For answer Dunning led McCloud off toward the Bend, and Dicksie was left alone with Whispering Smith.

He made a seat for her on the windward side of the big fire. When she had seated herself she looked up in great contentment to ask if he was not going to sit down beside her. The brown coat, the high black hat, and the big eyes of Whispering Smith had already become a part of her mental store. She saw that he seemed preoccu-

Between Girlhood and Womanhood

pied, and sought to draw him out of his abstraction.

"I am so glad you and Mr. McCloud are getting acquainted with Cousin Lance," she said. "And do you mind my giving you a confidence, Mr. Smith? Lance has been so unreasonable about this matter of the railroad's coming up the valley and powwowing so much with lawyers and ranchers that he has been forgetting about everything at home. He is so much older than I am that he ought to be the sensible one of the family, don't you think so? It frightens me to have him losing at cards and drinking. I am afraid he will get into some shooting affair. I don't understand what has come over him, and I worry about it. I believe you could influence him if you knew him."

"What makes you think that?" asked Whispering Smith, but his eyes were on the fire.

"Because these men he spends his time with in town—the men who fight and shoot so much—are afraid of you. Don't laugh at me. I know it is quite true in spite of their talk. I was afraid of you myself until——"

"Until we made verse together."

"Until you made verse and I spoiled it. But I think it is because I don't understand things that I am so afraid. I am not naturally a coward.

Whispering Smith

I'm sure I could not be afraid of you if I understood things better. And there is Marion. She
puzzles me. She will never speak of her husband
—I don't know why. And I don't know why Mr.
McCloud is so hard on Mr. Sinclair—Mr. Sinclair seems so kind and good-natured."

Whispering Smith looked from the fire into
Dicksie's eyes. "What should you say if I gave
you a confidence?"

She opened her heart to his searching gaze.
"Would you trust me with a confidence?"

He answered without hesitation. "You shall
see. Now, I have many things I can't talk about,
you understand. But if I had to give you a secret
this instant that carried my life, I shouldn't fear to
do it—so much for trusting you. Only this, too,
as to what I say: don't ever quote me or let it
appear that you any more than know me. Can you
manage that? Really? Very good; you will
understand why in a minute. The man that is
stirring up all this trouble with your Cousin Lance
and in this whole country is your kind and good-
natured neighbor, Mr. Sinclair. I am prejudiced
against him; let us admit that on the start, and
remember it in estimating what I say. But Sinclair is the man who has turned your cousin's head,
as well as made things in other ways unpleasant
for several of us. Sinclair—I tell you so you will

Between Girlhood and Womanhood

understand everything, more than your cousin, Mr. McCloud, or Marion Sinclair understand— Sinclair is a train-wrecker and a murderer. That makes you breathe hard, doesn't it? but it is so. Sinclair is fairly educated and highly intelligent, capable in every way, daring to the limit, and, in a way, fascinating; it is no wonder he has a following. But his following is divided into two classes: the men that know all the secrets, and the men that don't—men like Rebstock and Du Sang, and men like your cousin and a hundred or so sports in Medicine Bend, who see only the glamour of Sinclair's pace. Your cousin sympathizes with Sinclair when he doesn't actually side with him. All this has helped to turn Sinclair's head, and this is exactly the situation you and McCloud and I and a lot of others are up against. They don't know all this, but I know it, and now you know it. Let me tell you something that comes close to home. You have a cowboy on the ranch named Karg—he is called Flat Nose. Karg was a railroad man. He is a cattle-thief, a train-robber, a murderer, and a spy. I should not tell you this if you were not game to the last drop of your blood. But I think I know you better than you know yourself, though you never saw me until last night. Karg is Sinclair's spy at your ranch, and you must never feel it or know it; but he is there to keep your cousin's sympathy with Sinclair, and to lure your cousin his way. And Karg will try to kill George McCloud every time he sets foot on this ranch, remember that."

" Then Mr. McCloud ought not to be here. I don't want him to stay if he is in danger!" exclaimed Dicksie.

" But I do want him to come here as if it mattered nothing, and I shall try to take care of him. I have a man among your own men, a cowboy named Wickwire, who will be watching Karg, and who is just as quick, and Karg, not knowing he was watched, would be taken unawares. If Wickwire goes elsewhere to work some one else will take his place here. Karg is not on the ranch now; he is up North, hunting up some of your steers that were run off last month by his own cronies. Now do you think I am giving you confidence?"

She looked at him steadily. " If I can only deserve it all." In the distance she heard the calling of the men at the river borne on the wind. The shock of what had been told her, the strangeness of the night and of the scene, left her calm. Fear had given way to responsibility and Dicksie seemed to know herself.

" You have nothing whatever to do to deserve it but keep your own counsel. But listen a moment longer—for this is what I have been leading up

to," he said. "Marion will get a message to-
morrow, a message from Sinclair, asking her to
come to see him at his ranch-house before she goes
back. I don't know what he wants—but she is
his wife. He has treated her infamously; that is
why she will not live with him and does not speak
of him. But you know how strange a woman is—
or perhaps you don't: she doesn't always cease to
care for a man when she ceases to trust him. I
am not in Marion's confidence, Miss Dicksie. She
is another man's wife. I cannot tell how she feels
toward him; I know she has often tried to reclaim
him from his deviltry. She may try again, that is,
she may, for one reason or another, go to him as
he asks. I could not interfere, if I would. I have
no right to if I could, and I will not. Now this is
what I'm trying to get up the courage to ask you.
Should you dare to go with her to Sinclair's ranch
if she decides to go to him?"

"Certainly I should dare."

"After all you know?"

"After all I know—why not?"

"Then in case she does go and you go with her,
you will know nothing whatever about anything, of
course, unless you get the story from her. What I
fear is that which possibly may come of their interview. He may try to kill her—don't be frightened. He will not succeed if you can only make

Whispering Smith

sure he doesn't lead her away on horseback from
the ranch-house or get her alone in a room. She
has few friends. I respect and honor her because
she and I grew up as children together in the
same little town in Wisconsin. I know her folks,
all of them, and I've promised them—you know
—to have a kind of care of her."

"I think I know."

He looked self-conscious even at her tone of
understanding. "I need not try to deceive you;
your instinct would be poor if it did not tell you
more than I ought to. He came along and turned
her head. You need fear nothing for yourself in
going with her, and nothing for her if you can
cover just those two points—can you remember?
Not to let her go away with him on horseback, and
not to leave her where she will be alone with him
in the house?"

"I can and will. I think as much of Marion as
you do. I am proud to be able to do something
for you. How little I have known you! I
thought you were everything I didn't want to
know."

"It's nothing," he returned easily, "except that
Sinclair has stirred up your cousin and the ranchers as well as the Williams Cache gang, and that
makes talk about me. I have to do what I can to
make this a peaceable country to live in. The

238

railroad wants decent people here and doesn't want the other kind, and it falls on me, unfortunately, to keep the other kind moving. I don't like it, but we can none of us do quite what we please in making a living. Let me tell you this"—he turned to fix his eyes seriously on hers: " Believe anything you hear of me except that I have ever taken human life willingly or save in discharge of my duty. But this kind of work makes my own life an uncertainty, as you can see. I do almost literally carry my life in my hand, for if my hand is not quicker every time than a man's eye, I am done for then and there."

" It is dreadful to think of."

" Not exactly that, but it is something I can't afford to forget."

" What would become of the lives of the friends you protect if you were killed? "

" You say you care for Marion Sinclair. I should like to think if anything should happen to me you wouldn't forget her? "

" I never will."

He smiled. " Then I put her in charge of the man closest to me, George McCloud, and the woman she thinks the most of in the world—except her mother. What is this, are they back? Yonder they come."

" We found nothing serious," McCloud said,

answering their questions as he approached with Lance Dunning. " The current is really swinging away, but the bank is caving in where it was undermined last night." He stopped before Dicksie. " I am trying to get your cousin to go to the house and go to bed. I am going to stay all night, but there is no necessity for his staying."

" Damn it, McCloud, it's not right," protested Lance, taking off his hat and wiping his forehead. " You need the sleep more than I do. I say he is the one to go to bed to-night," continued Lance, putting it up to Whispering Smith. " And I insist, by the Almighty, that you two take him back to the house with you now ! "

Whispering Smith raised his hand. " If this is merely a family quarrel about who shall go to bed, let us compromise. You two stay up all night and let me go to bed."

Lance, however, was obdurate.

" It seems to be a family characteristic of the Dunnings to have their own way," ventured Mc-Cloud, after some further dispute. " If you will have it so, Mr. Dunning, you may stand watch to-night and I will go to the house."

Riding back with McCloud, Dicksie and Whispering Smith discussed the flood. McCloud disclaimed credit for the improvement in the situation. " If the current had held against us as it did yesterday, nothing I could have done would have turned it," he said.

"Honesty is the best policy, of course," observed Whispering Smith. "I like to see a modest man —and you want to remind him of all this when he sends in his bill," he suggested, speaking to Dicksie in the dark. "But," he added, turning to McCloud, "admitting that you are right, don't take the trouble to advertise your view of it around here. It would be only decent strategy for us in the valley just now to take a little of the credit due to the wind."

CHAPTER XXV

THE MAN ON THE FRENCHMAN

SINCLAIR'S place on the Frenchman backed up on a sharp rise against the foothills of the Bridger range, and the ranch buildings were strung along the creek. The ranch-house stood on ground high enough to command the country for miles up and down the valley.

Only two roads lead from Medicine Bend and the south into the Frenchman country: one a wagon-road following Smoky Creek and running through Dale Canyon; the other a pack-road, known as the Gridley trail, crossing the Topah Topah Hills and making a short cut from the Dunning ranch on the Crawling Stone to the Frenchman. The entire valley is, in fact, so difficult of access, save by the long and roundabout wagon-road, that the sight of a complete outfit of buildings such as that put up by Sinclair always came as a surprise to the traveller who, reaching the crest of the hills, looked suddenly down a thousand feet on his well-ordered sheds and barns and corrals.

The rider who reaches the Topah Topah crest

The Man on the Frenchman

on the Gridley trail now sees in the valley below only traces of what was so laboriously planned and perfectly maintained a few years ago. But even the ruins left on the Frenchman show the herculean labor undertaken by the man in setting up a comfortable and even an elaborate establishment in so inaccessible a spot. His defiance of all ordinary means of doing things was shown in his preference for bringing much of his building-material over the trail instead of around by the Smoky Creek road. A good part of the lumber that went into his house was packed over the Gridley trail. His piano was brought through the canyon on a wagon, but the mechanical player for the piano and his wagons themselves were packed over the trail on the backs of mules. A heavy steel range for the kitchen had been brought over the same way. For Sinclair no work was hard enough, none went fast enough, and revelry never rose high enough. During the time of his activity in the Frenchman Valley Sinclair had the best-appointed place between Williams Cache and the Crawling Stone, and in the Crawling Stone only the Dunning ranch would bear comparison with his own. On the Frenchman Sinclair kept an establishment the fame of which is still foremost in mountain story. Here his cows ranged the canyons and the hills for miles, and his horses were known from

Whispering Smith

Medicine Bend to Fort Tracy. Here he rallied
his men, laid snares for his enemies, dispensed a
reckless hospitality, ruled his men with an oath and
a blow, and carried a six-shooter to explain orders
and answer questions with.

Over the Gridley trail from the Crawling Stone
Marion and Dicksie Dunning rode early in the
morning the day after McCloud and his men left
the Stone Ranch with their work done. The trail
is a good three hours long, and they reached Sinclair's place at about ten o'clock. He was waiting for Marion—she had sent word she should
come—and he came out of the front door into the
sunshine with a smile of welcome when he saw
Dicksie with her. Dicksie, long an admirer of Sinclair's, as women usually were, had recast somewhat violently her opinions of him. She faced him
now with a criminal consciousness that she knew
too much. The weight of the dreadful secret
weighed on her, and her responsibility in the issue
of the day ahead did not help to make her greeting an easy one. One thing only was fixed in her
mind and reflected in the tension of her lips and
her eyes: the resolve to keep at every cost the
promise she had given. For Dicksie had fallen
under the spell of a man even more compelling
than Sinclair, and felt strangely bounden to what
she had said.

The Man on the Frenchman

Sinclair, however, had spirit enough to smooth quite away every embarrassment. " Bachelor's quarters," he explained roughly and pleasantly, as he led the two women toward the house. " Cowmen make poor housekeepers, but you must feel at home." And when Dicksie, looking at his Indian rugs on the floors, the walls, and the couches, said she thought he had little to apologize for, Sinclair looked gratified and took off his hat again. " Just a moment," he said, standing at the side of the door. " I've never been able to get Marion over here before, so it happens that a woman's foot has never entered the new house. I want to watch one of you cross the threshold for the first time."

Dicksie, moving ahead, retreated with a laugh. " You first, then, Marion."

" No, Dicksie, you."

" Never! you first." So Marion, quite red and wretchedly ill at ease, walked into the ranch-house first.

Sinclair shone nowhere better than as a host. When he had placed his guests comfortably in the living-room he told them the story of the building of the house. Then he made a cicerone of himself, and explained, with running comments, each feature of his plan as he showed how it had been carried out through the various rooms. Surprised at the attractiveness of things, Dicksie found herself making mental notes for her own use, and began asking questions. Sinclair was superb in answering, but the danger of admiring things became at once apparent, for when Dicksie exclaimed over a handsome bearskin, a rich dark-brown grizzly-skin of unusual size, Sinclair told the story of the killing, bared his tremendous fore-arm to show where the polished claws had ripped him, and, disregarding Dicksie's protests, insisted on sending the skin over to Crawling Stone Ranch as a souvenir of her visit.

" I live a great deal alone over here," he said, waving Dicksie's continued refusal magnificently aside as he moved into the next room. " I've got a few good dogs, and I hunt just enough to keep my hand in with a rifle." Dicksie quailed a little at the smile that went with the words. " The men, at least the kind I mix with, don't care for grizzly-skins, and to enjoy anything you've got to have sympathetic company—don't you know that?" he asked, looking admiringly at Dicksie. " I've got another skin for you—a silver-tip," he added in deep, gentle tones, addressing Marion. " It has a fine head, as fine as I ever saw in the Smithsonian. It is down at Medicine Bend now, being dressed and mounted. By the way, I've forgotten to ask you, Miss Dicksie, about the high water. How did you get through at the ranch?"

The Man on the Frenchman

Dicksie, sitting on the piano-bench, looked up with resolution. " Bravely! " she exclaimed. " Mr. McCloud came to our rescue with bags and mattresses and a hundred men, and he has put in a revetement a thousand feet long. Oh, we are regular river experts at our house now! Had you any trouble here, Mr. Sinclair? "

" No, the Frenchman behaves pretty well in the rock. We had forty feet of water here one day, though; forty feet, that's right. McCloud, yes; able fellow, I guess, too, though he and I don't hit it off." Sinclair sat back in his chair, and as he spoke he spoke magnanimously. " He docsn't like me, but that is no fault of his; railroad men, and good ones, too, sometimes get started wrong with one another. Well, I'm glad he took care of you. Try that piano, Miss Dicksie, will you? I don't know much about pianos, but that ought to be a good one. I would wheel the player over for you, but any one that plays as beautifully as you do ought not to be allowed to use a player. Marion, I want to talk a few minutes with you, may I? Do you mind going out under the cotton-wood? "

Dicksie's heart jumped. " Don't be gone long, Marion," she exclaimed impulsively, " for you know, Mr. Sinclair, we *must* get back by two o'clock." And Dicksie, pale with apprehension, looked at them both. Marion, quite composed, nodded reassuringly and followed Sinclair out of doors into the sunshine.

For a few minutes Dicksie fingered wildly on the piano at some half-forgotten air, and in a fever of excitement walked out on the porch to see where they were. To her relief, she saw Marion sitting near Sinclair under the big tree in front of the house, where the horses stood. Dicksie, with her hands on her girdle, walked forlornly back and forth, hummed a tune, sat down in a rocking-chair, fanned herself, rose, walked back and forth again, and reflected that she was perfectly helpless, and that Sinclair might kill Marion a hundred times before she could reach her. And the thought that Marion was perhaps wholly unconscious of danger increased her anxiety.

She sat down in despair. How could Whispering Smith have allowed any one he had a care for to be exposed in this dreadful way? Trying to think what to do, Dicksie hurried back into the living-room, walked to the piano, took the pile of sheet-music from the top, and sat down to thumb it over. She threw song after song on the chair beside her. They were sheets of gaudy coon songs and ragtime with flaring covers, and they seemed to give off odors of cheap perfume. Dicksie hardly saw the titles as she passed them over, but of a

The Man on the Frenchman

sudden she stopped. Between two sheets of the music lay a small handkerchief. It was mussed, and in the corner of it " Nellie " was written conspicuously in a laundry mark. The odor of musk became in an instant sickening. Dicksie threw the music disdainfully aside, and sprang up with a flushed face to leave the room. Sinclair's remark about the first woman to cross his threshold came back to her. From that moment Dicksie hated him. But no sooner had she seated herself on the porch than she remembered she had left her hat in the house, and rose to go in after it. She was resolved not to leave it under the roof another moment, and she had resolved to go over and wait where her horse was tied. As she reëntered the doorway she stopped. In the room she had just left a cowboy sat at the table, taking apart a revolver to clean it. The revolver was spread in its parts before him, but across the table lay a rifle. The man had not been in the room when she left it a moment before.

Dicksie passed behind him. He paid no attention to her; he had not looked up when she entered the room. Passing behind him once more to go out, Dicksie looked through the open window before which he sat. Sinclair and Marion sitting under the cottonwood tree were in plain sight, and the muzzle of the rifle where it lay covered them.

Dicksie thrilled, but the man was busy with his work. Breathing deeply, she walked out on the porch again. Sinclair, she thought, was looking straight at her, and in her anxiety to appear unconscious she turned, walked to the end of the house, and at the corner almost ran into a man sitting out of doors in the shade mending a saddle. He had removed his belt to work, and his revolver lay in the holster on the bench, its grip just within reach of his hand. Dicksie walked in front of him, but he did not look up. She turned as if changing her mind, and with a little flirt of her riding-skirt sat down in the porch chair, feeling a faint moisture upon her forehead.

"I am going to leave this country, Marion," Sinclair was saying. "There's nothing here for me; I can see that. What's the use of my eating my heart out over the way I've been treated? I've given the best years of my life to this railroad, and now they turn me down with a kick and a curse. It's the old story of the Indian and his dog, only I don't propose to let them make soup of me. I'm going to the coast, Marion. I'm going to California, where I wanted to go when we were married, and I wish to God we had gone there then. All our troubles might never have been if I had got in with a different crowd from these cow-boozers on the start. And, Marion, I want to know whether you'll give me another chance and go with me."

Sinclair, on the bench and leaning against the tree, sat with folded arms looking at his wife. Marion in a hickory chair faced him.

" No one would like to see you be all you ought to be more than I, Murray; but you are the only one in the world that can ever give yourself another chance to be that."

" The fellows in the saddle here now have denied me every chance to make a man of myself again on the railroad—you know that, Marion. In fact, they never did give me the show I was entitled to. I ought to have had Hailey's place. Bucks never treated me right in that; he never pushed me in the way he pushed other men that were just as bad as I ever was. It discouraged me; that's the reason I went to pieces."

" It could be no reason for treating me as you treated me: for bringing drunken men and drunken women into our house, and driving me out of it unless I would be what you were and what they were."

" I know I haven't treated you right; I've treated you shamefully. I will do anything on earth you say to square it. I will! Recollect, I had lived among men and in the same country

with women like that for years before I knew you.
I didn't know how to treat you; I admit it. Give
me another chance, Marion."

"I gave you all that I had when I married you,
Murray. I haven't anything more to give to any
man. You would be disappointed in me if I could
ever live with you again, and I could not do that
without living a lie every day."

He bent forward, looking at the ground. He
talked of their first meeting in Wisconsin; of the
happiness of their little courtship; he brought up
California again, and the Northwest coast, where,
he told her, a great railroad was to be built and
he should find the chance he needed to make a
record for himself—it had been promised him—
a chance to be the man his abilities entitled him to
be in railroading. "And I've got a customer for
the ranch and the cows, Marion. I don't care for
this business—damn the cows! let somebody else
chase after 'em through the sleet. I've done well;
I've made money—a lot of money—the last two
years in my cattle deals, and I've got it put away,
Marion; you need never lift your hand to work
in our house again. We can live in California,
and live well, under our own orange trees, whether
I work or not. All I want to know is, will you go
with me?"

"No! I will not go with you, Murray."

The Man on the Frenchman

He moved in his seat and threw his head up appealingly. " Why not ? "

" I will never be dishonest with you; I never have been and I never will be. I have nothing in my heart to give you, and I will not live upon your money. I am earning my own living. I am as content as I ever can be, and I shall stay where I am and do what I am doing till I die, probably. And this is why I came when you asked me to; to tell you the exact truth. I am not a girl any longer—I never can be again. I am a woman. What I was before I married you I never can be again, and you have no right to ask me to be a hypocrite and say I can love you—for that is what it all comes to—when I have no such thing in my heart or life for you. It is dead and gone, and I cannot help it."

" That sounds pretty hard, Marion."

" It is only the truth. It sounded fearfully hard to me when you told me that woman was your friend—that you knew her before you knew me and would know her after I was dead; that she was as good as I, and that if I didn't entertain her you would. But it was the truth; you told me the truth, and it was better that you told it—as it is better now that I tell it to you."

" I was drunk. I didn't tell you the truth. A man is a pretty tough animal sometimes, but you

253

are a woman and a pure one, and I care more for
you than for all the other women in the world, and
it is not your nature to be unforgiving."

" It is to be honest."

He looked suddenly up at her and spoke
sharply: " Marion, I know why you won't go."

" I have honestly told you."

" No; you have not honestly told me. The real
reason is Gordon Smith."

" If he were I should not hesitate to tell you,
Murray, but he is not," she said coldly.

Sinclair spoke harshly: " Do you think you can
fool me? Don't you suppose I know he spends
his time loafing around your shop? "

Marion flushed indignantly. " It is not true! "

" Don't you suppose I know he writes letters
back to Wisconsin to your folks? "

" What have I to do with that? Why shouldn't
he write to my mother? Who has a better right? "

" Don't drive me too far. By God! if I go
away alone I'll never leave you here to run off with
Whispering Smith—remember that! " She sat in
silence. His rage left her perfectly quiet, and her
unmoved expression shamed and in part silenced
him. " Don't drive me too far," he muttered
sullenly. " If you do you will be responsible,
Marion."

She did not move her eyes from the blue hills

The Man on the Frenchman

on the horizon. "I expect you to kill me sometime; I feel sure you will. And that you may do." Then she bent her look on him. "You may do it now if you want to."

His face turned heavy with rage. "Marion," he cried, with an oath, "do you know how close you are to death at this moment?"

"You may do it now."

He clinched the bench-rail and rose slowly to his feet. Marion sat motionless in the hickory chair; the sun was shining in her face and her hands were folded in her lap. Dicksie rocked on the porch. In the shadow of the house the man was mending the saddle.

CHAPTER XXVI

TOWER W

A T the end of a long and neglected hall on the second floor of the old bank block in Hill Street, Whispering Smith had a room in which he made headquarters at Medicine Bend; it was in effect Whispering Smith's home. A man's room is usually a forlorn affair in spite of any effort to make it home-like. If he neglects his room it looks barren, and if he ornaments it it looks fussy. Boys can do something with a den because they are not yet men, and some tincture of woman's nature still clings to a boy. Girls are born to the deftness that is to become all theirs in the touch of a woman's hand; but men, if they walk alone, pay the penalty of loneliness.

Whispering Smith, being logical, made no effort to decorate his domestic poverty. All his belongings were of a simple sort and his room was as bare as a Jesuit's. Moreover, his affairs, being at times highly particular, did not admit of the presence of a janitor in his quarters, and he was of necessity his own janitor. His iron bed was spread

Tower W

with a pair of Pullman blankets, his toilet arrangements included nothing more elaborate than a shaving outfit, and the mirror above his washstand was only large enough to make a hurried shave, with much neck-stretching, possible. The table was littered with letters, but it filled up one corner of the room, and a rocking-chair and a trunk filled up another. The floor was spread with a Navajo blanket, and near the head of the bed stood an old-fashioned wardrobe. This served not to ward Whispering Smith's robes, which hung for the most part on his back, but to accommodate his rifles, of which it contained an array that only a practised man could understand. The wardrobe was more, however, than an armory. Beside the guns that stood racked in precision along the inner wall, McCloud had once, to his surprise, seen a violin. It appeared out of keeping in such an atmosphere and rather the antithesis of force and violence than a complement for it. And again, though the rifles were disquietingly bright and effective-looking, the violin was old and shabby, hanging obscurely in its corner, as if, whatever it might have in common with its master, it had nothing in common with its surroundings.

The door of the room in the course of many years had been mutilated with keyholes and reënforced with locks until it appeared difficult to

Whispering Smith

choose an opening that would really afford entrance; but two men besides Whispering Smith carried keys to the room—Kennedy and George McCloud. They had right of way into it at all hours, and knew how to get in.

McCloud had left the bridge camp on the river for Medicine Bend on the Saturday that Marion Sinclair—whose husband had finally told her he would give her one more chance to think it over—returned with Dicksie safely from their trip to the Frenchman ranch.

Whispering Smith, who had been with Bucks and Morris Blood, got back to town the same day. The president and general manager were at the Wickiup during the afternoon, and left for the East at nine o'clock in the evening, when their car was attached to an east-bound passenger train. McCloud took supper afterward with Whispering Smith at a Front Street chop-house, and the two men separated at eleven o'clock. It was three hours later when McCloud tapped on the door of Smith's room, and in a moment opened it. "Awake, Gordon?"

"Sure: come in. What is it?"

"The second section of the passenger train—Number Three, with the express cars—was stopped at Tower W to-night. Oliver Sollers was pulling; he is badly shot up, and one of the messengers was

shot all to pieces. They cracked the through safe,
emptied it, and made a clean get-away."

" Tower W—two hundred and seventy-six miles.
Have you ordered up an engine? "

" Yes."

" Where's Kennedy? "

A second voice answered: " Right here."

" Strike a light, Farrell. What about the
horses? "

" They're being loaded."

" Is the line clear? "

" Rooney Lee is clearing it."

" Spike it, George, and leave every west-bound
train in siding, with the engine cut loose and plenty
of steam, till we get by. It's now or never this
time. Two hundred and seventy-six miles; they're
giving us our money's worth. Who's going with
us, Farrell? "

" Bob Scott, Reed Young, and Brill, if Reed can
get him at Sleepy Cat. Dancing is loading the
horses."

" I want Ed Banks to lead a *posse* straight from
here for Williams Cache; Dancing can go with
him. And telephone Gene and Bob Johnson to sit
down in Canadian Pass till they grow to the rocks,
but not to let anybody through if they want to live
after I see them. They've got all the instructions;
all they need is the word. It's a long chance,

Whispering Smith

but I think these are our friends. You can head
Banks off by telephone somewhere if we change
our minds when we get a trail. Start Brill Young
and a good man from Sleepy Cat ahead of us,
George, if you can, in a baggage car with any
horses that they can get there. They can be at
Tower W by daybreak and perhaps pick up a trail
before we reach there, and we shall have fresh
horses for them. I'm ready, I guess; let's go.
Slam the door, George!" In the hall Whispering
Smith threw a pocket-light on his watch. " I want
you to put us there by seven o'clock."

" Charlie Sollers is going to pull you," answered
McCloud. " Have you got everything? Then
we're off." The three men tiptoed down the dark
hall, down the stairs, and across the street on a
noiseless run for the railroad yard.

The air was chill and the sky clear, with a moon
more than half to the full. " Lord, what a night
to ride!" exclaimed Whispering Smith, looking
mournfully at the stars. " Well planned, well
planned, I must admit."

The men hastened toward the yard, where lan
terns were moving about the car of the train-
guards near the Blue Front stables. The load
ing board had been lowered, and the horses were
being carefully led into the car. From a switch
engine behind the car a shrill cloud of steam bil-

Tower W

lowed into the air. Across the yard a great passenger engine, its huge white side-rod rising and
falling slowly in the still light of the moon—one
of the mountain racers, thick-necked like an ath-
lete and deep-chested—was backing down for the
run with the single car almost across the west end
of the division. Trainmen were running to and
from the Wickiup platform. By the time the
horses were loaded the conductor had orders.
Until the last minute, Whispering Smith was in
consultation with McCloud, and giving Dancing
precise instructions for the *posse* into the Cache
country. They were still talking at the side door
of the car, McCloud and Dancing on the ground
and Whispering Smith squatting on his haunches
inside the moving car, when the engine signalled
and the special drew away from the chute, pounded
up the long run of the ladder switch, and moved
with gathering speed into the canyon. In the cab
Charlie Sollers, crushing in his hand the tissue that
had brought the news of his brother's death, sat
at the throttle. He had no speed orders. They
had only told him he had a clear track.

CHAPTER XXVII

PURSUIT

BRILL YOUNG picked up a trail Sunday morning at Tower W before the special from Medicine Bend reached there. The wrecked express car, which had been set out, had no story to tell. " The only story," said Whispering Smith, as the men climbed into their saddles, " is in the one from the hoofs, and the sooner we get after it the better."

The country around Tower W, which is itself an operating point on the western end of the division, a mere speck on the desert, lies high and rolling. To the south, sixty miles away, rise the Grosse Terre Mountains, and to the north and west lie the solitudes of the Heart range, while in the northeast are seen the three white Saddle peaks of the Missions. The cool, bright sunshine of a far and lonely horizon greets the traveller here, and ten miles away from the railroad, in any direction, a man on horseback and unacquainted with the country would wish himself—mountain men

Pursuit

will tell you—in hell, because it would be easier to ride out of.

To the railroad men the country offered no unusual difficulties. The Youngs were as much at home on a horse as on a hand car. Kennedy, though a large and powerful man, was inured to hard riding, and Bob Scott and Whispering Smith in the saddle were merely a part—though an important part—of their horses; without killing their mounts, they could get out of them every mile in their legs. The five men covered twenty miles on a trail that read like print. One after another of the railroad party commented on the carelessness with which it had been left. But twenty miles south of the railroad, in an open and comparatively easy country, it was swallowed completely up in the tracks of a hundred horses. The railroad men circled far and wide, only to find the herd tracks everywhere ahead of them.

"This is a beautiful job," murmured Whispering Smith as the party rode together along the edge of a creek-bottom. "Now who is their friend down in this country? What man would get out a bunch of horses like this and work them this hard so early in the morning? Let's hunt that man up. I like to meet a man that is a friend in need."

Bob Scott spoke: "I saw a man with some

Whispering Smith

horses in a canyon across the creek a few minutes
ago, and I saw a ranch-house behind those buttes
when I rode around them."

" Stop! Here's a man riding right into our
jaws," muttered Kennedy. " Divide up among the
rocks." A horseman from the south came galloping up the creek, and Kennedy rode out with an
ivory smile to meet him. The two men parleyed
for a moment, disputed each other sharply, and
rode together back to the railroad party.

" Haven't seen any men looking for horses this
morning, have you?" asked Whispering Smith,
eying the stranger, a squat, square-jawed fellow
with a cataract eye.

" I'm looking for horses myself. I ain't seen
anybody else. What are you looking for?"

" Is this your bunch of horses that got loose
here?" asked Smith.

" No."

" I thought," said Kennedy, smiling, " you said
a minute ago they were."

The stranger fixed his cataract on him like a
flash-light. " I changed my mind."

Whispering Smith's brows rose protestingly, but
he spoke with perfect amiability as he raised his
finger to bring the good eye his way. " You ought
to change your hat when you change your mind.
I saw you driving a bunch of horses up that canyon

Pursuit

a few minutes ago. Now, Rockstro, do you still drag your left leg?"

The rancher looked steadily at his new inquisitor, but blinked like a gopher at the sudden onslaught. "Which of you fellows is Whispering Smith?" he demanded.

"The man with the dough is Whispering Smith every time," was the answer from Smith himself. "You have about seven years to serve, Rockstro, haven't you? Seven, I think. Now what have I ever done to you that you should turn a trick like this on me? I knew you were here, and you knew I knew you were here, and I call this a pretty country; a little smooth right around here, like the people, but pretty. Have I ever bothered you? Now tell me one thing—what did you get for covering this trail? I stand to give you two dollars for every one you got last night for the job, if you'll put us right on the game. Which way did they go?"

"What are you talking about?"

"Get off your horse a minute," suggested Whispering Smith, dismounting, "and step over here toward the creek." The man, afraid to refuse and unwilling to go, walked haltingly after Smith.

"What is it, Rockstro?" asked his tormentor. "Don't you like this country? What do you want to go back to the penitentiary for? Aren't you

Whispering Smith

happy here? Now tell me one thing—will you give up the trail?"

"I don't know the trail."

"I believe you; we shouldn't follow it anyway. Were you paid last night or this morning?"

"I ain't seen a man hereabouts for a week."

"Then you can't tell me whether there were five men or six?"

"You've got one eye as good as mine, and one a whole lot better."

"So it was fixed up for cash a week ago?"

"Everything is cash in this country."

"Well, Rockstro, I'm sorry, but we'll have to take you back with us."

The rancher whipped out a revolver. Whispering Smith caught his wrist. The struggle lasted only an instant. Rockstro writhed, and the pistol fell to the ground.

"Now, shall I break your arm?" asked Smith, as the man cursed and resisted. "Or will you behave? We are going right back and you'll have to come with us. We'll send some one down to round up your horses and sell them, and you can serve out your time—with allowances, of course, for good conduct, which will cut it down. If I had ever done you a mean turn I would not say a word. If you could name a friend of yours I had ever done a mean turn to I would not say a word.

Pursuit

Can you name one? I guess not. I have left you as free as the wind here, making only the rule I make for everybody—to let the railroad alone. This is my thanks. Now, I'll ask you just one question. I haven't killed you, as I had a perfect right to when you pulled; I haven't broken your arm, as I would have done if there had been a doctor within twenty-five miles; and I haven't started you for the pen—not yet. Now I ask you one fair question only: Did you need the money?"

"Yes, I did need it."

Whispering Smith dropped the man's wrist. "Then I don't say a word. If you needed the money, I'm not going to send you back—not for mine."

"How can a man make a living in this country," asked the rancher, with a bitter oath, "unless he picks up everything that's going?"

"Pick up your gun, man! I'm not saying anything, am I?"

"But I'm damned if I can give a double-cross to any man," added Rockstro, stooping for his revolver.

"I should think less of you, Rockstro, if you did. You don't need money anyway now, but sometime you may need a friend. I'm going to leave you here. You'll hear no more of this, and I'm going to ask you a question: Why did you go against this when you knew you'd have to square yourself with me?"

"They told me you'd be taken care of before it was pulled off."

"They lied to you, didn't they? No matter, you've got their stuff. Now I am going to ask you one question that I don't know the answer to; it's a fair question, too. Was Du Sang in the penitentiary with you at Fort City? Answer fair."

"Yes."

"Thank you. Behave yourself and keep your mouth shut. I say nothing this time. Hereafter leave railroad matters alone, and if the woman should fall sick or you have to have a little money, come and see me." Smith led the way back to the horses.

"Look here!" muttered Rockstro, following, with his good eye glued on his companion. "I pulled on you too quick, I guess—quicker'n I'd ought to."

"Don't mention it. You didn't pull quick enough; it is humiliating to have a man that's as slow as you are pull on me. People that pull on me usually pull and shoot at the same time. Two distinct movements, Rockstro, should be avoided; they are fatal to success. Come down to the Bend sometime, and I'll get you a decent gun and give you a few lessons."

Pursuit

Whispering Smith drew his handkerchief as the one-eyed man rode away and he rejoined his companions. He was resigned, after a sickly fashion. " I like to play blind-man's-buff," he said, wiping his forehead, " but not so far from good water. They have pulled us half-way to the Grosse Terre Mountains on a beautiful trail, too beautiful to be true, Farrell—too beautiful to be true. They have been having fun with us, and they've doubled back through the Topah Topahs toward the Mission Mountains and Williams Cache—that is my judgment. And aren't we five able-bodied jays, gentlemen? Five strong-arm suckers? It is an inelegant word; it is an inelegant feeling. No matter, we know a few things. There are five good men and a led horse; we can get out of here by Goose River, find out when we cross the railroad how much they got, and pick them up somewhere around the Saddle peaks, *if* they've gone north. That's only a guess, and every man's guess is good now. What do you think, all of you? "

" If it's the crowd we think it is, would they go straight home? That doesn't look reasonable, does it? " asked Brill Young.

" If they could put one day between them and pursuit, wouldn't they be safer at home than anywhere else? And haven't they laid out one day's work for us, good and plenty? Farrell, remember one thing: there is sometimes a disadvantage in knowing too much about the men you are after. We'll try Goose River."

It was noon when they struck the railroad. They halted long enough to stop a freight train, send some telegrams, and ask for news. They got orders from Rooney Lee, had an empty box car set behind the engine for a special, and, loading their horses at the chute, made a helter-skelter run for Sleepy Cat. At three o'clock they struck north for the Mission Mountains.

CHAPTER XXVIII

THE SUNDAY MURDER

BANKS'S *posse,* leaving Medicine Bend before daybreak, headed northwest. Their instructions were explicit: to scatter after crossing the Frenchman, watch the trails from the Goose River country and through the Mission Mountains, and intercept everybody riding north until the *posse* from Sleepy Cat or Whispering Smith should communicate with them from the southwest. Nine men rode in the party that crossed the Crawling Stone Sunday morning at sunrise with Ed Banks.

After leaving the river the three white-capped Saddles of the Mission range afford a landmark for more than a hundred miles, and toward these the party pressed steadily all day. The southern pass of the Missions opens on the north slope of the range into a pretty valley known as Mission Springs Valley, and the springs are the head-waters of Deep Creek. The *posse* did not quite obey the instructions, and following a natural instinct of safety five of them, after Banks and his three deputies had scattered, bunched again, and at dark crossed Deep Creek at some distance below the springs. It was afterward known that these five men had been seen entering the valley from the east at sundown just as four of the men they wanted rode down South Mission Pass toward the springs. That they knew they would soon be cut off, or must cut their way through the line which Ed Banks, ahead of them, was posting at every gateway to Williams Cache, was probably clear to them. Four men rode that evening from Tower W through the south pass; the fifth man had already left the party. The four men were headed for Williams Cache and had reason to believe, until they sighted Banks's men, that their path was open.

They halted to take counsel on the suspicious-looking *posse* far below them, and while their cruelly exhausted horses rested, Du Sang, always in Sinclair's absence the brains of the gang, planned the escape over Deep Creek at Baggs's crossing. At dusk they divided: two men lurking in the brush along the creek rode as close as they could, unobserved, toward the crossing, while Du Sang and the cowboy Karg, known as Flat Nose, rode down to Baggs's ranch at the foot of the pass.

At that point Dan Baggs, an old locomotive engineer, had taken a homestead, got together a

The Sunday Murder

little bunch of cattle, and was living alone with his son, a boy of ten years. It was a hard country and too close to Williams Cache for comfort, but Dan got on with everybody because the toughest man in the Cache country could get a meal, a feed for his horse, and a place to sleep at Baggs's, without charge, when he needed it.

Ed Banks, by hard riding, got to the crossing at five o'clock, and told Baggs of the hold-up and the shooting of Oliver Sollers. The news stirred the old engineman, and his excitement threw him off his guard. Banks rode straight on for the middle pass, leaving word that two of his men would be along within half an hour to watch the pass and the ranch crossing, and asking Baggs to put up some kind of a fight for the crossing until more of the *posse* came up—at the least, to make sure that nobody got any fresh horses.

The boy was cooking supper in the kitchen, and Baggs had done his milking and gone back to the corral, when two men rode around the corner of the barn and asked if they could get something to eat. Poor Baggs sold his life in six words: " Why, yes; be you Banks's men? "

Du Sang answered: " No; we're from Sheriff Coon's office at Oroville, looking up a bunch of Duck Bar steers that's been run somewhere up Deep Creek. Can we stay here all night? "

Whispering Smith

They dismounted and disarmed Baggs's suspicions, though the condition of their horses might have warned him had he had his senses. The unfortunate man had probably fixed it in his mind that a ride from Tower W to Deep Creek in sixteen hours was a physical impossibility.

"Stay here? Sure! I want you to stay," said Baggs bluffly. "Looks to me like I seen you down at Crawling Stone, ain't I?" he asked of Karg.

Karg was lighting a cigarette. "I used to mark at the Dunning ranch," he answered, throwing away his match.

"That's hit. Good! The boy's cooking supper. Step up to the kitchen and tell him to cut ham for four more."

"Four?"

"Two of Ed Banks's men will be here by six o'clock. Heard about the hold-up? They stopped Number Three at Tower W last night and shot Ollie Sollers, as white a boy as ever pulled a throttle. Boys, a man that'll kill a locomotive engineer is worse'n an Indian; I'd help skin him."

"The hell you would!" cried Du Sang. "Well, don't you want to start in on me? I killed Sollers. Look at me; ain't I handsome? What you going to do about it?"

Before Baggs could think Du Sang was shooting

The Sunday Murder

him down. It was wanton. Du Sang stood in no need of the butchery; the escape could have been made without it. His victim had pulled an engine throttle too long to show the white feather, but he was dying by the time he had dragged a revolver from his pocket. Du Sang did the killing alone. At least, Flat Nose, who alone saw all of the murder, afterward maintained that he did not draw because he had no occasion to, and that Baggs was dead before he, Karg, had finished his cigarette. With his right arm broken and two bullets through his chest, Baggs fell on his face. That, however, did not check his murderer. Rising to his knees, Baggs begged for his life. " For God's sake! I'm helpless, gentlemen! I'm helpless. Don't kill me like a dog! " But Du Sang, emptying his pistol, threw his rifle to his shoulder and sent bullet after bullet crashing through the shapeless form writhing and twitching before him until he had beaten it in the dust soft and flat and still.

Banks's men came up within an hour to find the ranch-house deserted. They saw a lantern in the yard below, and near the corral gate they found the little boy in the darkness, screaming beside his father's body. The sheriff's men carried the old engineman to the house; others of the *posse* crossed the creek during the evening, and at eleven o'clock

Whispering Smith

Whispering Smith rode down from the south pass to find that four of the men they were after had taken fresh horses, after killing Baggs, and passed safely through the cordon Banks had drawn around the pass and along Deep Creek. Bill Dancing, who had ridden with Banks's men, was at the house when Whispering Smith arrived. He found some supper in the kitchen, and the tired man and the giant ate together.

Whispering Smith was too experienced a campaigner to complain. His party had struck a trail fifty miles north of Sleepy Cat and followed it to the Missions. He knew now who he was after, and knew that they were bottled up in the Cache for the night. The sheriff's men were sleeping on the floor of the living-room when Smith came in from the kitchen. He sat down before the fire. At intervals sobs came from the bedroom where the body lay, and after listening a moment, Whispering Smith got stiffly up, and, tiptoeing to still the jingle of his spurs, took the candle from the table, pushed aside the curtain, and entered the bedroom.

The little boy was lying on his face, with his arm around his father's neck, talking to him. Whispering Smith bent a moment over the bed, and, setting the candle on the table, put his hand on the boy's shoulder. He disengaged the hand

The Sunday Murder

from the cold neck, and sitting down took it in his own. Talking low to the little fellow, he got his attention after much patient effort and got him to speak. He made him, though struggling with terror, to understand that he had come to be his friend, and after the child had sobbed his grief into a strange heart he ceased to tremble, and told his name and his story, and described the two horsemen and the horses they had left. Smith listened quietly. " Have you had any supper, Dannie? No? You must have something to eat. Can't you eat anything? But there is a nice pan of fresh milk in the kitchen."

A burst of tears interrupted him. " Daddie just brought in the milk, and I was frying the ham, and I heard them shooting."

" See how he took care of you till the last minute, and left something for you after he was gone. Suppose he could speak now, don't you think he would want you to do as I say? I am your next friend now, for you are going to be a railroad man and have a big engine."

Dannie looked up. " Dad wasn't afraid of those men."

" Wasn't he, Dannie? "

" He said we would be all right and not to be afraid."

" Did he? "

Whispering Smith

"He said Whispering Smith was coming."

"My poor boy."

"He is coming, don't be afraid. Do you know Whispering Smith? He is coming. The men to-night all said he was coming."

The little fellow for a long time could not be coaxed away from his father, but his companion at length got him to the kitchen. When they came back to the bedroom the strange man was talking to him once more about his father. "We must try to think how he would like things done now, mustn't we? All of us felt so bad when we rode in and had so much to do we couldn't attend to taking care of your father. Did you know there are two men out at the crossing now, guarding it with rifles? But if you and I keep real quiet we can do something for him while the men are asleep; they have to ride all day to-morrow. We must wash his face and hands, don't you think so? And brush his hair and his beard. If you could just find the basin and some water and a towel— you couldn't find a brush, could you? Could you, honestly? Well! I call that a good boy—we shall have to have you on the railroad, sure. We must try to find some fresh clothes—these are cut and stained; then I will change his clothes, and we shall all feel better. Don't disturb the men; they are tired."

The Sunday Murder

They worked together by the candle-light. When they had done, the boy had a violent crying spell, but Whispering Smith got him to lie down beside him on a blanket spread on the floor, where Smith got his back against the sod wall and took the boy's head in his arm. He waited patiently for the boy to go to sleep, but Dan was afraid the murderers would come back. Once he lifted his head in a confidence. " Did you know my daddy used to run an engine? "

" No, I did not; but in the morning you must tell me all about it."

Whenever there was a noise in the next room the child roused. After some time a new voice was heard; Kennedy had come and was asking questions. " Wake up here, somebody! Where is Whispering Smith? "

Dancing answered: " He's right there in the bedroom, Farrell, staying with the boy."

There was some stirring. Kennedy talked a little and at length stretched himself on the floor. When all was still again, Dannie's hand crept slowly from the breast of his companion up to his chin, and the little hand, feeling softly every feature, stole over the strange face.

" What is it, Dannie? "

" Are you Whispering Smith? "

" Yeş, Dannie. Shut your eyes."

Whispering Smith

At three o'clock, when Kennedy lighted a candle and looked in, Smith was sitting with his back against the wall. The boy lay on his arm. Both were fast asleep. On the bed the dead man lay with a handkerchief over his face.

CHAPTER XXIX

WILLIAMS CACHE

ED BANKS had been recalled before daybreak from the middle pass. Two of the men wanted were now known to have crossed the creek, which meant they must work out of the country through Williams Cache.

" If you will take your best two men, Ed," said Whispering Smith, sitting down with Banks at breakfast, " and strike straight for Canadian Pass to help Gene and Bob Johnson, I'll undertake to ride in and talk to Rebstock while Kennedy and Bob Scott watch Deep Creek. The boy gives a good description, and the two men that did the job here are Du Sang and Flat Nose. Did I tell you how we picked up the trail yesterday? Magpies. They shot a scrub horse that gave out on them and skinned the brand. It hastened the banquet, but we got there before the birds were all seated. Great luck, wasn't it? And it gave us a beautiful trail. One of the party crossed the Goose River at American Fork, and Brill Young and Reed followed him. Four came through the Mission Mountains; that is a cinch and they are in the Cache—and if they get out it is our fault personally, Ed, and not the Lord's."

Williams Cache lies in the form of a great horn, with a narrow entrance at the lower end known as the Door, and a rock fissure at the upper end leading into Canadian Pass; but this fissure is so narrow that a man with a rifle could withstand a regiment. For a hundred miles east and west rise the granite walls of the Mission range, broken nowhere save by the formation known as the Cache. Even this does not penetrate the range; it is a pocket, and runs not over half-way into it and out again. But no man really knows the Cache; the most that may be said is that the main valley is known, and it is known as the roughest mountain fissure between the Spanish Sinks and the Mantrap country. Williams Cache lies between walls two thousand feet high, and within it is a small labyrinth of canyons. A generation ago, when Medicine Bend for one winter was the terminus of the overland railroad, vigilantes mercilessly cleaned out the town, and the few outlaws that escaped the shotgun and the noose at Medicine Bend found refuge in a far-away and unknown mountain gorge once named by French trappers the Cache. Years after these outcasts had come to infest it came one desperado more ferocious than all that had gone before. He made a frontier retreat of the Cache, and left to it the legacy of his evil name, Williams. Since his day it has served, as it served before, for the haunt of outlawed men. No honest man lives in Williams Cache, and few men of any sort live there long, since their lives are lives of violence; neither the law nor a woman crosses Deep Creek. But from the day of Williams to this day the Cache has had its ruler, and when Whispering Smith rode with a little party through the Door into the Cache the morning after the murder in Mission Valley he sent an envoy to Rebstock, whose success as a cattle-thief had brought its inevitable penalty. It had made Rebstock a man of consequence and of property and a man subject to the anxieties and annoyances of such responsibility.

Sitting once in the Three Horses at Medicine Bend, Rebstock had talked with Whispering Smith. "I used to have a good time," he growled. "When I was rustling a little bunch of steers, just a small bunch all by myself, and hadn't a cent in the world, no place to sleep and nothing to eat, I had a good time. Now I have to keep my money in the bank; that ain't pleasant—you know that. Every man that brings a bunch of cattle across Deep Creek has stole 'em, and expects me to buy 'em or lend him money. I'm busy with in-

Whispering Smith

spectors all the time, deviling with brands, standing off the Stock Association and all kinds of trouble. I've got too many cows, too much money. I'm afraid somebody will shoot me if I go to sleep, or poison me if I take a drink. Whispering Smith, I'd like to give you a half-interest in my business. That's on the square. You're a young man, and handy; it wouldn't cost you a cent, and you can have half of the whole shooting-match if you'll cross Deep Creek and help me run the gang." Such was Rebstock free from anxiety and in a confidential moment. Under pressure he was, like all men, different.

Whispering Smith had acquaintance even in the Cache, and after a little careful reconnoitring he found a crippled-up thief, driving a milch cow down the Cache, who was willing to take a message to the boss.

Whispering Smith gave his instructions explicitly, facing the messenger, as the two sat in their saddles, with an importunate eye. " Say to Rebstock exactly these words," he insisted. " This is from Whispering Smith: I want Du Sang. He killed a friend of mine last night at Mission Springs. I happened to be near there and know he rode in last night. He can't get out; the Canadian is plugged. I won't stand for the killing, and it is Du Sang or a clean-up in the Cache all

284

around, and then I'll get Du Sang anyway. Regards."

Riding circumspectly in and about the entrance to the Cache, the party waited an hour for an answer. When the answer came, it was unsatisfactory. Rebstock declined to appear upon so trivial a matter, and Whispering Smith refused to specify a further grievance. More parley and stronger messages were necessary to stir the Deep Creek monarch, but at last he sent word asking Whispering Smith to come to his cabin accompanied only by Kennedy.

The two railroad men rode up the canyon together. "And now I will show you a lean and hungry thief grown monstrous and miserly, Farrell," said Whispering Smith.

At the head of a short pocket between two sheer granite walls they saw Rebstock's weather-beaten cabin, and he stood in front of it smoking. He looked moodily at his visitors out of eyes buried between rolls of fat. Whispering Smith was a little harsh as the two shook hands, but he dismounted and followed Rebstock into the house.

"What are you so high and mighty about?" he demanded, throwing his hat on the table near which Rebstock had seated himself. "Why don't you come out when I send a man to you, or send word what you will do? What have you got to kick about? Haven't you been treated right?"

Being in no position to complain, but shrewdly aware that much unpleasantness was in the wind, Rebstock beat about the bush. He had had rheumatism; he couldn't ride; he had been in bed three weeks and hadn't seen Du Sang for three months. "You ain't chasing up here after Du Sang because he killed a man at Mission Springs. I know better than that. That ain't the first man he's killed, and it ain't a' goin' to be the last."

Whispering Smith lifted his finger and for the first time smiled. "Now there you err, Rebstock —it is 'a goin' to be' the last. So you think I'm after you, do you? Well, if I were, what are you going to do about it? Rebstock, do you think, if I wanted *you*, I would send a message for you to come out and meet me? Not on your life! When I want you I'll come to your shack and drag you out by the hair of the head. Sit down!" roared Whispering Smith.

Rebstock, who weighed at least two hundred and seventy-five pounds, had lifted himself up to glare and swear freely. Now he dropped angrily back into his chair. "Well, who do you want?" he bellowed in kind.

A smile softened the asperity of the railroad man's face. "That's a fair question and I give you a straight answer. I'm not bluffing: I want Du Sang."

Rebstock squirmed. He swore with shortened breath that he knew nothing about Du Sang; that Du Sang had stolen his cattle; that hanging was too good for him; that he would join any *posse* in searching for him; and that he had not seen him for three months.

"Likely enough," assented Whispering Smith, "but this is wasting time. He rode in here last night after killing old Dan Baggs. Your estimable nephew Barney is with him, and Karg is with him, and I want them; but, in especial and particular, I want Du Sang."

Rebstock denied, protested, wheezed, and stormed, but Whispering Smith was immovable. He would not stir from the Cache upon any promises. Rebstock offered to surrender any one else in the Cache—hinted strongly at two different men for whom handsome rewards were out; but every compromise suggested was met with the same good-natured words: "I want Du Sang."

At last the smile changed on Whispering Smith's face. It lighted his eyes still, but with a different expression. "See here, Rebstock, you and I have always got along, haven't we? I've no desire to crowd any man to the wall that is a man. Now I am going to tell you the simple truth. Du Sang

Whispering Smith

has got you scared to death. That man is a faker,
Rebstock. Because he kills men right and left
without any provocation, you think he is dangerous. He isn't; there are a dozen men in the Cache
just as good with a gun as Du Sang is. Don't
shake your head. I know what I'm talking about.
He is a jay with a gun, and you may tell him I
said so; do you hear? Tell him to come out if he
wants me to demonstrate it. He has got everybody, including you, scared to death. Now, I say,
don't be silly. I want Du Sang."

Rebstock rose to his feet solemnly and pointed
his finger at Whispering Smith. "Whispering
Smith, you know me—"

"I know you for a fat rascal."

"That's all right. You know me, and, just as
you say, we always get along because we both got
sense."

"You're hiding yours to-day, Rebstock."

"No matter; I'll tell you what I'll do. I'll give
you all the horseflesh you can kill and all the men
you can hire to go after him, and I'll bury your
dead myself. You think he can't shoot? I give
you a tip on the square." Whispering Smith
snorted. "He'll shoot the four buttons off your
coat in four shots." Smith kicked Rebstock's dog
contemptuously. "And do it while you are falling down. I've seen him do it," persisted Reb-

288

Williams Cache

stock, moist with perspiration. "I'm not looking for a chance to go against a sure thing; I wash my hands of the job."

Whispering Smith rose. "It was no trick to see he had you scared to death. You are losing your wits, old man. The albino is a faker, and I tell you I am going to run him out of the country." Whispering Smith reached for his hat. "Our treaty ends right here. You promised to harbor no man in your sink that ever went against our road. You know as well as I do that this man, with four others, held up our train night before last at Tower W, shot our engineman to death for mere delight, killed a messenger, took sixty-five thousand dollars out of the through safe, and made his good get-away. Now, don't lie; you know every word of it, and you thought you could pull it out of me by a bluff. I track him to your door. He is inside the Cache this minute. You know every curve and canyon and pocket and wash-out in it, and every cut-throat and jail-bird in it, and they pay you blood-money and hush-money every month; and when I ask you not to give up a dozen men the company is entitled to, but merely to send this pink-eyed lobster out with his guns to talk with me, you wash your hands of the job, do you? Now listen. If you don't send Du Sang into the open before noon to-morrow, I'll run every

Whispering Smith

living steer and every living man out of Williams
Cache before I cross the Crawling Stone again, so
help me God! And I'll send for cowboys within
thirty minutes to begin the job. I'll scrape your
Deep Creek canyons till the rattlesnakes squeal.
I'll make Williams Cache so wild that a timber-
wolf can't follow his own trail through it. You'll
break with me, will you, Rebstock? Then wind
up your bank account; before I finish with you
I'll put you in stripes and feed buzzards off your
table."

Rebstock's face was apoplectic. He choked with
a torrent of oaths. Whispering Smith, paying
no attention, walked out to where Kennedy was
waiting. He swung into the saddle, ignoring
Rebstock's abjurations, and with Kennedy rode
away.

"It is hard to do anything with a man that is
scared to death," said Smith to his companion.
"Then, too, Rebstock's nephew is probably in
this. In any case, when Du Sang has got Rebstock scared, he is a dangerous man to be abroad.
We have got to smoke him out, Farrell. Lance
Dunning insisted the other day he wanted to do
me a favor. I'll see if he'll lend me Stormy Gorman and some of his cowpunchers for a round-up.
We've got to smoke Du Sang out. A round-up is
the thing. But, by Heaven, if that round-up is

Williams Cache

actually pulled off it will be a classic when you and I are gone."

Thirty minutes afterward, messengers had taken the Frenchman trail for Lance Dunning's cowboys.

CHAPTER XXX

THE FIGHT IN THE CACHE

A CLEAR night and a good moon made a long ride possible, and the Crawling Stone contingent, headed by Stormy Gorman, began coming into the railroad camp by three o'clock the next morning. With them rode the two Youngs, who had lost the trail they followed across Goose River and joined the cowboys on the road to the north.

The party divided under Kennedy and Smith, who rode through the Door into the Cache just before daybreak.

" I don't know what I am steering you against this morning, Farrell," said Whispering Smith. " Certainly I should hate to run you into Du Sang, but we can't tell where we shall strike him. If we have laid out the work right I ought to see him as soon as anybody does. Accidents do happen, but remember he will never be any more dangerous than he is at the first moment. Get him to talk. He gets nervous if he can't shoot right away. When you pull, get a bullet into his stom-

The Fight in the Cache

ach at the start, if you possibly can, to spoil his aim. We mustn't make the mistake of underestimating him. Rebstock is right: he is a fright with a revolver, and Sinclair and Seagrue are the only men in the mountains that can handle a rifle with him. Now we split here; and good luck!"

"Don't you want to take Brill Young with you?"

"You take both the Youngs, Farrell. We shall be among rocks, and if he tries to rush us there is cover."

Stormy Gorman with four Crawling Stone cowboys followed Whispering Smith. Every rider on the range had a grievance against Williams Cache, and any of them would have been glad to undertake reprisals against the rustlers under the wing of Whispering Smith.

Just how in the mountains—without telegraph, newspapers, and all ordinary means of publicity —news travels so fast may not certainly be said. The scattered lines of telephone wires help, but news outstrips the wires. Moreover, there are no telephones in the Mission Mountains. But on the morning that the round-up party rode into the Cache it was known in the streets of Medicine Bend that the Tower W men had been tracked into the north country; that some, if not all, of them were in Williams Cache; that an ultimatum

Whispering Smith

had been given, and that Whispering Smith and Kennedy had already ridden in with their men to make it good.

Whispering Smith, with the cowboys, took the rough country to the left, and Kennedy and his party took the south prong of the Cache Creek. The instructions were to make a clean sweep as the line advanced. Behind the centre rode three men to take stock driven in from the wings. Word that was brief but reasonable had been sent everywhere ahead. Every man, it was promised, that could prove property should have a chance to do so at the Door that day and the next; but any brands that showed stolen cattle, or that had been skinned or tampered with in any way, were to be turned over to the Stock Association for the benefit of owners.

The very first pocket raided started a row and uncovered eighty head of five-year-old steers bearing a mutilated Duck Bar brand. It was like poking at rattlesnakes to undertake to clean out the grassy retreats of the Cache, but the work was pushed on in spite of protests, threats, and resistance. Every man that rode out openly to make a protest was referred calmly to Rebstock, and before very long Rebstock's cabin had more men around it than had been seen together in the Cache for years. The impression that the whole jig was

The Fight in the Cache

up, and that the refugees had been sold out by their own boss, was one that no railroad man undertook to discourage. The cowboys insisted on the cattle, with the assurance that Rebstock could explain everything. By noon the Cache was in an uproar. The cowboys were riding carefully, and their guards, rifles in hand, were watching the corners. Ahead of the slowly moving line with the growing bunch of cattle behind it, flourished as it were rather conspicuously, fugitive riders dashed back and forth with curses and yells across the narrow valley. If it had been Whispering Smith's intention to raise a large-sized row it was apparent that he had been successful. Rebstock, driven to desperation, held council after council to determine what to do. Sorties were discussed, ambushes considered, and a pitched battle was planned. But, while ideas were plentiful, no one aspired to lead an attack on Whispering Smith.

Moreover, Williams Cache, it was conceded, would in the end be worsted if the company and the cowmen together seriously undertook with men and unlimited money to clean it out. Whispering Smith's party had no explanation to offer for the round-up, but when Rebstock made it known that the fight was over sending out Du Sang, the rage of the rustlers turned on Du Sang. Again, however, no man wanted to take up personally with

Whispering Smith

Du Sang the question of the reasonableness of Whispering Smith's demand. Instead of doing so, they fell on Rebstock and demanded that if he were boss he make good and send Du Sang out.

Of all this commotion the railroad men saw only the outward indications. As the excitement grew on both sides there was perhaps a little more of display in the way the cattle were run in, especially when some long-lost bunch was brought to light and welcomed with yells from the centre. A steer was killed at noon, everybody fed, and the line moved forward. The wind, which had slept in the sunshine of the morning, rose in the afternoon, and the dust whirled in little clouds where men or animals moved. From the centre two men had gone back with the cattle gathered up to that time, and Bill Dancing, with Smith, Stormy Gorman, and two of the cowboys, were heading a draw to cross to the north side of the Cache, when three men rode out into the road five hundred yards ahead, and halted.

Whispering Smith spoke: "There come our men; stop here. This ground in front of us looks good to me; they may have chosen something over there that suits them better. Feel your guns and we'll start forward slowly; don't take your eyes off the bunch, whatever you do. Bill, you go back

The Fight in the Cache

and help the men with the cattle; there will be four of us against three then."

"Not for mine!" said Bill Dancing bluntly. "You may need help from an old fool yet. I'll see you through this and look after the cattle afterward."

"Then, Stormy, one or two of you go back," urged Whispering Smith, speaking to the cowboy foreman without turning his eyes. "There's no need of five of us in this."

But Stormy swore violently. "You go back yourself," exclaimed Stormy, when he could control his feelings. "We'll bring them fellows in for you in ten minutes with their hands in the air."

"I know you would; I know it. But I'm paid for this sort of thing and you are not, and I advise no man to take unnecessary chances. If you all want to stay, why, stay; but don't ride ahead of the line, and let me do all the talking. See that your guns are loose—you'll never have but one chance to pull, and don't pull till you're ready. The albino is riding in the middle now, isn't he? And a little back, playing for a quick drop. Watch him. Who is that on the right? Can it be George Seagrue? Well, this is a bunch. And I guess Karg is with them."

Holding their horses to a slow walk, the two

parties gingerly approached each other. When the Cache riders halted the railroad riders halted; and when the three rode the five rode: but the three rode with absolute alignment and acted as one, while Whispering Smith had trouble in holding his men back until the two lines were fifty feet apart.

By this time the youngest of the cowboys had steadied and was thinking hard. Whispering Smith halted. In perfect order and sitting their horses as if they were riding parade, the horses ambling at a snail's pace, the Cache riders advanced in the sunshine like one man. When Du Sang and his companions reined up, less than twelve feet separated the two lines.

In his tan shirt, Du Sang, with his yellow hair, his white eyelashes, and his narrow face, was the least impressive of the three men. The Norwegian, Seagrue, rode on the right, his florid blood showing under the tan on his neck and arms. He spoke to the cowboys from the ranch, and on the left the young fellow Karg, with the broken nose, black-eyed and alert, looked the men over in front of him and nodded to Dancing. Du Sang and his companions wore short-armed shirts; rifles were slung at their pommels, and revolvers stuck in their hip-scabbards. Whispering Smith, in his dusty suit of khaki, was the only man in either line who

The Fight in the Cache

showed no revolver, but a hammerless or muley Savage rifle hung beside his pommel.

Du Sang, blinking, spoke first: " Which of you fellows is heading this round-up? "

" I am heading the round-up," said Whispering Smith. " Why? Have we got some of your cattle? "

The two men spoke as quietly as school-teachers. Whispering Smith's expression in no way changed, except that as he spoke he lifted his eyebrows a little more than usual.

Du Sang looked at him closely as he went on: " What kind of a way is this to treat anybody? To ride into a valley like this and drive a man's cows away from his door without notice or papers? Is your name Smith? "

" My name is Smith; yours is Du Sang. Yes, I'll tell you, Du Sang. I carry an inspector's card from the Mountain Stock Association—do you want to see it? When we get these cattle to the Door, any man in the Cache may come forward and prove his property. I shall leave instructions to that effect when we go, for I want you to go to Medicine Bend with me, Du Sang, as soon as convenient, and the men that are with me will finish the round-up."

" What do you want me for? There's no papers out against me, is there? "

Whispering Smith

" No, but I'm an officer, Du Sang. I'll see to
the papers; I want you for murder."

" So they tell me. Well, you're after the wrong
man. But I'll go with you; I don't care about
that."

" Neither do I, Du Sang; and as you have some
friends along, I won't break up the party. They
may come, too."

" What for? "

" For stopping a train at Tower W Saturday
night."

The three men looked at one another and
laughed.

Du Sang with an oath spoke again: " The men
you want are in Canada by this time. I can't
speak for my friends; I don't know whether they
want to go or not. As far as I am concerned, I
haven't killed anybody that I know of. I suppose
you'll pay my expenses back? "

" Why, yes, Du Sang, if you were coming back
I would pay your expenses; but you are not coming
back. You are riding down Williams Cache for
the last time; you've ridden down it too many
times already. This round-up is especially for
you. Don't deceive yourself; when you ride with
me this time out of the Cache, you won't come
back."

Du Sang laughed, but his blinking eyes were as

300

The Fight in the Cache

steady as a cat's. It did not escape Whispering Smith's notice that the mettlesome horses ridden by the outlaws were continually working around to the right of his party. He spoke amiably to Karg: "If you can't manage that horse, Karg, I can. Play fair. It looks to me as if you and Du Sang were getting ready to run for it, and leave George Seagrue to shoot his way through alone."

Du Sang, with some annoyance, intervened: "That's all right; I'll go with you. I'd rather see your papers, but if you're Whispering Smith it's all right. I'm due to shoot out a little game sometime with you at Medicine Bend, anyway."

"Any time, Du Sang; only don't let your hand wabble next time. It's too close to your gun now to pull right."

"Well, I told you I was going to come, didn't I? And I'm coming—now!"

With the last word he whipped out his gun. There was a crash of bullets. Questioned once by McCloud and reproached for taking chances, Whispering Smith answered simply. "I have to take chances," he said. "All I ask is an even break."

But Kennedy had said there was no such thing as an even break with Whispering Smith. A few men in a generation amuse, baffle, and mystify other men with an art based on the principle that the action of the hand is quicker than the action of the eye. With Whispering Smith the drawing of a revolver and the art of throwing his shots instantly from wherever his hand rested was pure sleight-of-hand. To a dexterity so fatal he added a judgment that had not failed when confronted with deceit. From the moment that Du Sang first spoke, Smith, convinced that he meant to shoot his way through the line, waited only for the moment to come. When Du Sang's hand moved like a flash of light, Whispering Smith, who was holding his coat lapels in his hands, struck his pistol from the scabbard over his heart and threw a bullet at him before he could fire, as a conjurer throws a vanishing coin into the air. Spurring his horse fearfully as he did so, he dashed at Du Sang and Karg, leaped his horse through their line and, wheeling at arm's length, shot again. Bill Dancing jumped in his saddle, swayed, and toppled to the ground. Stormy Gorman gave a single whoop at the spectacle and, with his two cowboys at his heels, fled for life.

More serious than all, Smith found himself among three fast revolvers, working from an unmanageable horse. The beast tried to follow the fleeing cowboys, and when faced sharply about showed temper. The trained horses of the outlaws stood like statues, but Smith had to fight with

Wheeling at arm's length, shot again.

The Fight in the Cache

his horse bucking at every shot. He threw his
bullets as best he could first over one shoulder and
then over the other, and used the last cartridge in
his revolver with Du Sang, Seagrue, and Karg
shooting at him every time they could fire without
hitting one another.

It was not the first time the Williams Cache
gang had sworn to get him and had worked together to do it, but for the first time it looked as
if they might do it. A single chance was left to
Whispering Smith for his life, and with his coat
slashed with bullets, he took it. For an instant
his life hung on the success of a trick so appal-
lingly awkward that a cleverer man might have
failed in turning it. If his rifle should play free
in the scabbard as he reached for it, he could
fall to the ground, releasing it as he plunged from
the saddle, and make a fight on his feet. If the
rifle failed to release he was a dead man. To
so narrow an issue are the cleverest combinations
sometimes brought by chance. He dropped his
empty revolver, ducked like a mud-hen on his
horse's neck, threw back his leg, and, with all the
precision he could summon, caught the grip of his
muley in both hands. He made his fall heavily to
the ground, landing on his shoulder. But as he
keeled from the saddle the last thing that rolled
over the saddle, like the flash of a porpoise fin, was

the barrel of the rifle, secure in his hands. Karg, on horseback, was already bending over him, revolver in hand, but the shot was never fired. A thirty-thirty bullet from the ground knocked the gun into the air and tore every knuckle from Karg's hand. Du Sang spurred in from the right. A rifle-slug like an axe at the root caught him through the middle. His fingers stiffened. His six-shooter fell to the ground and he clutched his side. Seagrue, ducking low, put spurs to his horse, and Whispering Smith, covered with dust, rose on the battle-field alone.

Hats, revolvers, and coats lay about him. Face downward, the huge bulk of Bill Dancing was stretched motionless in the road. Karg, crouching beside his fallen horse, held up the bloody stump of his gun hand, and Du Sang, fifty yards away, reeling like a drunken man in his saddle, spurred his horse in an aimless circle. Whispering Smith, running softly to the side of his own trembling animal, threw himself into the saddle, and, adjusting his rifle sights as the beast plunged down the draw, gave chase to Seagrue.

CHAPTER XXXI

THE DEATH OF DU SANG

WHISPERING SMITH, with his horse in a lather, rode slowly back twenty minutes later with Seagrue disarmed ahead of him. The deserted battle-ground was alive with men. Stormy Gorman, hot for blood, had come back, captured Karg, and begun swearing all over again, and Smith listened with amiable surprise while he explained that seeing Dancing killed, and not being able to tell from Whispering Smith's peculiar tactics which side he was shooting at, Gorman and his companions had gone for help. While they angrily surrounded Karg and Seagrue, Smith slipped from his horse where Bill Dancing lay, lifted the huge head from the dust, and tried to turn the giant over. A groan greeted the attempt.

" Bill, open your eyes! Why would you not do as I wanted you to? " he murmured bitterly to himself. A second groan answered him. Smith called for water, and from a canteen drenched the pallid forehead, talking softly meanwhile; but his efforts to restore consciousness were unavailing.

Whispering Smith

He turned to where two of the cowboys had dragged Karg to the ground and three others had their old companion Seagrue in hand. While two held huge revolvers within six inches of his head, the third was adjusting a rope-knot under his ear.

Whispering Smith became interested. "Hold on!" said he mildly, "what is loose? What are you going to do?"

"We're going to hang these fellows," answered Stormy, with a volley of hair-raising imprecations.

"Oh, no! Just put them on horses under guard."

"That's what we're going to do," exclaimed the foreman. "Only we're going to run 'em over to those cottonwoods and drive the horses out from under 'em. Stand still, you tow-headed cow-thief!" he cried, slipping the noose up tight on George Seagrue's neck.

"See here," returned Whispering Smith, showing some annoyance, "you may be joking, but I am not. Either do as I tell you or release those men."

"Well, I guess we are not joking very much. You heard me, didn't you?" demanded Stormy angrily. "We are going to string these damned critters up right here in the draw on the first tree."

Whispering Smith drew a pocket-knife and walked to Flat Nose, slit the rope around his neck,

The Death of Du Sang

pushed him out of the circle, and stood in front of him. "You can't play horse with my prisoners," he said curtly. "Get over here, Karg. Come, now, who is going to walk in first? You act like a school-boy, Gorman."

Hard words and a wrangle followed, but Smith did not change expression, and there was a backdown. "Have you fellows let Du Sang get away while you were playing fool here?" he asked.

"Du Sang's over the hill there on his horse, and full of fight yet," exclaimed one.

"Then we will look him up," suggested Smith. "Come, Seagrue."

"Don't go over there. He'll get you if you do," cried Gorman.

"Let us see about that. Seagrue, you and Karg walk ahead. Don't duck or run, either of you. Go on."

Just over the brow of the hill near which the fight had taken place, a man lay below a ledge of granite. The horse from which he had fallen was grazing close by, but the man had dragged himself out of the blinding sun to the shade of the sagebrush above the rock—the trail of it all lay very plain on the hard ground. Watching him narrowly, Smith, with his prisoners ahead and the cowboys riding in a circle behind, approached.

"Du Sang?"

Whispering Smith

The man in the sagebrush turned his head.

Smith walked to him and bent down. "Are you suffering much, Du Sang?"

The wounded man, sinking with shock and internal hemorrhage, uttered a string of oaths.

Smith listened quietly till he had done; then he knelt beside him and put his hand on Du Sang's hand. "Tell me where you are hit, Du Sang. Put your hand to it. Is it the stomach? Let me turn you on your side. Easy. Does your belt hurt? Just a minute, now; I can loosen that."

"I know you," muttered Du Sang thickly. Then his eyes—terrible, rolling, pink eyes—brightened and he swore violently.

"Du Sang, you are not bleeding much, but I'm afraid you are badly hit," said Whispering Smith. "Is there anything I can do for you?"

"Get me some water."

A creek flowed at no great distance below the hill, but the cowboys refused to go for water. Whispering Smith would have gone with Seagrue and Karg, but Du Sang begged him not to leave him alone lest Gorman should kill him. Smith canvassed the situation a moment. "I'll put you on my horse," said he at length, "and take you down to the creek."

He turned to the cowboys and asked them to help, but they refused to touch Du Sang.

The Death of Du Sang

Whispering Smith kept his patience. " Karg, take that horse's head," said he. " Come here, Seagrue; help me lift Du Sang on the horse. The boys seem to be afraid of getting blood on their hands."

With Whispering Smith and Seagrue supporting Du Sang in the saddle and Karg leading the horse, the cavalcade moved slowly down to the creek, where a tiny stream purled among the rocks. The water revived the injured man for a moment; he had even strength enough, with some help, to ride again; and, moving in the same halting order, they took him to Rebstock's cabin. Rebstock, at the door, refused to let the sinking man be brought into the house. He cursed Du Sang as the cause of all the trouble. But Du Sang cursed him with usury, and, while Whispering Smith listened, told Rebstock with bitter oaths that if he had given the boy Barney anything but a scrub horse they never would have been trailed. More than this concerning the affair Du Sang would not say, and never said. The procession turned from the door. Seagrue led the way to Rebstock's stable, and they laid Du Sang on some hay.

Afterward they got a cot under him. With surprising vitality he talked a long time to Whispering Smith, but at last fell into a stupor. At nine o'clock that night he sat up. Ed Banks and

Whispering Smith

Kennedy were standing beside the cot. Du Sang became delirious, and in his delirium called the name of Whispering Smith; but Smith was at Baggs's cabin with Bill Dancing. In a spasm of pain, Du Sang, opening his eyes, suddenly threw himself back. The cot broke, and the dying man rolled under the feet of the frightened horses. In the light of the lanterns they lifted him back, but he was bleeding slowly at the mouth, quite dead.

The surgeon, afterward, found two fatal wounds upon him. The first shot, passing through the stomach, explained Du Sang's failure to kill at a distance in which, uninjured, he could have placed five shots within the compass of a silver dollar. Firing for Whispering Smith's heart, he had, despite the fearful shock, put four bullets through his coat before the rifle-ball from the ground, tearing at right angles across the path of the first bullet, had cut down his life to a question of hours.

Bill Dancing, who had been hit in the head and stunned, had been moved back to the cabin at Mission Spring, and lay in the little bedroom. A doctor at Oroville had been sent for, but had not come. At midnight of the second day, Smith, who was beside his bed, saw him rouse up, and noted the brightness of his eyes as he looked around. " Bill," he declared hopefully, as he sat beside the

The Death of Du Sang

bed, "you are better, hang it! I know you are. How do you feel?"

"Ain't that blamed doctor here yet? Then give me my boots. I'm going back to Medicine Bend to Doc Torpy."

In the morning Whispering Smith, who had cleansed and dressed the wound and felt sure the bullet had not penetrated the skull, offered no objection to the proposal beyond cautioning him to ride slowly. "You can go down part way with the prisoners, Bill," suggested Whispering Smith. "Brill Young is going to take them to Oroville, and you can act as chairman of the guard."

Before the party started, Smith called Seagrue to him. "George, you saved my life once. Do you remember—in the Pan Handle? Well, I gave you yours twice in the Cache day before yesterday. I don't know how badly you are into this thing. If you kept clear of the killing at Tower W I will do what I can for you. Don't talk to anybody."

CHAPTER XXXII

NEWS of the fight in Williams Cache reached Medicine Bend in the night. Horsemen, filling in the gaps between telephones leading to the north country, made the circuit complete, but the accounts, confused and colored in the repeating, came in a cloud of conflicting rumors. In the streets, little groups of men discussed the fragmentary reports as they came from the railroad offices. Toward morning, Sleepy Cat, nearer the scene of the fight, began sending in telegraphic reports in which truth and rumor were strangely mixed. McCloud waited at the wires all night, hoping for trustworthy advices as to the result, but received none. Even during the morning nothing came, and the silence seemed more ominous than the bad news of the early night. Routine business was almost suspended and McCloud and Rooney Lee kept the wires warm with inquiries, but neither the telephone nor the telegraph would yield any definite word as to what had actually

McCloud and Dicksie

happened in the Williams Cache fight. It was easy to fear the worst.

At the noon hour McCloud was signing letters when Dicksie Dunning walked hurriedly up the hall and hesitated in the passageway before the open door of his office. He gave an exclamation as he pushed back his chair. She was in her riding-suit just as she had slipped from her saddle. "Oh, Mr. McCloud, have you heard the awful news? Whispering Smith was killed yesterday in Williams Cache by Du Sang."

McCloud stiffened a little. "I hope that can't be true. We have had nothing here but rumors; perhaps it is these that you have heard."

"No, no! Blake, one of our men, was in the fight and got back at the ranch at nine o'clock this morning. I heard the story myself, and I rode right in to—to see Marion, and my courage failed me—I came here first. Does she know, do you think? Blake saw him fall from the saddle after he was shot, and everybody ran away, and Du Sang and two other men were firing at him as he lay on the ground. He could not possibly have escaped with his life, Blake said; he must have been riddled with bullets. Isn't it terrible?" She sobbed suddenly, and McCloud, stunned at her words, led her to his chair and bent over her.

Whispering Smith

"If his death means this to you, think of what it means to me!"

A flood of sympathy bore them together. The moment was hardly one for interruption, but the despatcher's door opened and Rooney Lee halted, thunderstruck, on the threshold.

Dicksie's hand disappeared in her handkerchief. McCloud had been in wrecks before, and gathered himself together unmoved. "What is it, Rooney?"

The very calmness of the two at the table disconcerted the despatcher. He held the message in his hand and shuffled his feet. "Give me your despatch," said McCloud impatiently.

Quite unable to take his hollow eyes off Dicksie, poor Rooney advanced, handed the telegram to McCloud, and beat an awkward retreat.

McCloud devoured the words of the message at a glance.

"Ah!" he cried, "this is from Gordon himself, sent from Sleepy Cat. He must be safe and unhurt! Listen:

"Three of the Tower W men trailed into Williams Cache. In resisting arrest this morning, Du Sang was wounded and is dying to-night. Two prisoners, Karg and Seagrue. G. S.

"Those are Gordon's initials; it is the signature over which he telegraphs me. You see, this

McCloud and Dicksie

was sent last night long after Blake left. He is safe; I will stake my life on it."

Dicksie sank back while McCloud re-read the message. " Oh, isn't that a relief? " she exclaimed. " But how can it be? I can't understand it at all; but he *is* safe, isn't he? I was heartbroken when I heard he was killed. Marion ought to know of this," she said, rising. " I am going to tell her."

" And may I come over after I tell Rooney Lee to repeat this to headquarters? "

" Why, of course, if you want to."

When McCloud reached the cottage Dicksie met him. " Katie Dancing's mother is sick, and she has gone home. Poor Marion is all alone this morning, and half dead with a sick headache," said Dicksie. " But I told her, and she said she shouldn't mind the headache now at all."

" But what are you going to do? "

" I am going to get dinner; do you want to help? "

" I'm going to help."

" Oh, you are? That would be very funny."

" Funny or not, I'm going to help."

" You would only be in the way."

" You don't know whether I should or not."

" I know *I* should do much better if you would go back and run the railroad a few minutes."

315

"The railroad be hanged. I am for dinner."

"But I will get dinner for you."

"You need not. I can get it for myself."

"You are perfectly absurd, and if we stand here disputing, Marion won't have anything to eat."

They went into the kitchen disputing about what should be cooked. At the end of an hour they had two fires going—one in the stove and one in Dicksie's cheeks. By that time it had been decided to have a luncheon instead of a dinner. Dicksie attempted some soup, and McCloud found a strip of bacon, and after he had cooked it, Dicksie, with her riding-skirt pinned up and her sleeves delightfully rolled back, began frying eggs. When Marion, unable longer to withstand the excitement, appeared, the engineer, flushed with endeavor, was making toast.

The three sat down at table together. They found they had forgotten the coffee, but Marion was not allowed to move from her chair. When the coffee was made ready the bacon had been eaten and more had to be fried. McCloud proved able for any part of the programme, and when they rose it was four o'clock and too late, McCloud declared, to go back to the office that afternoon.

Marion and Dicksie, after a time, attempted jointly to get rid of him, but they found they could not, so the three talked about Whispering Smith.

McCloud and Dicksie

When the women tried to discourage McCloud by talking hats he played the wheezy piano, and when Dicksie spoke about going home he declared he would ride home with her. But Dicksie had no mind that he should, and when he asked to know why, without realizing what a flush lingered in his face, she said only, no; if she had reasons she would give none. McCloud persisted, because under the flush about his eyes was the resolve that he would take one long ride that evening, in any event. He had made up his mind for that ride— a longer one than he had ever taken before or expected ever to take again—and would not be balked.

Dicksie, insisting upon going home, went so far as to have her horse brought from the stable. To her surprise, a horse for McCloud came over with it. Quiet to the verge of solemnity, but with McCloud following, Dicksie walked with admirable firmness out of the shop to the curb. Mc-Cloud gave her rein to her, and with a smile stood waiting to help her mount.

She was drawing on her second glove. " You are not going with me."

" You'll let me ride the same road, won't you —even if I can't keep up? "

Dicksie looked at his mount. " It would be difficult to keep up, with that horse."

Whispering Smith

"Would you ride away from me just because you have a better horse?"

"No, not *just* because I have a better horse."

He looked steadily at her without speaking.

"Why must you ride home with me when I don't want you to?" she asked reproachfully. Fear had come upon her and she did not know what she was saying. She saw only the expression of his eyes and looked away, but she knew that his eyes followed her. The sun had set. The deserted street lay in the white half-light of a mountain evening, and the day's radiance was dying in the sky. In lower tones he spoke again, and she turned deadly white.

"I've wanted so long to say this, Dicksie, that I might as well be dead as to try to keep it back any longer. That's why I want to ride home with you if you are going to let me." He turned to stroke her horse's head. Dicksie stood seemingly helpless. McCloud slipped his finger into his waistcoat pocket and held something out in his hand. "This shell pin fell from your hair that night you were at camp by the bridge—do you remember? I couldn't bear to give it back."

Dicksie's eyes opened wide. "Let me see it. I don't think that is mine."

"Great Heaven! Have I been carrying Marion Sinclair's pin for a month?" exclaimed Mc-

McCloud and Dicksie

Cloud. "Well, I won't lose any time in returning it to her, at any rate."

"Where are you going?" Dicksie's voice was faint.

"I'm going to give Marion her pin."

"Do nothing of the sort! Come here! Give it to me."

"Dicksie, dare you tell me, after a shock like that, it really *is* your pin?"

"Oh, I don't know whose pin it is!"

"Why, what is the matter?"

"Give me the pin!" She put her hands unsteadily up under her hat. "Here, for Heaven's sake, if you must have something, take this comb!" She slipped from her head the shell that held her knotted hair. He caught her hand and kissed it, and she could not get it away.

"You are dear," murmured Dicksie, "if you are silly. The reason I wouldn't let you ride home with me is because I was afraid you might get shot. How do you suppose I should feel if you were killed? Or don't you think I have any feeling?"

"But, Dicksie, is it all right?"

"How do I know? What do you mean? I will not let you ride home with me, and you *will* not let me ride home alone. Tie Jim again. I am going to stay with Marion all night."

CHAPTER XXXIII

THE LAUGH OF A WOMAN

WITHIN an hour, Marion, working over a hat in the trimming-room, was startled to hear the cottage door open, and to see Dicksie quite unconcernedly walk in. To Marion's exclamation of surprise she returned only a laugh. " I have changed my mind, dear. I am going to stay all night."

Marion kissed her approvingly. " Really, you are getting so sensible I shan't know you, Dicksie. In fact, I believe this is the most sensible thing you were ever guilty of."

" Glad you think so," returned Dicksie dryly, unpinning her hat. " I certainly hope it is. Mr. McCloud persuaded me it wasn't right for me to ride home alone, and I knew better than he what danger there was for him in riding home with me —so here I am. He is coming over for supper, too, in a few minutes."

When McCloud arrived he brought with him a porterhouse steak, and Marion was again driven

The Laugh of a Woman

from the kitchen. At the end of an hour, Dicksie, engrossed over the broiler, was putting the finishing touches to the steak, and McCloud, more engrossed, was watching her, when a diffident and surprised-looking person appeared in the kitchen doorway and put his hand undecidedly on the casing. While he stood, Dicksie turned abruptly to McCloud.

"Oh, by the way, I have forgotten something! Will you do me a favor?"

"Certainly! Do you want money or a pass?"

"No, not money," said Dicksie, lifting the steak on her forks, "though you might give me a pass."

"But I should hate to have you go away anywhere——"

"I don't want to go anywhere, but I never had a pass, and I think it would be kind of nice to have one just to keep. Don't you?"

"Why, yes; you might put it in the bank and have it drawing interest."

"This steak is. Do they give interest on passes?"

"Well, a good deal of interest is felt in them—on this division at least. What is the favor?"

"Yes, what is it? How can I think? Oh, I know! If they don't put Jim in a box stall to-night he will kill some of the horses over there. Will you telephone the stables?"

Whispering Smith

"Won't you give me the number and let me telephone?" asked a voice behind them. They turned in astonishment and saw Whispering Smith. "I am surprised," he added calmly, "to see a man of your intelligence, George, trying to broil a steak with the lower door of your stove wide open. Close the lower door and cut out the draft through the fire. Don't stare, George; put back the broiler. And haven't you made a radical mistake to start with?" he asked, stepping between the confused couple. "Are you not trying to broil a roast of beef?"

"Where did you come from?" demanded McCloud, as Marion came in from the dining-room.

"Don't search me the very first thing," protested Whispering Smith.

"But we've been frightened to death here for twenty-four hours. Are you really alive and unhurt? This young lady rode in twenty miles this morning and came to the office in tears to get news of you."

Smith looked mildly at Dicksie. "Did you shed a tear for me? I should like to have seen just one! Where did I come from? I reported in wild over the telephone ten minutes ago. Didn't Marion tell you? She is so forgetful. That is what causes wrecks, Marion. I have been in the saddle since three o'clock this morning, thank you, and

322

The Laugh of a Woman

have had nothing for five days but raw steer garnished with sunshine."

The four sat down to supper, and Whispering Smith began to talk. He told the story of the chase to the Cache, the defiance from Rebstock, and the tardy appearance of the men he wanted. " Du Sang meant to shoot his way through us and make a dash for it. There really was nothing else for him to do. Banks and Kennedy were up above, even if he could have ridden out through the upper canyon, which is very doubtful with all the water now. After a little talk back and forth, Du Sang drew, and of course then it was every man for himself. He was hit twice and he died Sunday night, but the other two were not seriously hurt. What can you do? It is either kill or get killed with those fellows, and, of course, I talked plainly to Du Sang. He had butchered a man at Mission Springs just the night before, and deserved hanging a dozen times over. He meant from the start, he told me afterward, to get me. Oh, Miss Dunning, may I have some more coffee? Haven't I an agreeable part of the railroad business, don't you think? I shouldn't have pushed in here to-night, but I saw the lights when I rode by awhile ago; they looked so good I couldn't resist."

McCloud leaned forward. " You call it pushing in, do you, Gordon? Do you know what this

Whispering Smith

young lady did this morning? One of her cowboys came down from the Cache early with the word that you had been killed in the fight by Du Sang. He said he saw you drop from your saddle to the ground with Du Sang shooting at you. She ordered up her horse, without a word, and rode twenty miles in an hour and a half to find out here what we had heard. She 'pushed in' at the Wickiup, where she never had been before in her life, and wandered through it alone looking for my office, to find out from me whether I hadn't something to contradict the bad news. While we talked, in came your despatch from Sleepy Cat. Never was one better timed! And when she knew you were safe her eyes filled again."

Whispering Smith looked at Dicksie quizzically. Her confusion was delightful. He rose, lifted her hand in his own, and, bending, kissed it.

They talked till late, and when Dicksie walked out on the porch McCloud followed to smoke. Whispering Smith still sat at the table talking to Marion, and the two heard the sound of the low voices outside. At intervals Dicksie's laugh came in through the open door.

Whispering Smith, listening, said nothing for some time, but once she laughed peculiarly. He pricked up his ears. " What has been happening since I left town?"

324

The Laugh of a Woman

"What do you mean?" asked Marion Sinclair. He nodded toward the porch. "McCloud and Dicksie out there. They have been fixing things up."

"Nonsense! What do you mean?"

"I mean they are engaged."

"Never in the world!"

"I may be slow in reading a trail," said Smith modestly, "but when a woman laughs like that I think there's something doing. Don't you believe it? Call them in and ask them. You won't? Well, I will. Take them in separate rooms. You ask her and I'll ask him."

In spite of Marion's protests the two were brought in. "I am required by Mr. Smith to ask you a very silly question, Dicksie," said Marion, taking her into the living-room. "Answer yes or no. Are you engaged to anybody?"

"What a question! Why, no!"

"Marion Sinclair wants to know just one thing, George," said Whispering Smith to McCloud after he had taken him into the dark shop. "She feels she ought to know because she is in a way Dicksie's chaperone, you know, and she feels that you are willing she should know. I don't want to be too serious, but answers yes or no. Are you engaged to Dicksie?"

"Why, yes. I——"

Whispering Smith

"That's all; go back to the porch," directed Whispering Smith. McCloud obeyed orders.

Marion, alone in the living-room, was waiting for the inquisitor, and her face wore a look of triumph. "You are not such a mind-reader after all, are you? I told you they weren't."

"I told you they were," contended Whispering Smith.

"She says they are *not*," insisted Marion.

"He says they are," returned Whispering Smith. "And, what's more, I'll bet my saddle against the shop they are. I could be mistaken in anything but that laugh."

CHAPTER XXXIV

A MIDNIGHT VISIT

THE lights, but one, were out. McCloud and Whispering Smith had gone, and Marion was locking up the house for the night, when she was halted by a knock at the shop door. It was a summons that she thought she knew, but the last in the world that she wanted to hear or to answer. Dicksie had gone to the bedroom, and standing between the portières that curtained the workroom from the shop, Marion in the half-light listened, hesitating whether to ignore or to answer the midnight intruder. But experience, and bitter experience, had taught her there was only one way to meet that particular summons, and that was to act, whether at noon or at midnight, without fear. She waited until the knocking had been twice repeated, turned up the light, and going to the door drew the bolt; Sinclair stood before her, and she drew back for him to enter. " Dicksie Dunning is with me to-night," said Marion, with her hand on the latch, " and we shall have to talk here."

Sinclair took off his hat. " I knew you had company," he returned in the low, gentle tone that Marion knew very well, " so I came late. And I heard to-night, for the first time, that this railroad crowd is after me—God knows why; but they have to earn their salary somehow. I want to keep out of trouble if I can. I won't kill anybody if they don't force me to it. They've scared nearly all my men away from the ranch already; one crippled-up cowboy is all I have got to help me look after the cattle. But I won't quarrel with them, Marion, if I can get away from here peaceably, so I've come to talk it over once more with you. I'm going away and I want you to go with me; I've got enough to keep us as well as the best of them and as long as we live. You've given me a good lesson. I needed it, girlie——"

" Don't call me that ! "

He laughed kindly. " Why, that's what it used to be; that's what I want it to be again. I don't blame you. You're worth all the women I ever knew, Marion. I've learned to appreciate some few things in the lonely months I've spent up on the Frenchman; but I've felt while I was there as if I were working for both of us. I've got a buyer in sight now for the cattle and the land. I'm ready to clean up and say good-by to trouble—all I want is for you to give me the one chance I've asked for and go along."

A Midnight Visit

They stood facing each other under the dim light. She listened intently to every word, though in her terror she might not have heard or understood all of them. One thing she did very clearly understand, and that was why he had come and what he wanted. To that she held her mind tenaciously, and for that she shaped her answer. " I cannot go with you—now or ever."

He waited a moment. " We always got along, Marion, when I behaved myself."

" I hope you always will behave yourself; but I could no more go with you than I could make myself again what I was years ago, Murray. I wish you nothing but good; but our ways parted long ago."

" Stop and think a minute, Marion. I offer you more and offer it more honestly than I ever offered it before, because I know myself better. I am alone in the world—strong, and better able to care for you than I was when I undertook to——"

" I have never complained."

" That's what makes me more anxious to show you now that I can and will do what's right."

" Oh, you multiply words! It is too late for you to be here. You are in danger, you say; for the love of Heaven, leave me and go away! "

" You know me, Marion, when my mind is made

up. I won't leave without you." He leaned with one hand against the ribbon showcase. " If you don't want to go I will stay right here and pay off the scores I owe. Two men here have stirred this country up too long, anyway. I don't care much how soon anybody gets me after I round them up. But to-night I felt like this: you and I started out in life together, and we ought to live it out or die together, whether it's to-night, Marion, or twenty years from to-night."

" If you want to kill me to-night, I have no resistance to make."

Sinclair sat down on a low counter-stool, and, bending forward, held his head between his hands. " It oughtn't all to end here. I know you, and I know you want to do what's right. I couldn't kill you without killing myself; you know that." He straightened up slowly. "Here!" He slipped his revolver from his hip-holster and held the grip of the gun toward her. " Use it on me if you want to. It is your chance to end everything; it may save several lives if you do. I won't leave McCloud here to crow over me, and, by God, I won't leave you here for Whispering Smith! I'll settle with him anyhow. Take the pistol! What are you afraid of? Take it! Use it! I don't want to live without you. If you make me do it, you're to blame for the consequences."

A Midnight Visit

She stood with wide-open eyes, but uttered no word.

"You won't touch it—then you care a little for me yet," he murmured.

"No! Do not say so. But I will not do murder."

"Think about the other, then. Go with me and everything will be all right. I will come back some evening soon for my answer. And until then, if those two men have any use for life, let them keep in the clear. I heard to-night that Du Sang is killed. Do you know whether it is true?"

"It is true."

An oath half escaping showed how the confirmation cut him. "And Whispering Smith got away! It is Du Sang's own fault; I told him to keep out of that trap. I stay in the open; and I'm not Du Sang. I'll choose my own ground for the finish when they want it with me, and when I go I'll take company—I'll promise you that. Good-night, Marion. Will you shake hands?"

"No."

"Damn it, I like your grit, girl! Well, good-night, anyway."

She closed the door. She had even strength enough to bolt it before his footsteps died away. She put out the light and felt her way blindly back to the work-room. She staggered through it,

clutching at the curtains, and fell in the darkness
into Dicksie's arms.

"Marion dear, don't speak," Dicksie whispered. "I heard everything. Oh, Marion!"
she cried, suddenly conscious of the inertness of
the burden in her arms. "Oh, what shall I do?"

Moved by fright to her utmost strength, Dicksie
drew the unconscious woman back to her room and
managed to lay her on the bed. Marion opened
her eyes a few minutes later to see the lights burning, to hear the telephone bell ringing, and to find
Dicksie on the edge of the bed beside her.

"Oh, Marion, thank Heaven, you are reviving!
I have been frightened to death. Don't mind the
telephone; it is Mr. McCloud. I didn't know
what to do, so I telephoned him."

"But you had better answer him," said Marion
faintly. The telephone bell was ringing wildly.

"Oh, no! he can wait. How are you, dear? I
don't wonder you were frightened to death. Marion, he means to kill us—every one!"

"No, Dicksie. He will kill me and kill himself;
that is where it will end. Dicksie, do answer the
telephone. What are you thinking of? Mr. Mc-
Cloud will be at the door in five minutes. Do you
want him in the street to-night?"

Dicksie fled to the telephone, and an excited conference over the wire closed in seeming reassur-

A Midnight Visit

ance at both ends. By that time Marion had regained her steadiness, but she could not talk of
what had passed. At times, as the two lay together
in the darkness, Marion spoke, but it was not to
be answered. " I do not know," she murmured
once wearily. " Perhaps I am doing wrong; perhaps I ought to go with him. I wish, oh, I wish
I knew what I ought to do!"

CHAPTER XXXV

THE CALL

BEYOND receiving reports from Kennedy and Banks, who in the interval rode into town and rode out again on their separate and silent ways, Whispering Smith for two days seemed to do nothing. Yet instinct keener than silence kept the people of Medicine Bend on edge during those two days, and when President Bucks's car came in on the evening of the second day, the town knew from current rumors that Banks had gone to the Frenchman ranch with a warrant on a serious charge for Sinclair. In the president's car Bucks and McCloud, after a late dinner, were joined by Whispering Smith, and the president heard the first connected story of the events of the fortnight that had passed. Bucks made no comment until he had heard everything. " And they rode Sinclair's horses," he said in conclusion.

" Sinclair's horses," returned Whispering Smith, " and they are all accounted for. One horse supplied by Rebstock was shot where they crossed Stampede Creek. It had given out and they had

The Call

a fresh horse in the willows, for they shot the scrub half a mile up one of the canyons near the crossing. The magpies attracted my attention to it. A piece of skin a foot square had been cut out of the flank."

" You got there before the birds."

" It was about an even thing," said Smith. " Anyway, we were there in time to see the horse."

" And Sinclair was away from the ranch from Saturday noon till Sunday night? "

" A rancher living over on Stampede Creek saw the five men when they crossed Saturday afternoon. The fellow was scared and lied to me about it, but he told Wickwire who they were."

" Now, who is Wickwire? " asked Bucks.

" You ought to remember Wickwire, George," remarked Whispering Smith, turning to McCloud. " You haven't forgotten the Smoky Creek wreck? Do you remember the tramp who had his legs crushed and lay in the sun all morning? You put him in your car and sent him down here to the railroad hospital and Barnhardt took care of him. That was Wickwire. Not a bad fellow, either; he can talk pretty straight and shoot pretty straight. How do I know? Because he has told me the story and I've seen him shoot. There, you see, is one friend that you never reckoned on. He used to be a cowboy, and I got him a job working for

Whispering Smith

Sinclair on the Frenchman; he has worked at Dunning's and other places on the Crawling Stone. He hates Sinclair with a deadly hatred for some reason. Just lately Wickwire set up for himself on Little Crawling Stone."

"I have noticed that fellow's ranch," remarked McCloud.

"I couldn't leave him at Sinclair's," continued Whispering Smith frankly. "The fellow was on my mind all the time. I felt certain he would kill Sinclair or get killed if he stayed there. And then, when I took him away they sprang Tower W on me! That is the price, not of having a conscience, for I haven't any, but of listening to the voice that echoes where my conscience used to be," said the railroad man, moving uneasily in his chair.

Bucks broke the ash from his cigar into the tray on the table. "You are restless to-night, Gordon —and it isn't like you, either."

"It is in the air. There has been a dead calm for two days. Something is due to happen to-night. I wish I could hear from Banks; he started with the papers for Sinclair's yesterday while I went to Oroville to sweat Karg. Blood-poisoning has set in and it is rather important to us to get a confession. There's a horse!" He stepped to the window. "Coming fast, too. Now, I wonder —no, he's gone by."

The Call

Five minutes later a messenger came to the car from the Wickiup with word that Kennedy was looking for Whispering Smith. Bucks, McCloud, and Smith left the car together and walked up to McCloud's office.

Kennedy, sitting on the edge of the table, was tapping his leg nervously with a ruler. "Bad news, Gordon."

"Not from Ed Banks?"

"Sinclair got him this morning."

Whispering Smith sat down. "Go on."

"Banks and I picked up Wickwire on the Crawling Stone early, and we rode over to the Frenchman. Wickwire said Sinclair had been up at Williams Cache the day before, and he didn't think he was home. Of course I knew the Cache was watched and he wouldn't be there long, so Ed asked me to stay in the cottonwoods and watch the creek for him. He and Wickwire couldn't find anybody home when they got to the ranch-house and they rode down the corral together to look over the horses."

Whispering Smith's hand fell helplessly on the table. "Rode down together! For God's sake, why didn't *one* of them stay at the house?"

"Sinclair rode out from behind the barn and hit Wickwire in the arm before they saw him. Banks turned and opened on him, and Wickwire

337

ducked for the creek. Sinclair put a soft bullet through Banks's shoulder—tore it pretty bad, Gordon—and made his get-away before Wickwire and I could reach the barn again. I got Ed on his horse and back to Wickwire's, and we sent one of the boys to Oroville for a doctor. After Banks fell out of the saddle and was helpless Sinclair talked to him before I came up. ' You ought to have kept out of this, Ed,' he said. ' This is a railroad fight. Why didn't they send the head of their own gang after me? '—naming you." Kennedy nodded toward Whispering Smith.

" Naming me."

" Banks says, ' I'm sheriff of this county, and will be a long time yet! ' I took the papers from his breast pocket," continued Kennedy. " You can see where he was hit." Kennedy laid the sheriff's packet on the table. Bucks drew his chair forward and, with his cigar between his fingers, picked the packet up and opened it. Kennedy went on: " Ed told Sinclair if he couldn't land him himself that he knew a man who could and would before he was a week older. He meant you, Gordon, and the last thing Ed told me was that he wanted you to serve the papers on Sinclair."

A silence fell on the company. One of the documents passing under Bucks's hand caught his eye and he opened it. It was the warrant for Sinclair.

The Call

He read it without comment, folded it, and, looking at Whispering Smith, pushed it toward him. "Then this, I guess, Gordon, belongs to you."

Starting from a revery, Whispering Smith reached for the warrant. He looked for a moment at the blood-stained caption. "Yes," he said, "this, I guess, belongs to me."

CHAPTER XXXVI

DUTY

THE stir of the town over the shooting of Banks seemed to Marion, in her distress, to point an accusing finger at her. The disgrace of what she had felt herself powerless to prevent now weighed on her mind, and she asked herself whether, after all, the responsibility of this murder was not upon her. Even putting aside this painful doubt, she bore the name of the man who had savagely defied accountability and now, it seemed to her, was dragging her with him through the slough of blood and dishonor into which he had plunged.

The wretched thought would return that had she listened to him, had she consented to go away, this outbreak might have been prevented. And what horror might not another day bring—what lives still closer to her life be taken? For herself she cared less; but she knew that Sinclair, now that he had begun, would not stop. In whichever way her thoughts turned, wretchedness was upon them, and the day went in one of those de-

Duty

spairing and indecisive battles that each one within his own heart must fight at times with heaviness and doubt.

McCloud called her over the telephone in the afternoon to say that he was going West on the evening train and would not be over for supper. She wished he could have come, for her loneliness began to be insupportable.

Toward sunset she put on her hat and started for the post-office. In the meantime, Dicksie, at home, had called McCloud up and told him she was coming down for the night. He immediately cancelled his plans for going West, and when Marion returned at dusk she found him with Dicksie at the cottage. The three had supper. Afterward Dicksie and McCloud went out for a walk, and Marion was alone in the house when the shop door opened and Whispering Smith walked in. It was dusk.

" Don't light the lamps, Marion," he said, sitting down on a counter-stool as he took off his hat. " I want to talk to you just a minute, if you don't mind. You know what has happened. I am called on now to go after Sinclair. I have tried to avoid it, but my hand has been forced. To-day I've been placing horses. I am going to ride to-night with the warrant. I have given him a start of twenty-four hours, hoping he may get out of the country. To stay here means only death to him in the end, and, what is worse, the killing of more and innocent men. But he won't leave the country; do you think he will? "

" Oh, I do not know! I am afraid he will not."

" I do not think I have ever hesitated before at any call of this kind; nor at what such a call will probably sometime mean; but this man I have known since we were boys."

" If I had never seen him! "

" That brings up another point that has been worrying me all day. I could not help knowing what you have had to go through in this country. It is a tough country for any woman. Your people and mine were always close together and I have felt bound to do what I could to——"

" Don't be afraid to say it—make my path easier."

" Something like that, though there's been little real doing. What this situation in which Sinclair is now placed may still mean to you I do not know, but I would not add a straw to the weight of your troubles. I came to-night to ask a plain question. If he doesn't leave the country I have got to meet him. You know what, in all human probability, that will mean. From such a meeting only one of us can come back. Which shall it be? "

" I'm afraid I don't understand you—do you

Duty

ask me this question? How can I know which it shall be? What is it you mean?"

" I mean I will not take his life in a fight—if it comes to that—if you would rather he should come back."

A sob almost refused an answer to him. " How can you ask me so terrible a question?"

" It is a question that means a good deal to me, of course, and I don't know just what it means to you: that is the point I am up against. I may have no choice in the matter, but I must decide what to try to do if I have one. Am I to remember first that he is your husband?"

There was a silence. " What shall I say—what can I say? God help me, how am I to answer a question like that?"

" How am I to answer it?"

Her voice was low and pitiful when her answer came: " You must do your duty."

" What is my duty then? To serve the paper that has been given to me, I know—but not necessarily to defend my life at the price of his. The play of a chance lies in deciding that; I can keep the chance or give it away; that is for you to say. Or take the question of duty again. You are alone and your friends are few. Haven't I any duty toward you, perhaps? I don't know a woman's heart. I used to think I did, but I don't.

343

Whispering Smith

My duty to this company that I work for is only the duty of a servant. If I go, another takes my place; it means nothing except taking one name off the pay-roll and putting another on. Whatever he may have done, this man is your husband; if his death would cause you a pang, it shall not be laid at my door. We ought to understand each other on that point fairly before I start to-night."

" Can you ask me whether you ought not to take every means to defend your own life? or whether any consideration ought to come before that? I think not. I should be a wicked woman if I were to wish evil to him, wretched as he has made me. I am a wretched woman, whichever way I turn. But I should be less than human if I could say that to me your death would not be a cruel, cruel blow."

There was a moment of silence. " Dicksie understood you to say that you were in doubt as to whether you ought to go away with him when he asked you to go. That is why I was unsettled in my mind."

" The only reason why I doubted was that I thought by going I might save better lives than mine. I could willingly give up my life to do that. But to stain it by going back to such a man— God help me!"

" I think I understand. If the unfortunate

Duty

should happen before I come back I hope only
this: that you will not hate me because I am the
man on whom the responsibility has fallen. I
haven't sought it. And if I should not come back
at all, it is only—good-by."

He saw her clasp her hands convulsively. "I
will not say it! I will pray on my knees that you
do come back."

"Good-night, Marion. Some one is at the cottage door."

"It is probably Mr. McCloud and Dicksie. I
will let them in."

CHAPTER XXXVII

McCLOUD and Dicksie met them at the porch door. Marion, unnerved, went directly to her room. Whispering Smith stopped to speak to Dicksie and McCloud interposed. " Bob Scott telephoned the office just now he had a man from Oroville who wanted to see you right away, Gordon," said he. " I told him to send him over here. It is Wickwire."

" Wickwire," repeated Whispering Smith. " Wickwire has no business here that I know of; no doubt it is something I ought to know of. And, by the way, you ought to see this man," he said, turning again to Dicksie. " If McCloud tells the story right, Wickwire is a sort of protégé of yours, Miss Dicksie, though neither of you seems to have known it. He is the tramp cowboy who was smashed up in the wreck at Smoky Creek. He is not a bad man, but whiskey, you know, beats some decent men." A footstep fell on the porch. " There he comes now, I reckon. Shall I let him in a minute? "

346

Wickwire

"Oh, I should like to see him! He has been at the ranch at different times, you know."

Smith opened the door and stepping out on the porch, talked with the new-comer. In a moment he brought him in. Dicksie had seated herself on the sofa, McCloud stood in the doorway of the dining-room, and Whispering Smith laid one arm on the table as he sat down beside it with his face above the dark shade of the lamp. Before him stood Wickwire. The half-light threw him up tall and dark, but it showed the heavy shock of black hair falling over his forehead, and the broad, thin face of a mountain man.

"He has just been telling me that Seagrue is loose," Whispering Smith explained pleasantly. "Who turned the trick, Wickwire?"

"Sheriff Coon and a deputy jailer started with Seagrue for Medicine Bend this morning. Coming through Horse Eye Canyon, Murray Sinclair and Barney Rebstock got a clean drop on them, took Seagrue, and they all rode off together. They didn't make any bones about it, either. Their gang has got lots of friends over there, you know. They rode into Atlantic City and stayed over an hour. Coon tracked them there and got up a *posse* of six men. The three were standing in front of the bank when the sheriff rode into town. Sinclair and Seagrue got on their horses and started off. Reb-

Whispering Smith

stock went back to get another drink. When he came out of the saloon he gave the *posse* a gun-fight all by himself, and wounded two men and made his get-away."

Whispering Smith shook his head, and his hand fell on the table with a tired laugh. "Barney Rebstock," he murmured, "of all men! Coward, skate, filler-in! Barney Rebstock—stale-beer man, sneak, barn-yard thief! Hit two men!" He turned to McCloud. "What kind of a wizard is Murray Sinclair? What sort of red-blood toxin does he throw into his gang to draw out a spirit like that? Murray Sinclair belongs to the race of empire-builders. By Heaven, it is pitiful a man like that should be out of a job! England, Mc-Cloud, needs him. And here he is holding up trains on the mountain division!"

"They are all up at Oroville with the Williams Cache gang, celebrating," continued Wickwire.

Whispering Smith looked at the cowboy. "Wickwire, you made a good ride and I thank you. You are all right. This is the young lady and this is the man who had you sent to the hospital from Smoky Creek," he added, rising. "You can thank them for picking you up. When you leave here tell Bob Scott to meet me at the Wickiup with the horses at eleven o'clock, will you?" He turned to Dicksie in a gentle aside. "I

Wickwire

am riding north to-night—I wish you were going part way."

Dicksie looked at him intently. " You are worried over something," she murmured; " I can see it in your face."

" Nothing more than usual. I thrive, you know, on trouble—and I'm sorry to say good-night so early, but I have a long ride ahead." He stepped quietly past McCloud and out of the door.

Wickwire was thanking Dicksie when unwillingly she let Whispering Smith's hand slip out of her own. " I shore wouldn't have been here to-night if you two hadn't picked me up," laughed Wickwire, speaking softly to Dicksie when she turned to him. " I've knowed my friends a long time, but I reckon they all didn't know me."

" I've known you longer than you think," returned Dicksie with a smile. " I've seen you at the ranch-house. But now that we really do know each other, please remember you are always sure of a home at the ranch—whenever you want one, Mr. Wickwire, and just as long as you want one. We never forget our friends on the Crawling Stone."

" If I may make so bold, I thank you kindly. And if you all will let me run away now, I want to catch Mr. Whispering Smith for just one minute."

Whispering Smith

Wickwire overtook Smith in Fort Street. "Talk quick, Wickwire," he said; "I'm in a hurry. What do you want?"

"Partner, I've always played fair with you."

"So far as I know, Wickwire, yes. Why?"

"I've got a favor to ask."

"What is it—money?"

"No, partner, not money this time. You've always been more than liberal with me. But so far I've had to keep under cover; you asked me to. I want to ask the privilege now of coming out into the open. The jig is up so far as watching anybody goes."

"Yes."

"There's nobody to watch any more—they're all to chase, I reckon, now. The open is my kind of a fight, anyway. I want to ride out this manhunt with you."

"How is your arm?"

"My arm is all right, and there ought to be a place for me in the chase now that Ed Banks is out of it. I want to cut loose up on the range, anyhow; if I'm a man I want to know it, and if I ain't I want to know it. I want to ride with you after Seagrue and Sinclair and Barney Rebstock."

Whispering Smith spoke coldly: "You mean, Wickwire, you want to get killed."

Wickwire

" Why, partner, if it's coming to me, I don't mind—yes."

" What's the use, Wickwire? "

" If I'm a man I want to know it; if I ain't, it's time my friends knowed it. Anyhow, I'm man enough to work out with some of that gang. Most of them have put it over me one time or another; Sinclair pasted me like a blackbird only the other day. They all say I'm nothing but a damned tramp. You say I have done you service—give me a show."

Whispering Smith stopped a minute in the shadow of a tree and looked keenly at him. " I'm too busy to-night to say much, Wickwire," he said after a moment. " You go over to the barn and report to Bob Scott. If you want to take the chances, it is up to you; and if Bob Scott is agreeable, I'll use you where I can—that's all I can promise. You will probably have more than one chance to get killed."

CHAPTER XXXVIII

INTO THE NORTH

THE moon had not yet risen, and in the darkness of Boney Street Smith walked slowly
toward his room. The answer to his question had
come. The rescue of Seagrue made it clear that
Sinclair would not leave the country. He well
knew that Sinclair cared no more for Seagrue than
for a prairie-dog. It was only that he felt strong
enough, with his friends and sympathizers, to defy
the railroad force and Whispering Smith, and
planned now, probably, to kill off his pursuers or
wear them out. There was a second incentive for
remaining: nearly all the Tower W money had
been hidden at Rebstock's cabin by Du Sang.
That Kennedy had already got hold of it Sinclair
could not know, but it was certain that he would
not leave the country without an effort to recover
the booty from Rebstock.

Whispering Smith turned the key in the door of
his room as he revolved the situation in his mind.
Within, the dark was cheerless, but he made no
effort to light a lamp. Groping his way to the side

of the low bed, he sat down and put his head between his hands to think.

There was no help for it that he could see: he must meet Sinclair. The situation he had dreaded most, from the moment Bucks asked him to come back to the mountains, had come.

He thought of every phase of the outcome. If Sinclair should kill him the difficulties were less. It would be unpleasant, certainly, but something that might happen any time and at any man's hands. He had cut into the game too long ago and with his eyes too wide open to complain at this time of the possibility of an accident. They might kill each other; but if, escaping himself, he should kill Sinclair——

He came back in the silence always to that if. It rose dark between him and the woman he loved —whom he had loved since she was a child with school-girl eyes and braided hair. After he had lost her, only to find years afterward that she was hardly less wretched in her life than he in his, he had dreamed of the day when she might again be free and he free to win a love long hoped for.

But to slay this man—her husband—in his inmost heart he felt it would mean the raising of a bar as impalpable as fate, and as undying, to all his dreams. Deserved or not, whatever she should say or not say, what would she feel? How could

her husband's death in that encounter, if it ever
came, be other than a stain that must shock and
wound her, no matter how much she should try
not to see. Could either of them ever quite forget it?

Kennedy and his men were guarding the Cache.
Could they be sent against Sinclair? That would
be only a baser sort of murder—the murder of
his friends. He himself was leader, and so looked
upon; the post of danger was his.

He raised his head. Through the window came
a faint light. The moon was rising, and against
the inner wall of the room the straight, hard lines
of the old wardrobe rose dimly. The rifles were
within. He must choose.

He walked to the window and pushed the curtain aside. It was dark everywhere across the
upper town, but in the distance one light burned.
It was in Marion's cottage. He had chosen this
room because from the window he could see her
home. He stood for a few moments with his
hands in his pockets, looking. When he turned
away he drew the shade closely, lighted a lamp,
and unlocked the wardrobe door.

Scott left the barn at half-past ten with a led
horse for Whispering Smith. He rode past

Into the North

Smith's room in Fort Street, but the room was dark, and he jogged down to the Wickiup square, where he had been told to meet him. After waiting and riding about for an hour, he tied the horses and went up to McCloud's office. McCloud was at his desk, but knew nothing of Whispering Smith except that he was to come in before he started. " He's a punctual man," murmured Bob Scott, who had the low voice of the Indian. " Usually he is ahead of time."

" Is he in his room, do you think? " asked McCloud.

" I rode around that way about fifteen minutes ago; there was no light."

" He must be there," declared McCloud. " Have you the horses below? We will ride over and try the room again."

Fort Street back of Front is so quiet after eleven o'clock at night that a footfall echoes in it. McCloud dismounted in front of the bank building and, throwing the reins to Bob Scott, walked upstairs and back toward Smith's room. In the hallway he paused. He heard faint strains of music. They came from within the room—fragments of old airs played on a violin, and subdued by a mute, in the darkness. Instinct stayed McCloud's hand at the door. He stood until the music ceased and footsteps moved about in the

Whispering Smith

room; then he knocked, and a light appeared within. Whispering Smith opened the door. He stood in his trousers and shirt, with his cartridge-belt in his hand. " Come in, George. I'm just getting hooked up."

" Which way are you going to-night, Gordon? " asked McCloud, sitting down on the chair.

" I am going to Oroville. The crowd is celebrating there. It is a défi, you know."

" Who are you going to take with you? "

" Nobody."

McCloud moved uneasily. " I don't like that."

" There will be nothing doing. Sinclair may be gone by the time I arrive, but I want to see Bob and Gene Johnson, and scare the Williams Cache coyotes, just to keep their tails between their legs."

" I'd like to kill off half a dozen of that gang."

Whispering Smith said nothing for a moment. " Did you ever have to kill a man, George? " he asked buckling his cartridge-belt.

" No. Why? "

There was no reply. Smith had taken a rifle from the rack and was examining the firing mechanism. He worked the lever for a moment with lightning-like speed, laid the gun on the bed, and sat down beside it.

" You would hardly believe, George, how I hate to go after Murray Sinclair. I've known him all

Into the North

my life. His folks and mine lived across the street from one another for twenty years. Which is the older? Murray is five years older than I am; he was always a big, strong, good-looking fellow." Whispering Smith put his hands on the side of the bed. " It is curious how you remember things that happened when you were a boy, isn't it? I thought of something to-night I hadn't thought of for twenty years. A little circus came to town. While they were setting up the tent the lines for the gasolene tank got fouled in the block at the top of the centre pole. The head canvasman offered a quarter to any boy that would climb the pole and free the block. One boy after another tried it, but they couldn't climb half-way up. Then Murray sailed in. I was seven years old and Murray was twelve, and he wore a vest. He gave me the vest to hold while he went up. I felt like a king. There was a lead-pencil in one pocket, beautifully sharpened, and I showed it to the other boys. Did he make good? He always made good," said Whispering Smith gloomily. " The canvasman gave him the quarter and two tickets, and he gave one of the. tickets to me. I got to thinking about that to-night. As boys, Murray and I never had a quarrel." He stopped. Mc-Cloud said nothing, and, after an interval, Smith spoke again:

Whispering Smith

"He was an oracle for all the small boys in town, and could advise us on any subject on earth —whether he knew anything about it or nothing about it made no difference. I told him once I wanted to be a California stage-robber, and he replied without an instant's hesitation that I ought to begin to practise running. I was so upset at his grasp of the subject that I hadn't the nerve to ask him why I needed to practise running to be a stage-robber. I was ashamed of appearing green and to this day I've never understood what he meant. Whether it was to run after the stage or to run away from it I couldn't figure out. Perhaps my being too proud to ask the question changed my career. He went away for a long time, and we heard he was in the Black Hills. When he came back, my God! what a hero he was."

Bob Scott knocked at the door and Whispering Smith opened it. "Tired of waiting, Bob? Well, I guess I'm ready. Is the moon up? This is the rifle I'm going to take, Bob. Did Wickwire have a talk with you? He's all right. Suppose you send him to the mouth of Little Crawling Stone to watch things a day or two. They may try to work north that way or hide in the wash."

Walking down to the street, Whispering Smith continued his suggestions. "And by the way, Bob, I want you to pass this word for me up and

358

Into the North

down Front Street. Sinclair has his friends in town and it's all right—I know them and expect them to stay by him. I expect Murray's friends to do what they can for him. I've got my friends and expect them to stay by me. But there is one thing that I will not stand for on any man's part, and that is hiding Sinclair anywhere in Medicine Bend. You keep him out of Medicine Bend, Bob; will you do it? And remember, I will never let up on the man who hides him in town while this fight is on. There are good reasons for drawing the line on that point, and there I draw it hard and fast. Now Bob and Gene Johnson were at Oroville when you left, were they, Bob?" He was fastening his rifle in the scabbard. "Which is deputy sheriff this year, Bob or Gene? Gene— very good." He swung into the saddle.

"Have you got everything?" murmured Scott.

"I think so. Stop! I'm riding away without my salt-bag. That would be a pretty piece of business, wouldn't it? Take the key, Bob. It's hanging between the rifles and the clock. Here's the wardrobe key, too."

There was some further talk when Scott came back with the salt, chiefly about horses and directions as to telephoning. Whispering Smith took up a notch again in his belt, pulled down his hat, and bent over the neck of his horse to lay his

Whispering Smith

hand a moment in McCloud's. It was one o'clock. Across the foot-hills the moon was rising, and Whispering Smith straightening up in the saddle wheeled his horse and trotted swiftly up the street into the silent north.

CHAPTER XXXIX

AMONG THE COYOTES

OROVILLE once marked farthest north for the Peace River gold camps, but with mining long ago abandoned it now marks farthest south for a rustler's camp, being a favorite resort for the people of the Williams Cache country. Oroville boasts that it has never surrendered and that it has never been cleaned out. It has moved, and been moved, up stream and down, and from bank to bank; it has been burned out and blown away and lived on wheels: but it has never suffered the loss of its identity. Oroville is said to have given to its river the name of Peace River—either wholly in irony or because in Oroville there was for many years no peace save in the river. However, that day, too, is past, and Peace County has its sheriff and a few people who are not habitually "wanted."

Whispering Smith, well dusted with alkali, rode up to the Johnson ranch, eight miles southwest of Oroville, in the afternoon of the day after he left Medicine Bend. The ranch lies in a valley wa-

Whispering Smith

tered by the Rainbow, and makes a pretty little oasis of green in a limitless waste of sagebrush. Gene and Bob Johnson were cutting alfalfa when Whispering Smith rode into the field, and, stopping the mowers, the three men talked while the seven horses nibbled the clover.

"I may need a little help, Gene, to get him out of town," remarked Smith, after he had told his story; "that is, if there are too many Cache men there for me."

Bob Johnson was stripping a stalk of alfalfa in his fingers. "Them fellows are pretty sore."

"That comes of half doing a job, Bob. I was in too much of a hurry with the round-up. They haven't had dose enough yet," returned Whispering Smith. "If you and Gene will join me sometime when I have a week to spare, we will go in there, clean up the gang and burn the hair off the roots of the chapparal—what? I've hinted to Rebstock he could get ready for something like that."

"Tell us about that fight, Gordon."

"I will if you will give me something to eat and have this horse taken care of. Then, Bob, I want you to ride into Oroville and reconnoitre. This is mail day and I understand some of the boys are buying postage stamps to put on my coffin."

Among the Coyotes

They went to the house, where Whispering Smith talked as he ate. Bob took a horse and rode away, and Gene, with his guest, went back to the alfalfa, where Smith took Bob's place on the mower. When they saw Bob riding up the valley, Whispering Smith, bringing in the machine, mounted his horse.

"Your man is there all right," said Bob, as he approached. "He and John Rebstock were in the Blackbird saloon. Seagrue isn't there, but Barney Rebstock and a lot of others are. I talked a few minutes with John and Murray. Sinclair didn't say much; only that the railroad gang was trying to run him out of the country, and he wanted to meet a few of them before he went. I just imagined he held up a little before me; maybe not. There's a dozen Williams Cache men in town."

"But those fellows are not really dangerous, Bob, though they may be troublesome," observed Smith reflectively.

"Well, what's your plan?" blurted Gene Johnson.

"I haven't any, Gene," returned Smith, with perfect simplicity. "My only plan is to ride into town and serve my papers, if I can. I've got a deputyship—and that I'm going to do right away. If you, Bob, or both of you, will happen in about thirty minutes later you'll get the news and perhaps see the fun. Much obliged for your feed, Gene; come down to Medicine Bend any time and I'll fill you up. I want you both for the elk hunt next fall, remember that. Bucks is coming, and is going to bring Brown and Henson and perhaps Atterbury and Gibbs and some New Yorkers; and McCloud's brother, the preacher, is coming out and they are all right—all of them."

The only street in Oroville faces the river, and the buildings string for two or three blocks along modest bluffs. Not a soul was anywhere in sight when Whispering Smith rode into town, save that across the street from where he dismounted and tied his horse three men stood in front of the Blackbird.

They watched the new arrival with languid interest. Smith walked stiffly over toward the saloon to size up the men before he should enter it. The middle man of the group, with a thin red face and very blue eyes, was chewing tobacco in an unpromising way. Before Smith was half-way across the street he saw the hands of the three men falling to their hips. Taking care, however, only to keep the men between him and the saloon door, Smith walked directly toward them. " Boys, have you happened to see Gene or Bob Johnson to-day, any of you? " He threw back the brim of his Stetson as he spoke.

Among the Coyotes

"Hold your hand right there—right where it is," said the blue-eyed man sharply.

Whispering Smith smiled, but held his hand rather awkwardly upon his hat-brim.

"No," continued the spokesman, "we ain't none of us happened to see Bob or Gene Johnson to-day; but we happen to seen Whispering Smith, and we'll blow your face off if you move it an inch."

Smith laughed. "I never quarrel with a man that's got the drop on me, boys. Now, this is sudden but unexpected. Do I know any of you?" He looked from one face to another before him, with a wide reach in his field of vision for the three hands that were fast on three pistol-butts. "Hold on! I've met you somewhere," he said with easy confidence to the blue-eyed man with the weather-split lip. "Williams Cache, wasn't it? All right, we're placed. Now what have you got in for me?"

"I've got forty head of steers in for you," answered the man in the middle, with a splitting oath. "You stole forty head of my steers in that round-up, and I'm going to fill you so full of lead you'll never run off no more stock for nobody. Don't look over there to your horse or your rifle. Hold your hands right where they are."

"Certainly, certainly!"

"When I pull, I shoot!"

"I don't always do it, but it is business, I ac-

Whispering Smith

knowledge. When a man pulls he ought to shoot —very often it's the only chance he ever gets to shoot. Well, it isn't every man gets the drop on me that easy, but you boys have got it," continued Whispering Smith in frank admiration. " Only I want to say you're after the wrong man. That round-up was all Rebstock's fault, and Rebstock is bound to make good all loss and damage."

" You'll make good my share of it right now and here," said the man with the wash-blue eyes.

" Why, of course," assented Whispering Smith, " if I must, I must. I suppose I may light a cigarette, boys, before you turn loose the fireworks? "

" Light it quick! "

Laughing at the humor of the situation, Whispering Smith, his eyes beaming with good-nature, put the finger and thumb of his right hand into his waistcoat pocket, drew out a package of cigarette paper, and, bantering his captors innocently the while, tore out a sheet and put the packet back. Folding the paper in his two hands, he declared he believed his tobacco was in his saddle-pocket, and asked leave to step across the street to get it. The trick was too transparent, and leave was refused with scorn and some hard words. Whispering Smith begged the men in front of him in turn for tobacco. They cursed him and shook their heads.

Among the Coyotes

For an instant he looked troubled. Still appealing to them with his eyes, he tapped lightly the lower outside pockets of his coat with his fingers, shifting the cigarette paper from hand to hand as he hunted. The outside pockets seemed empty. But as he tapped the inside breast pocket on the left side of the coat—the three men, lynx-eyed, watching—his face brightened. " Stop! " said he, his voice sinking to a relieved whisper as his hand rested lightly on the treasure. " There's the tobacco. I suppose one of you will give me a match ? "

All that the three before him could ever afterward recollect—and for several years afterward they cudgelled their brains pretty thoroughly about that moment—was that Whispering Smith took hold of the left lapel of his coat to take the tobacco out of the breast pocket. An excuse to take that lapel in his left hand was, in fact, all that Whispering Smith needed to put not alone the three men before him but all Oroville at his mercy. The play of his right hand in crossing the corduroy waistcoat to pull his revolver from its scabbard and throw it into their faces was all too quick for better eyes than theirs. They saw only the muzzle of the heavy Colt's playing like a snake's tongue under their surprised noses, with the good-natured smile still behind it. " Or will

Whispering Smith

one of you roll a cigarette?" asked Whispering Smith, without a break between the two questions. " I don't smoke. Now don't make faces; go right ahead. Do anything you want to with your hands. I wouldn't ask a man to keep his hands or feet still on a hot day like this," he insisted, the revolver playing all the time. " You won't draw? You won't fight? Pshaw! Then disengage your hands gently from your guns. You fellows really ought not to attempt to pull a gun in Oroville, and I will tell you why—there's a reason for it." He looked confidential as he put his head forward to whisper among the crestfallen faces. " At this altitude it is too fast work. I know you now," he went on as they continued to wilt. " You are Fatty Filber," he said to the thin chap. " Don't work your mouth like that at me; don't do it. You seem surprised. Really, have you the asthma? Get over it, because you are wanted in Pound County for horse-stealing. Why, hang it, Fatty, you're good for ten years, and of course, since you have reminded me of it, I'll see that you get it. And you, Baxter," said he to the man on the right, " I know I spoke to you once when I was inspector about altering brands; that's five years, you know. You," he added, scrutinizing the third man to scare him to death—" I think you were at Tower W. No? No matter; you two boys may go, any-

Among the Coyotes

way. Fatty, you stay; we'll put some state cow on your ribs. By the way, are you a detective, Fatty? Aren't you? See here! I can get you into an association. For ten dollars, they give you a German-silver star, and teach the Japanese method of pulling, by correspondence. Or you might get an electric battery to handle your gun with. You can get pocket dynamos from the mail-order houses. Sure! Read the big book!"

When Gene and Bob Johnson rode into town, Whispering Smith was sitting in a chair outside the Blackbird, still chatting with Filber, who stood with his arms around a hitching-post, holding fast a mail-order house catalogue. A modest crowd of hangers-on had gathered.

"Here we are, Gene," exclaimed Smith to the deputy sheriff. "I was looking for steers, but some calves got into the drive. Take him away."

While the Johnsons were laughing, Smith walked into the Blackbird. He had lost thirty minutes, and in losing them had lost his quarry. Sinclair had disappeared, and Whispering Smith made a virtue of necessity by taking the upsetting of his plans with an unruffled face. There was but one thing more, indeed, to do, and that was to eat his supper and ride away. The street encounter had made so much talk in Oroville that Smith declined Gene Johnson's invitation to go back to the

Whispering Smith

house. It seemed a convenient time to let any
other ambitious rustlers make good if they were
disposed to try, and Whispering Smith went for
his supper to the hotel where the Williams Cache
men made their headquarters.

There was a rise in the atmospheric pressure the
moment he entered the hotel office door, and when
he walked into the dining-room, some minutes
later, the silence was oppressive. Smith looked
for a seat. The only vacant place chanced to be
at a table where nine men from the Cache sat busy
with ham and eggs. It was a trifle awkward, but
the only thing to do was to take the vacant chair.

The nine men were actively engaged with knives
and forks and spoons when Whispering Smith
drew out the empty chair at the head of the table;
but nine pairs of hands dropped modestly under
the table when he sat down. Coughing slightly to
hide his embarrassment and to keep his right hand
in touch with his necktie, Whispering Smith looked
around the table with the restrained air of a man
who has bowed his head and resolved to ask the
blessing, but wants to make reasonably sure that
the family is listening. A movement at the other
tables, among the regular boarders of the hostelry,
was apparent almost at once. Appetites began to
fail all over the dining-room. Whispering Smith
gave his order genially to the confused waitress:

Among the Coyotes

" Bring me two eggs—one fried on one side and one on the other—and coffee."

There was a general scraping of chairs on the floor as they were pushed back and guests not at the moment interested in the bill of fare started, modestly but firmly, to leave the dining-room. At Whispering Smith's table there were no second calls for coffee. To stimulate the eating he turned the conversation into channels as reassuring as possible. Unfortunately for his endeavor, the man at the far end of the table reached for a toothpick. It seemed a pleasant way out of the difficulty, and when the run on toothpicks had once begun, all Whispering Smith's cordiality could not check it. Every man appeared to want a toothpick, and one after another of Whispering Smith's company deserted him. He was finally left alone with a physician known as " Doc," a forger and a bigamist from Denver. Smith tried to engage Doc in medical topics. The doctor was not alone frightened but tipsy, and when Smith went so far as to ask him, as a medical man, whether in his opinion the high water in the mountains had any direct connection with the prevalence of falling of the spine among old " residenters " in Williams Cache, the doctor felt of his head as if his brain were turning turtle.

When Whispering Smith raised his knife osten-

Whispering Smith

tatiously to bring out a feature of his theory, the doctor raised his knife higher to admit the force of it; and when Whispering Smith leaned his head forward impressively to drive home a point in his assertion, the doctor stretched his neck till his face grew apoplectic. Releasing him at length from the strain, Whispering Smith begged of the staring maid-servant the recipe for the biscuit. When she came back with it he sat all alone, pouring catsup over his griddle-cakes in an abstracted manner, and it so flurried her that she had to go out again to ask whether the gasolene went into the dough or under it.

He played out the play to the end, but when he rode away in the dusk his face was careworn. John Rebstock had told him why Sinclair dodged: there were others whom Sinclair wanted to meet first; and Whispering Smith was again heading on a long, hard ride, and after a man on a better horse, back to the Crawling Stone and Medicine Bend. "There's others he wants to see first or you'd have no trouble in talking business to-day. You nor no other man will ever get him alive." But Whispering Smith knew that.

"See that he doesn't get you alive, Rebstock," was his parting retort. "If he finds out Kennedy has got the Tower W money, the first thing he does will be to put the Doxology all over you."

CHAPTER XL

WHEN Whispering Smith rode after Sinclair, Crawling Stone Ranch, in common with the whole countryside, had but one interest in life, and that was to hear of the meeting. Riders across the mountain valleys met with but one question; mail-carriers brought nothing in their pouches of interest equal to the last word concerning Sinclair or his pursuer. It was commonly agreed through the mountains that it would be a difficult matter to overhaul any good man riding Sinclair's steel-dust horses, but with Sinclair himself in the saddle, unless it pleased him to pull up, the chase was sure to be a stern one. Against this to feed speculation stood one man's record—that of the man who had ridden alone across Deep Creek and brought Chuck Williams out on a buckboard.

Business in Medicine Bend, meantime, was practically suspended. As the centre of all telephone lines the big railroad town was likewise the centre of all rumors. Officers and soldiers to and from the Fort, stage-drivers and cowmen, homesteaders and rustlers, discussed the apprehension of Sinclair. Moreover, behind this effort to arrest one man who had savagely defied the law were ranged all of the prejudices, sympathies, and hatreds of the high country, and practically the whole population tributary to Medicine Bend and the Crawling Stone Valley were friends either to Sinclair or to his pursuer. Behind Sinclair were nearly all the cattlemen, not alone because he was on good terms with the rustlers and protected his friends, but because he warred openly on the sheepmen. The big range interests, as a rule, were openly or covertly friendly to Sinclair, while against him were the homesteaders, the railroad men, the common people, and the men who everywhere hate cruelty and outrage and the making of a lie.

Lance Dunning had never concealed his friendliness for Sinclair, even after hard stories about him were known to be true, and it was this confidence of fellowship that made Sinclair, twenty-four hours after he had left Oroville, ride down the hill trail to Crawling Stone ranch-house.

The morning had been cold, with a heavy wind and a dull sky. In the afternoon the clouds lowered over the valley and a misting rain set in. Dicksie had gone into Medicine Bend on the stage

A Sympathetic Ear

in the morning, and, after a stolen half-hour with McCloud at Marion's, had ridden home to escape the storm. Not less, but much more, than those about her she was alive to the situation in which Sinclair stood and its danger to those closest to her. In the morning her one prayer to McCloud had been to have a care of himself, and to Marion to have a care of herself; but even when Dicksie left them it seemed as if neither quite felt the peril as she felt it.

In the afternoon the rain, falling steadily, kept her in the house, and she sat in her room sewing until the light failed. She went downstairs. Puss had lighted the grate in the living-room, and Dicksie threw herself into a chair. The sound of hoofs aroused her and she went to a window. To her horror, she saw Sinclair walking with her cousin up to the front door. She ran into the dining-room, and the two men entered the hall and walked into the office. Choking with excitement, Dicksie ran through the kitchen and upstairs to master her agitation.

In the office Sinclair was sitting down before the hot stove with a tumbler of whiskey. " Lance " —he shook his head as he spoke hoarsely—" I want to say my friends have stood by me to a man, but there's none of them treated me squarer through thick and thin than you have. Well,

Whispering Smith

I've had some bad luck. It can't be helped.
Regards!"

He drank, and shook his wet hair again. Four
days of hard riding had left no trace on his iron
features. Wet to the bone, his eyes flashed with
fire. He held the glassful of whiskey in a hand
as steady as a spirit-level and tossed it down a
throat as cool as dew.

" I want to say another thing, Lance: I had no
more intention than a child of hurting Ed Banks.
I warned Ed months ago to keep out of this fight,
and I never knew he was in it till it was too late.
But I'm hoping he will pull through yet, if they
don't kill him in the hospital to spite me. I never
recognized the men at all till it was too late.
Why, one of them used to work for me! A man
with the whole railroad gang in these mountains
after him has got to look out for himself or
his life ain't worth a glass of beer. Thank you,
Lance, not any more. I saw two men, with their
rifles in their hands, looking for me. I hollered
at them; but, Lance, I'm rough and ready, as all
my friends know, and I will let no man put a drop
on me—that I will never do. Ed, before I ever
recognized him, raised his rifle; that's the only
reason I fired. Not so full, Lance, not so full, if
you please. Well," he shook his black hair as he
threw back his head, " here's to better luck in

A Sympathetic Ear

worse countries!" He paused as he swallowed, and set the tumbler down. "Lance, I'm saying good-by to the mountains."

"You're not going away for good, Murray?"

"I'm going away for good. What's the use? For two years these railroad cutthroats have been trying to put something on me; you know that. They've been trying to mix me up with that bridge-burning at Smoky Creek; Sugar Buttes, they had me there; Tower W—nothing would do but I was there, and they've got one of the men in jail down there now, Lance, trying to sweat enough perjury out of him to send me up. What show has a poor man got against all the money there is in the country? I wouldn't be afraid of a jury of my own neighbors—the men that know me, Lance—any time. What show would I·have with a packed jury in Medicine Bend? I could explain anything I've done to the satisfaction of any reasonable man. I'm human, Lance; that's all I say. I've been mistreated and I don't forget it. They've even turned my wife against me—as fine a woman as ever lived."

Lance swore sympathetically. "There's good stuff in you yet, Murray."

"I'm going to say good-by to the mountains," Sinclair went on grimly, "but I'm going to Medicine Bend to-night and tell the man that has

377

hounded me what I think of him before I leave. I'm going to give my wife a chance to do what is right and go with me. She's been poisoned against me—I know that; but if she does what's fair and square there'll be no trouble—no trouble at all. All I want, Lance, is a square deal. What? "

Dicksie with her pulses throbbing at fever-heat heard the words. She stood half-way down the stairs, trembling as she listened. Anger, hatred, the spirit of vengeance, choked in her throat at the sinister words. She longed to stride into the room and confront the murderer and call down retribution on his head. It was no fear of him that restrained her, for the Crawling Stone girl never knew fear. She would have confronted him and denounced him, but prudence checked her angry impulse. She knew what he meant to do— to ride into Medicine Bend under cover of the storm, murder the two he hated, and escape in the night; and she resolved he should never succeed. If she could only get to the telephone! But the telephone was in the room where he sat. He was saying good-by. Her cousin was trying to dissuade him from riding out into the storm, but he was going. The door opened; the men went out on the porch, and it closed. Dicksie, lightly as a shadow, ran into the office and began ringing Medicine Bend on the telephone.

CHAPTER XLI

DICKSIE'S RIDE

WHEN Lance Dunning entered the room ten minutes later, Dicksie stood at the telephone; but the ten minutes of that interval had made quite another creature of his cousin. The wires were down and no one from any quarter gave a response to her frantic ringing. Through the receiver she could hear only the sweep of the rain and the harsh crackle of the wind. Sometimes praying, sometimes fainting, and sometimes despairing, she stood clinging to the instrument, ringing and pounding upon it like one frenzied. Lance looked at her in amazement. " Why, God a'mighty, Dicksie, what's the matter? "

He called twice to her before she turned, and her words almost stunned him: " Why did you not detain Sinclair here to-night? Why did you not arrest him? "

Lance's sombrero raked heavily to one side of his face, and one end of his mustache running up much higher on the other did not begin to express

Whispering Smith

his astonishment. "Arrest him? Arrest Sinclair? Dicksie, are you crazy? Why the devil should I arrest Sinclair? Do you suppose I am going to mix up in a fight like this? Do you think *I* want to get killed? The level-headed man in this country, just at present, is the man who can keep out of trouble, and the man who succeeds, let me tell you, has got more than plenty to do."

Lance, getting no answer but a fierce, searching gaze from Dicksie's wild eyes, laid his hand on a chair, lighted a cigar, and sat down before the fire. Dicksie dropped the telephone receiver, put her hand to her girdle, and looked at him. When she spoke her tone was stinging. "You know that man is going to Medicine Bend to kill his wife!"

Lance took the cigar from his mouth and returned her look. "I know no such thing," he growled curtly.

"And to kill George McCloud, if he can."

He stared without reply.

"You heard him say so," persisted Dicksie vehemently.

Lance crossed his legs and threw back the brim of his hat. "McCloud is nobody's fool. He will look out for himself."

"These fiendish wires to Medicine Bend are down. Why hasn't this line been repaired?" she

380

cried, wringing her hands. "There is no way to give warning to any one that he is coming, and you have let him go!"

Lance whirled in his chair. "Damnation! Could I keep him from going?"

"You did not want to; you are keeping out of trouble. What do you care whom he kills to-night!"

"You've gone crazy, Dicksie. Your imagination has upset your reason. Whether he kills anybody to-night or not, it's too late now to make a row about it," exclaimed Lance, throwing his cigar angrily away. ": He won't kill us."

"And you expect me to sit by and fold my hands while that wretch sheds more blood, do you?"

"It can't be helped."

"I say it can be helped! I can help it—I will help it—as you could have done if you had wanted to. I will ride to Medicine Bend to-night and help it."

Lance jumped to his feet, with a string of oaths. "Well this is the limit!" He pointed his finger at her. "Dicksie Dunning, you won't stir out of this house to-night."

Her face hardened. "How dare you speak in that way to me? Who are you, that you order me

Whispering Smith

what to do, where to stay? Am I your cowboy, to be defiled with your curses?"

He looked at her in amazement. She was only eighteen; he would still face her down. "I'll tell you who I am. I am master here, and you will do as I tell you. You will ride to Medicine Bend to-night, will you?" He struck the table with his clinched fist. "Do you hear me? I say, by God, not a horse shall leave this ranch in this storm to-night to go anywhere for anybody or with anybody!"

"Then I say to you this ranch is my ranch, and these horses are my horses! From this hour forth I will order them to go and come when and where I please!" She stepped toward him. "Henceforward I am mistress here. Do you hear me? Henceforward *I* give orders in Crawling Stone House, and every one under this roof takes orders from me!"

"Dicksie, what do you mean? For God's sake, you're not going to try to ride——"

She swept from the room. What happened afterward she could never recall. Who got Jim for her or whether she got the horse up herself, what was said to her in low, kindly words of warning by the man at Jim's neck when she sprang into the saddle, who the man was, she could not have told. All she felt at last was that she was free

382

Dicksie's Ride

and out under the black sky, with the rain beating
her burning face and her horse leaping fearfully
into the wind.

No man could have kept the trail to the pass
that night. The horse took it as if the path flashed
in sunshine, and swung into the familiar stride that
had carried her so many times over the twenty
miles ahead of them. The storm driving into
Dicksie's face cooled her. Every moment she rec-
ollected herself better, and before her mind all the
aspects of her venture ranged themselves. She
had set herself to a race, and against her rode the
hardest rider in the mountains. She had set herself to what few men on the range would have
dared and what no other woman on the range
could do. "Why have I learned to ride," went
the question through her mind, " if not for this—
for those I love and for those who love me? "
Sinclair had a start, she well knew, but not so much
for a night like this night. He would ride to kill
those he hated; she would ride to save those she
loved. Her horse already was on the Elbow
grade; she knew it from his shorter spring—a lithe,
creeping spring that had carried her out of deep
canyons and up long draws where other horses
walked. The wind lessened and the rain drove
less angrily in her face. She patted Jim's neck
with her wet glove, and checked him as tenderly

Whispering Smith

as a lover, to give him courage and breath. She
wanted to be part of him as he strove, for the
horror of the night began to steal on the edge
of her thoughts. A gust drove into her face.
They were already at the head of the pass,
and the horse, with level ground underfoot, was
falling into the long reach; but the wind was
colder.

Dicksie lowered her head and gave Jim the rein.
She realized how wet she was; her feet and her
knees were wet. She had no protection but her
skirt, though the meanest rider on all her countless acres would not have braved a mile on such a
night without leather and fur. The great lapels
of her riding-jacket, reversed, were buttoned tight
across her shoulders, and the double fold of fur
lay warm and dry against her heart and lungs;
but her hands were cold, and her skirt dragged
leaden and cold from her waist, and water soaked
in upon her chilled feet. She knew she ought to
have thought of these things. She planned, as
thought swept in a moving picture across her brain,
how she would prepare again for such a ride—
with her cowboy costume that she had once mas-
queraded in for Marion, with leggings of buck-
skin and " chaps " of long white silken wool. It
was no masquerade now—she was riding in deadly
earnest; and her lips closed to shut away a creepy

Dicksie's Ride

feeling that started from her heart and left her shivering.

She became conscious of how fast she was going. Instinct, made keen by thousands of saddle miles, told Dicksie of her terrific pace. She was riding faster than she would have dared go at noonday and without thought or fear of accident. In spite of the sliding and the plunging down the long hill, the storm and the darkness brought no thought of fear for herself; her only fear was for those ahead. In supreme moments a horse, like a man when human efforts become superhuman, puts the lesser dangers out of reckoning, and the faculties, set on a single purpose, though strained to the breaking-point, never break. Low in her saddle, Dicksie tried to reckon how far they had come and how much lay ahead. She could feel her skirt stiffening about her knees, and the rain beating at her face was sharper; she knew the sleet as it stung her cheeks, and knew what next was coming—the snow.

There was no need to urge Jim. He had the rein and Dicksie bent down to speak to him, as she often spoke when they were alone on the road, when Jim, bolting, almost threw her. Recovering instantly, she knew they were no longer alone. She rose alert in her seat. Her straining eyes could see nothing. Was there a sound in the wind?

Whispering Smith

She held her breath to listen, but before she could apprehend Jim leaped violently ahead. Dicksie screamed in an agony of terror. She knew then that she had passed another rider, and so close she might have touched him.

Fear froze her to the saddle; it lent wings to her horse. The speed became wild. Dicksie knit herself to her dumb companion and a prayer choked in her throat. She crouched lest a bullet tear her from her horse; but through the darkness no bullet came, only the sleet, stinging her face, stiffening her gloves, freezing her hair, chilling her limbs, and weighting her like lead on her struggling horse. She knew not even Sinclair could overtake her now—that no living man could lay a hand on her bridle-rein—and she pulled Jim in down the winding hills to save him for the long flat. When they struck it they had but four miles to go.

Across the flat the wind drove in fury. Reflection, thought, and reason were beginning to leave her. She was crying to herself quietly as she used to cry when she lost herself, a mere child, riding among the hills. She was praying meaningless words. Snow purred softly on her cheeks. The cold was soothing her senses. Unable at last to keep her seat on the horse, she stopped him, slipped stiffly to the ground, and, struggling through the

Dicksie's Ride

wind as she held fast to the bridle and the horn, half walked and half ran to start the blood through her benumbed veins. She struggled until she could drag her mired feet no farther, and tried to draw herself back into the saddle. It was almost beyond her. She sobbed and screamed at her helplessness. At last she managed to climb flounderingly back into her seat, and, bending her stiffened arms to Jim's neck, she moaned and cried to him. When again she could hold her seat no longer, she fell to the horse's side, dragged herself along in the frozen slush, and, screaming with the pain of her freezing hands, drew herself up into the saddle.

She knew that she dare not venture this again—that if she did so she could never remount. She felt now that she should never live to reach Medicine Bend. She rode on and on and on—would it never end? She begged God to send a painless death to those she rode to save, and when the prayer passed her failing senses a new terror awakened her, for she found herself falling out of the saddle. With excruciating torment she recovered her poise. Reeling from side to side, she fought the torpor away. Her mind grew clearer and her tears had ceased. She prayed for a light. The word caught between her stiffened lips and she mumbled it till she could open them wide and scream it out. Then came a sound like the beating of great drums in her ears. It was the crash of Jim's hoofs on the river bridge, and she was in Medicine Bend.

A horse, galloping low and heavily, slued through the snow from Fort Street into Boney, and, where it had so often stopped before, dashed up on the sidewalk in front of the little shop. The shock was too much for its unconscious rider, and, shot headlong from her saddle, Dicksie was flung bruised and senseless against Marion's door.

CHAPTER XLII

S HE woke in a dream of hoofs beating at her
brain. Distracted words fell from her lips,
and when she opened her swollen eyes and saw
those about her she could only scream.

Marion had called up the stable, but the stable-
men could only tell her that Dicksie's horse, in
terrible condition, had come in riderless. While
Barnhardt, the railway surgeon, at the bedside ad-
ministered restoratives, Marion talked with him of
Dicksie's sudden and mysterious coming. Dicksie,
lying in pain and quite conscious, heard all, but,
unable to explain, moaned in her helplessness. She
heard Marion at length tell the doctor that Mc-
Cloud was out of town, and the news seemed to
bring back her senses. Then, rising in the bed,
while the surgeon and Marion coaxed her to lie
down, she clutched at their arms and, looking from
one to the other, told her story. When it was
done she swooned, but she woke to hear voices
at the door of the shop. She heard as if she

Whispering Smith

dreamed, but at the door the words were dread reality. Sinclair had made good his word, and had come out of the storm with a summons upon Marion and it was the surgeon who threw open the door and saw Sinclair standing in the snow.

No man in Medicine Bend knew Sinclair more thoroughly or feared him less than Barnhardt. No man could better meet him or speak to him with less of hesitation. Sinclair, as he faced Barnhardt, was not easy in spite of his dogged self-control; and he was standing, much to his annoyance, in the glare of an arc-light that swung across the street in front of the shop. He was well aware that no such light had ever swung within a block of the shop before and in it he saw the hand of Whispering Smith. The light was unexpected, Barnhardt was a surprise, and even the falling snow, which protected him from being seen twenty feet away, angered him. He asked curtly who was ill, and without awaiting an answer asked for his wife.

The surgeon eyed him coldly. " Sinclair, what are you doing in Medicine Bend? Have you come to surrender yourself? "

" Surrender myself? Yes, I'm ready any time to surrender myself. Take me along yourself, Barnhardt, if you think I've done worse than any

At the Door

man would that has been hounded as I've been hounded. I want to see my wife."

" Sinclair, you can't see your wife."

" What's the matter—is she sick? "

" No, but you can't see her."

" Who says I can't see her? "

" I say so."

Sinclair swept the ice furiously from his beard and his right hand fell to his hip as he stepped back. " You've turned against me too, have you, you gray-haired wolf? Can't see her! Get out of that door."

The surgeon pointed his finger at the murderer. " No, I won't get out of this door. Shoot, you coward! Shoot an unarmed man. You will not live to get a hundred feet away. This place is watched for you; you could not have got within a hundred yards of it to-night except for this snow." Barnhardt pointed through the storm. " Sinclair, you will hang in the court-house square, and I will take the last beat of your pulse with these fingers, and when I pronounce you dead they will cut you down. You want to see your wife. You want to kill her. Don't lie; you want to kill her. You were heard to say as much to-night at the Dunning ranch. You were watched and tracked, and you are expected and looked for here. Your best friends have gone back on you.

Whispering Smith

Ay, curse again and over again, but that will not put Ed Banks on his feet."

Sinclair stamped with frenzied oaths. "You're too hard on me," he cried, clenching his hands. "I say you're too hard. You've heard one side of it. Is that the way you put judgment on a man that's got no friends left because they start a new lie on him every day? Who is it that's watching me? Let them stand out like men in the open. If they want me, let them come like men and take me!"

"Sinclair, this storm gives you a chance to get away; take it. Bad as you are, there are men in Medicine Bend who knew you when you were a man. Don't stay here for some of them to sit on the jury that hangs you. If you can get away, get away. If I were your friend—and God knows whom you can call friend in Medicine Bend to-night—I couldn't say more. Get away before it is too late."

He was never again seen alive in Medicine Bend. They tracked him next day over every foot of ground he had covered. They found where he had left his spent horse and where afterward he had got the fresh one. They learned how he had eluded all the picketing planned for precisely such a contingency, got into the Wickiup, got upstairs and burst open the very door of McCloud's room.

At the Door

But Dicksie had on her side that night One greater than her invincible will or her faithful horse. McCloud was two hundred miles away.

Barnhardt lost no time in telephoning the Wickiup that Sinclair was in town, but within an hour, while the two women were still under the surgeon's protection, a knock at the cottage door gave them a second fright. Barnhardt answered the summons. He opened the door and, as the man outside paused to shake the snow off his hat, the surgeon caught him by the shoulder and dragged into the house Whispering Smith.

Picking the icicles from his hair, Smith listened to all that Barnhardt said, his eyes roving meantime over everything within the room and mentally over many things outside it. He congratulated Barnhardt, and when Marion came into the room he apologized for the snow he had brought in. Dicksie heard his voice and cried out from the bedroom. They could not keep her away, and she ran out to catch his hands and plead with him not to go away. He tried to assure her that the danger was over; that guards were now outside everywhere, and would be until morning. But Dicksie clung to him and would take no refusal.

Whispering Smith looked at her in amazement and in admiration. "You are captain to-night, Miss Dicksie, by Heaven. If you say the word

Whispering Smith

I'll lie here on a rug till morning. But that man will not be back to-night. You are a queen. If I had a mountain girl that would do as much as that for me I would——"

"What would you do?" asked Marion.

"Say good-by to this accursed country forever."

CHAPTER XLIII

CLOSING IN

IN the morning the sun rose with a mountain smile. The storm had swept the air till the ranges shone blue and the plain sparkled under a cloudless sky. Bob Scott and Wickwire, riding at daybreak, picked up a trail on the Fence River road. A consultation was held at the bridge, and within half an hour Whispering Smith, with unshaken patience, was in the saddle and following it.

With him were Kennedy and Bob Scott. Sinclair had ridden into the lines, and Whispering Smith, with his best two men, meant to put it up to him to ride out. They meant now to get him, with a trail or without, and were putting horseflesh against horseflesh and craft against craft.

At the forks of the Fence they picked up Wickwire, Kennedy taking him on the up road, while Scott with Whispering Smith crossed to the Crawling Stone. When Smith and Scott reached the Frenchman they parted to cover in turn each of the trails by which it is possible to get out of the river country toward the Park and Williams Cache.

By four o'clock in the afternoon they had all covered the ground so well that the four were able to make their rendezvous on the big Fence divide, south of Crawling Stone Valley. They then found, to their disappointment, that, widely separated as they had been, both parties were following trails they believed to be good. They shot a steer, tagged it, ate dinner and supper in one, and separated under Whispering Smith's counsel that both the trails be followed into the next morning —in the belief that one of them would run out or that the two would run together. At noon the next day Scott rode through the hills from the Fence, and Kennedy with Wickwire came through Two Feather Pass from the Frenchman with the report that the game had left their valleys.

Without rest they pushed on. At the foot of the Mission Mountains they picked up the tracks of a party of three horsemen. Twice within ten miles afterward the men they were following crossed the river. Each time their trail, with some little difficulty, was found again. At a little ranch in the Mission foot-hills, Kennedy and Scott, leaving Wickwire with Whispering Smith, took fresh horses and pushed ahead as far as they could

Closing In

ride before dark, but they brought back news. The trail had split again, with one man riding alone to the left, while two had taken the hills to the right, heading for Mission Pass and the Cache. With Gene Johnson and Bob at the mouth of the Cache there was little fear for that outlet. The turn to the left was the unexpected. Over the little fire in the ranch kitchen where they ate supper, the four men were in conference twenty minutes. It was decided that Scott and Kennedy should head for the Mission Pass, while Whispering Smith, with Wickwire to trail with him, should undertake to cut off, somewhere between Fence River and the railroad, the man who had gone south, the man believed to be Sinclair. It was a late moon, and when Scott and Kennedy saddled their horses Whispering Smith and Wickwire were asleep.

With the cowboy, Whispering Smith started at daybreak. No one saw them again for two days. During those two days and nights they were in the saddle almost continuously. For every mile the man ahead of them rode they were forced to ride two miles and often three. Late in the second night they crossed the railroad, and the first word from them came in long despatches sent by Whispering Smith to Medicine Bend and instructions to Kennedy and Scott in the north, which

were carried by hard riders straight to Deep
Creek.

On the morning of the third day Dicksie Dunning, who had gone home from Medicine Bend
and who had been telephoning Marion and George
McCloud two days for news, was trying to get
Medicine Bend again on the telephone when Puss
came in to say that a man at the kitchen door
wanted to see her.

" Who is it, Puss ? "

" I d'no, Miss Dicksie; 'deed, I never seen him
b'fore."

Dicksie walked around on the porch to the
kitchen. A dust-covered man sitting on a limp
horse threw back the brim of his hat as he touched
it, lifted himself stiffly out of the saddle, and
dropped to the ground. He laughed at Dicksie's
startled expression. " Don't you know me? " he
asked, putting out his hand. It was Whispering
Smith.

He was a fearful sight. Stained from head to
foot with alkali, saddle-cramped and bent, his face
scratched and stained, he stood with a smiling appeal in his bloodshot eyes.

Dicksie gave a little uncertain cry, clasped her
hands, and, with a scream, threw her arms impulsively around his neck. " Oh, I did not know
you! What has happened? I am so glad to

Closing In

see you! Tell me what has happened. Are you hurt?"

He stammered like a school-boy. "Nothing has happened. What's this? Don't cry; nothing at all has happened. I didn't realize what a tramp I look or I shouldn't have come. But I was only a mile away and I had heard nothing for four days from Medicine Bend. And how are you? Did your ride make you ill? No? By Heaven, you are a game girl. That was a ride! How are they all? Where's your cousin? In town, is he? I thought I might get some news if I rode up, and oh, Miss Dicksie—jiminy! some coffee. But I've got only two minutes for it all, only two minutes; do you think Puss has any on the stove?"

Dicksie with coaxing and pulling got him into the kitchen, and Puss tumbled over herself to set out coffee and rolls. He showed himself ravenously hungry, and ate with a simple directness that speedily accounted for everything in sight. "You have saved my life. Now I am going, and thank you a thousand times. There, by Heaven, I've forgotten Wickwire! He is with me—waiting down in the cottonwoods at the fork. Could Puss put up a lunch I could take to him? He hasn't had a scrap for twenty-four hours. But, Dicksie, your tramp is a hummer! I've tried to ride him down and wear him out and lose him, and, by Heaven, he turns up every time and has been of more use to me than two men."

She put her hand on Whispering Smith's arm. " I told him if he would stop drinking he could be foreman here next season." Puss was putting up the lunch. " Why need you hurry away? " persisted Dicksie. " I've a thousand things to say."

He looked at her amiably. " This is really a case of must."

" Then, tell me, what favor may I do for you? " She looked appealingly into his tired eyes. " I want to do something for you. I must! don't deny me. Only, what shall it be? "

" Something for me? What can I say? You'll be kind to Marion—I shouldn't have to ask that. What can I ask? Stop! there is one thing. I've got a poor little devil of an orphan up in the Deep Creek country. Du Sang murdered his father. You are rich and generous, Dicksie; do something for him, will you? Kennedy or Bob Scott will know all about him. Bring him down here, will you, and see he doesn't go to the dogs? You're a good girl. What's this, crying? Now you are frightened. Things are not so bad as that. You want to know everything—I see it in your eyes. Very well, let's trade. You tell me everything and I'll tell you everything. Now then: Are you engaged? "

Closing In

They were standing under the low porch with the sunshine breaking through the trees. She turned away her face and threw all of her happiness into a laugh. " I won't tell."

" Oh, that's enough. You have told ! " declared Whispering Smith. " I knew—why, of course I knew—but I wanted to make you own up. Well, here's the way things are. Sinclair has run us all over God's creation for two days to give his pals a chance to break into Williams Cache to get the Tower W money they left with Rebstock. For a fact, we have ridden completely around Sleepy Cat and been down in the Spanish Sinks since I saw you. He doesn't want to leave without the money, and doesn't know it is in Kennedy's hands, and can't get into the Cache to find out. Now the three—whoever the other two are—and Sinclair —are trying to join forces somewhere up this valley, and Kennedy, Scott, Wickwire, and I are after them; and every outlet is watched, and it must all be over, my dear, before sunset to-night. Isn't that fine ? I mean to have the thing wound up somehow. Don't look worried."

" Do not—do not let him kill you," she cried with a sob.

" He will not kill me; don't be afraid."

" I *am* afraid. Remember what your life is to all of us ! "

Whispering Smith

"Then, of course, I've got to think of what it is to myself—being the only one I've got. Sometimes I don't think much of it; but when I get a welcome like this it sets me up. If I can once get out of this accursed man-slaughtering business, Dicksie— How old are you? Nineteen? Well, you've got the finest chap in all these mountains, and George McCloud has the finest——"

With a bubbling laugh she shook her finger at him. "*Now* you are caught. Say the finest woman in these mountains if you dare! Say the finest woman!"

"The finest woman of nineteen in all creation!" He swung with a laugh into the saddle and waved his hat. She watched him ride down the road and around the hill. When he reappeared she was still looking and he was galloping along the lower road. A man rode out at the fork to meet him and trotted with him over the bridge. Riding leisurely across the creek, their broad hats bobbing unevenly in the sunshine, they spurred swiftly past the grove of quaking asps, and in a moment were lost beyond the trees.

CHAPTER XLIV

CRAWLING STONE WASH

WHERE the Little Crawling Stone River tears out of the Mission Mountains it has left a grayish-white gap that may be seen for many miles. This is the head of the North Crawling Stone Valley. Twenty miles to the right the big river itself bursts through the Mission hills in the canyon known as the Box. Between the confluence of Big and Little Crawling Stone, and on the east side of Little Crawling Stone, lies a vast waste. Standing in the midst of this frightful eruption from the heart of the mountains, one sees, as far as the eye can reach, a landscape utterly forbidding. North for sixty miles lie the high chains of the Mission range, and a cuplike configuration of the mountains close to the valley affords a resting-place for the deepest snows of winter and a precipitous escape for the torrents of June. Here, when the sun reaches its summer height or a sweet-grass wind blows soft or a cloudburst above the peaks strikes the southerly face of the range, winter unfrocks in a single night. A glacier of snow melts within twenty-four hours into a torrent of lava and bursts with incredible fury from a thousand gorges.

When this happens nothing withstands. Whatever lies in the path of the flood is swept from the face of the earth. The mountains, assailed in a moment with the ferocity of a hundred storms, are ripped and torn like hills of clay. The frosted scale of the granite, the desperate root of the cedar, the poised nest of the eagle, the clutch of the crannied vine, the split and start of the mountain-side, are all as one before the June thaw. At its height Little Crawling Stone, with a head of forty feet, is a choking flood of rock. Mountains, torn and bleeding, vomit bowlders of thirty, sixty, a hundred tons like pebbles upon the valley. Even there they find no permanent resting-place. Each succeeding year sees them torn groaning from their beds in the wash. New masses of rock are hurled upon them, new waters lift them in fresh caprice, and the crash and the grinding echo in the hills like a roar of mountain thunder.

Where the wash covers the valley nothing lives; the fertile earth has long been buried under the mountain *débris*. It supports no plant life beyond the scantiest deposit of weed-plant seed, and the rocky scurf, spreading like a leprosy over many miles, scars the face of the green earth. This is the

Crawling Stone Wash

Crawling Stone wash. Exhausted by the fury of its few yearly weeks of activity, Little Crawling Stone runs for the greater part of the year a winding, shallow stream through a bed of whitened bowlders where lizards sun themselves and trout lurk in shaded pools.

When Whispering Smith and his companions were fairly started on the last day of their ride, it was toward this rift in the Mission range that the trail led them. Sinclair, with consummate cleverness, had rejoined his companions; but the attempt to get into the Cache, and his reckless ride into Medicine Bend, had reduced their chances of escape to a single outlet, and that they must find up Crawling Stone Valley. The necessity of it was spelled in every move the pursued men had made for twenty-four hours. They were riding the pick of mountain horseflesh and covering their tracks by every device known to the high country. Behind them, made prudent by unusual danger, rode the best men the mountain division could muster for the final effort to bring them to account. The fast riding of the early week had given way to the pace of caution. No trail sign was overlooked, no point of concealment directly approached, no hiding-place left unsearched.

The tension of a long day of this work was drawing to a close when the sun set and left the

Whispering Smith

big wash in the shadow of the mountains. On the higher ground to the right, Kennedy and Scott were riding where they could command the gullies of the precipitous left bank of the river. High on the left bank itself, worming his way like a snake from point to point of concealment through the scanty brush of the mountain-side, crawled Wickwire, commanding the pockets in the right bank. Closer to the river on the right and following the trail itself over shale and rock and between scattered bowlders, Whispering Smith, low on his horse's neck, rode slowly.

It was almost too dark to catch the slight discolorations where pebbles had been disturbed on a flat surface or the calk of a horseshoe had slipped on the uneven face of a ledge, and he had halted under an uplift to wait for Wickwire on the distant left to advance, when, half a mile below him, a horseman crossing the river rode slowly past a gap in the rocks and disappeared below the next bend. He was followed in a moment by a second rider and a third. Whispering Smith knew he had not been seen. He had flushed the game, and, wheeling his horse, rode straight up the river-bank to high ground, where he could circle around widely below them. They had slipped between his line and Wickwire's, and were doubling back, following the dry bed of the stream. It was im-

406

Crawling Stone Wash

possible to recall Kennedy and Scott without giving an alarm, but by a quick *détour* he could at least hold the quarry back for twenty minutes with his rifle, and in that time Kennedy and Scott could come up.

Less than half an hour of daylight remained. If the outlaws could slip down the wash and out into the Crawling Stone Valley they had every chance of getting away in the night; and if the third man should be Barney Rebstock, Whispering Smith knew that Sinclair thought only of escape. Smith alone, of their pursuers, could now intercept them, but a second hope remained: on the left, Wickwire was high enough to command every turn in the bed of the river. He might see them and could force them to cover with his rifle even at long range. Casting up the chances, Whispering Smith, riding faster over the uneven ground than anything but sheer recklessness would have prompted, hastened across the waste. His rifle lay in his hand, and he had pushed his horse to a run. A single fearful instinct crowded now upon the long strain of the week. A savage fascination burned like a fever in his veins, and he meant that they should not get away. Taking chances that would have shamed him in cooler moments, he forced his horse at the end of the long ride to within a hundred paces of the river, threw his lines, slipped like a lizard from the saddle, and, darting with incredible swiftness from rock to rock, gained the water's edge.

From up the long shadows of the wash there came the wail of an owl. From it he knew that Wickwire had seen them and was warning him, but he had anticipated the warning and stood below where the hunted men must ride. He strained his eyes over the waste of rock above. For one half-hour of daylight he would have sold, in that moment, ten years of his life. What could he do if they should be able to secrete themselves until dark between him and Wickwire? Gliding under cover of huge rocks up the dry watercourse, he reached a spot where the floods had scooped a long, hollow curve out of a soft ledge in the bank, leaving a stretch of smooth sand on the bed of the stream. At the upper point great bowlders pushed out in the river. He could not inspect the curve from the spot he had gained without reckless exposure, but he must force the little daylight left to him. Climbing completely over the lower point, he advanced cautiously, and from behind a sheltering spur stepped out upon an overhanging table of rock and looked across the river-bottom. Three men had halted on the sand within the curve. Two lay on their rifles under the upper point, a hundred and twenty paces from Whispering Smith.

Crawling Stone Wash

The third man, Seagrue, less than fifty yards away, had got off his horse and was laying down his rifle, when the hoot-owl screeched again and he looked uneasily back. They had chosen for their halt a spot easily defended, and needed only darkness to make them safe, when Smith, stepping out into plain sight, threw forward his hand.

They heard his sharp call to pitch up, and the men under the point jumped. Seagrue had not yet taken his hand from his rifle. He threw it to his shoulder. As closely together as two fingers of the right hand can be struck twice in the palm of the left, two rifle-shots cracked across the wash. Two bullets passed so close in flight they might have struck. One cut the dusty hair from Smith's temple and slit the brim of his hat above his ear; the other struck Seagrue under the left eye, ploughed through the roof of his mouth, and, coming out below his ear, splintered the rock at his back.

The shock alone would have staggered a bullock, but Seagrue, laughing, came forward pumping his gun. Sinclair, at a hundred and twenty yards, cut instantly into the fight, and the ball from his rifle creased the alkali that crusted Whispering Smith's unshaven cheek. As he fired he sprang to cover.

Whispering Smith

For Seagrue and Smith there was no cover: for one or both it was death in the open and Seagrue, with his rifle at his cheek, walked straight into it. Taking for a moment the fire of the three guns, Whispering Smith stood, a perfect target, outlined against the sky. They whipped the dust from his coat, tore the sleeve from his wrist, and ripped the blouse collar from his neck; but he felt no bullet shock. He saw before him only the buckle of Seagrue's belt forty paces away, and sent bullet after bullet at the gleam of brass between the sights. Both men were using high-pressure guns, and the deadly shock of the slugs made Seagrue twitch and stagger. The man was dying as he walked. Smith's hand was racing with the lever, and had a cartridge jammed, the steel would have snapped like a match.

It was beyond human endurance to support the leaden death. The little square of brass between the sights wavered. Seagrue stumbled, doubled on his knees, and staggering plunged loosely forward on the sand. Whispering Smith threw his fire toward the bowlder behind which Sinclair and Barney Rebstock had disappeared.

Suddenly he realized that the bullets from the point were not coming his way. He was aware of a second rifle-duel above the bend. Wickwire, worming his way down the stream, had uncovered

Crawling Stone Wash

Sinclair and young Rebstock from behind. A yell between the shots rang across the wash, and the cringing figure of a man ran out toward Whispering Smith with his hands high in the air, and pitched headlong on the ground. It was the skulker, Barney Rebstock, driven out by Wickwire's fire.

The shooting ceased. Silence fell upon the gloom of the dusk. Then came a calling between Smith and Wickwire, and a signalling of pistol-shots for their companions. Kennedy and Bob Scott dashed down toward the river-bed on their horses. Seagrue lay on his face. Young Rebstock sat with his hands around his knees on the sand. Above him at some distance, Wickwire and Smith stood before a man who leaned against the sharp cheek of the bowlder at the point. In his hands his rifle was held across his lap just as he had dropped on his knee to fire. He had never moved after he was struck. His head, drooping a little, rested against the rock, and his hat lay on the sand; his heavy beard had sunk into his chest and he kneeled in the shadow, asleep. Scott and Kennedy knew him. In the mountains there was no double for Murray Sinclair.

When he jumped behind the point to pick Whispering Smith off the ledge he had laid himself directly under Wickwire's fire across the wash.

Whispering Smith

The first shot of the cowboy at two hundred yards had passed, as he knelt, through both temples.

They laid him at Seagrue's side. The camp was made beside the dead men in the wash. "You had better not take him to Medicine Bend," said Whispering Smith, sitting late with Kennedy before the dying fire. "It would only mean that much more unpleasant talk and notoriety for her. The inquest can be held on the Frenchman. Take him to his own ranch and telegraph the folks in Wisconsin—God knows whether they will want to hear. But his mother is there yet. But if half what Barney has told to-night is true it would be better if no one ever heard."

CHAPTER XLV

BACK TO THE MOUNTAINS

IN the cottage in Boney Street, one year later, two women were waiting. It was ten o'clock at night.

" Isn't it a shame to be disappointed like this? " complained Dicksie, pushing her hair impatiently back. " Really, poor George is worked to death. He was to be in at six o'clock, Mr. Lee said, and here it is ten, and all your beautiful dinner spoiled. Marion, are you keeping something from me? Look me in the eye. Have you heard from Gordon Smith? "

" No, Dicksie."

" Not since he left the mountains a year ago? "

" Not since he left the mountains a year ago. "

Dicksie, sitting forward in her chair, bent her eyes upon the fire. " It is so strange. I wonder where he is to-night. How he loves you, Marion! He told me everything when he said good-by. He made me promise not to tell then; but I didn't promise to keep it forever."

Whispering Smith

Marion smiled. " A year isn't forever, Dick-sie."

" Well, it's pretty near forever when you are in love," declared Dicksie energetically. " I know just how he felt," she went on in a quieter tone. " He felt that all the disagreeable excitement and talk we had here then bore heaviest on you. He said if he stayed in Medicine Bend the newspapers never would cease talking and people never would stop annoying you—and you know George did say they were asking to have passenger trains held here just so people could see Whispering Smith. And, Marion, think of it, he actually doesn't know yet that George and I are married! How could we notify him without knowing where he was? And he doesn't know that trains are running up the Crawling Stone Valley. Mercy! a year goes like an hour when you're in love, doesn't it? George said he *knew* we should hear from him within six months—and George has never yet been mistaken excepting when he said I should grow to like the railroad business—and now it is a year and no news from him." Dicksie sprang from her chair. " I am going to call up Mr. Rooney Lee and just demand my husband! I think Mr. Lee handles trains shockingly every time George tries to get home like this on Saturday nights—now don't you? And passenger trains ought to get out of the way,

Back to the Mountains

anyway, when a division superintendent is trying to get home. What difference does it make to a passenger, I'd like to know, whether he is a few hours less or longer in getting to California or Japan or Manila or Hongkong or Buzzard's Gulch, provided he is safe—and you know there has not been an accident on the division for a year, Marion. There's a step now. I'll bet that's George!"

The door opened and it was George.

"Oh, honey!" cried Dicksie softly, waving her arms as she stood an instant before she ran to him. "But haven't I been a-waitin' for you!"

"Too bad! and, Marion," he exclaimed, turning without releasing his wife from his arms, "how can I ever make good for all this delay? Oh, yes, I've had dinner. Never, for Heaven's sake, wait dinner for me! But wait, both of you, till you hear the news!"

Dicksie kept her hands on his shoulders. "You have heard from Whispering Smith!"

"I have."

"I knew it!"

"Wait till I get it straight. Mr. Bucks is here —I came in with him in his car. He has news of Whispering Smith. One of our freight-traffic men in the Puget Sound country, who has been in a hospital in Victoria, learned by the merest

Whispering Smith

accident that Gordon Smith was lying in the same hospital with typhoid fever."

Marion rose swiftly. " Then the time has come, thank God, when I can do something for him; and I am going to him to-night!"

" Fine!" cried McCloud. " So am I, and that is why I'm late."

" Then I am going, too," exclaimed Dicksie solemnly.

" Do you mean it?" asked her husband. " Shall we let her, Marion? Mr. Bucks says I am to take his car and take Barnhardt, and keep the car there till I can bring Gordon back. Mr. Bucks and his secretary will ride to-night as far as Bear Dance with us, and in the morning they join Mr. Glover there." McCloud looked at his watch. " If you are both going, can you be ready by twelve o'clock for the China Mail?"

" We can be ready in an hour," declared Dicksie, throwing her arm half around Marion's neck, " can't we, Marion?"

" I can be ready in thirty minutes."

" Then, by Heaven—" McCloud studied his watch.

" What is it, George?"

" We won't wait for the midnight train. We will take an engine, run special to Green River,

Back to the Mountains

overhaul the Coast Limited, and save a whole day."

"George, pack your suit-case—quick, dear; and you, too, Marion; suit-cases are all we can take," cried Dicksie, pushing her husband toward the bedroom. "I'll telephone Rooney Lee for an engine myself right away. Dear me, it is kind of nice, to be able to order up a train when you want one in a hurry, isn't it, Marion? Perhaps I *shall* come to like it if they ever make George a vice-president."

In half an hour they had joined Bucks in his car, and Bill Dancing was piling the baggage into the vestibule. Bucks was sitting down to coffee. Chairs had been provided at the table, and after the greetings, Bucks, seating Marion Sinclair at his right and Barnhardt and McCloud at his left, asked Dicksie to sit opposite and pour the coffee. "You are a railroad man's wife now and you must learn to assume responsibility."

McCloud looked apprehensive. "I am afraid she will be assuming the whole division if you encourage her too much, Mr. Bucks."

"Marrying a railroad man," continued Bucks, pursuing his own thought, "is as bad as marrying into the army; if you have your husband half the time you are lucky. Then, too, in the railroad business your husband may have to be set back

Whispering Smith

when the traffic falls off. It's a little light at this moment, too. How should you take it if we had to put him on a freight train for a while, Mrs. McCloud?"

"Oh, Mr. Bucks!"

"Or suppose he should be promoted and should have to go to headquarters—some of us are getting old, you know."

"Really," Dicksie looked most demure as she filled the president's cup, "really, I often say to Mr. McCloud that I can *not* believe Mr. Bucks is president of this great road. He always looks to me to be the youngest man on the whole executive staff. Two lumps of sugar, Mr. Bucks?"

The bachelor president rolled his eyes as he reached for his cup. "Thank you, Mrs. Mc-Cloud, only one after that." He looked toward Marion. "All I can say is that if Mrs. Mc-Cloud's husband had married her two years earlier he might have been general manager by this time. Nothing could hold a man back, even a man of his modesty, whose wife can say as nice things as that. By the way, Mrs. Sinclair, does this man keep you supplied with transportation?"

"Oh, I have my annual, Mr. Bucks!" Marion opened her bag to find it.

Bucks held out his hand. "Let me see it a moment." He adjusted his eye-glasses, looked at the

418

Back to the Mountains

pass, and called for a pen; Bucks had never lost his gracious way of doing very little things. He laid the card on the table and wrote across the back of it over his name: " Good on all passenger trains." When he handed the card back to Marion he turned to Dicksie. " I understand you are laying out two or three towns on the ranch, Mrs. McCloud? "

" Two or three! Oh, no, only one as yet, Mr. Bucks! They are laying out, oh, such a pretty town! Cousin Lance is superintending the street work—and whom do you think I am going to name it after? You! I think ' Bucks ' makes a dandy name for a town, don't you? And I am going to have one town named Dunning; there will be two stations on the ranch, you know, and I think, really, there *ought* to be three."

" As many as that? "

" I don't believe you can operate a line that long, Mr. Bucks, with stations fourteen miles apart." Bucks opened his eyes in benevolent surprise. Dicksie, unabashed, kept right on: " Well, do you know how traffic is increasing over there, with the trains running only two months now? Why, the settlers are fairly pouring into the country."

" Will you give me a corner lot if we put another station on the ranch? "

Whispering Smith

"I will give you two if you will give us excursions and run some of the Overland passenger trains through the valley."

Bucks threw back his head and laughed in his tremendous way. "I don't know about that; I daren't promise offhand, Mrs. McCloud. But if you can get Whispering Smith to come back you might lay the matter before him. He is to take charge of all the colonist business when he returns; he promised to do that before he went away for his vacation. Whispering Smith is really the man you will have to stand in with."

Whispering Smith, lying on his iron bed in the hospital, professed not to be able quite to understand why they had made such a fuss about it. He underwent the excitement of the appearance of Barnhardt and the first talk with McCloud and Dicksie with hardly a rise in his temperature, and, lying in the sunshine of the afternoon, he was waiting for Marion. When she opened the door his face was turned wistfully toward it. He held out his hands with the old smile. She ran half blinded across the room and dropped on her knee beside him.

"My dear Marion, why did they drag you away out here?"

"They did not drag me away out here. Did

Back to the Mountains

you expect me to sit with folded hands when I heard you were ill anywhere in the wide world?"

He looked hungrily at her. "I didn't suppose any one in the wide world would take it very seriously."

"Mr. McCloud is crushed this afternoon to think you have said you would not go back with him. You would not believe how he misses you."

"It has been pretty lonesome for the last year. I didn't think it *could* be so lonesome anywhere."

"Nor did I."

"Have you noticed it? I shouldn't think you could in the mountains. Was there much water last spring? Heavens, I'd like to see the Crawling Stone again!"

"Why don't you come back?"

He folded her hands in his own. "Marion, it is you. I've been afraid I couldn't stand it to be near you and not tell you——"

"What need you be afraid to tell me?"

"That I have loved you so long."

Her head sunk close to his. "Don't you know you have said it to me many times without words? I've only been waiting for a chance to tell you how happy it makes me to think it is true."